Acclaim for the Lake Erie Mysteries

"*Beatrice Ophelia is Flickering Out* is a delightful cozy mystery full of warmth and wit. Beyond the clever twists, the story reminds us that family itself is a great mystery—and the greatest treasure of all. A wonderful debut!"
-Stephanie Morrill, author of the Piper Sail Mysteries

"*Beatrice Ophelia is Flickering Out* is a strong, feel-good mystery with an undercurrent of love and loyalty. With a cozy harbor setting, Gerig's likeable protagonist navigates through complicated family dynamics, a tentative romance, and finding her life's path, all while solving a murder to bring her family back together and save her beloved town. You'll close the book supremely satisfied but anxiously awaiting the next installment in the series."
-Korina Moss, author of the Cheese Shop Mysteries

BEATRICE OPHELIA is FLICKERING OUT

BEATRICE OPHELIA is FLICKERING OUT

MEGAN GERIG

Copyright © 2026 by Megan Gerig

Published by Lamplighter Literary Creations.

All rights reserved.

No part of this publication may be reproduced, distributed, or transmitted in any form or by any means, including photocopying, recording, or other electronic or mechanical methods, without the prior written permission of the publisher, except as permitted by U.S. copyright law. For permission requests, contact Megan Gerig at megangerig.com.

This is a work of fiction. The characters and events portrayed in this book are the product of the author's imagination or are used fictitiously. Any similarity to actual people and/or events, unless otherwise specified by the author, is coincidental.

NO AI TRAINING: Without in any way limiting the author's [and publisher's] exclusive rights under copyright, any use of this publication to "train" generative artificial intelligence (AI) technologies to generate text is expressly prohibited. The author reserves all rights to license uses of this work for generative AI training and development of machine learning language models.

Library of Congress Control Number: 2025924752

Paperback ISBN: 978-1-969970-01-6

Hardcover ISBN: 978-1-969970-02-3

Ebook ISBN: 978-1-969970-00-9

Book Cover by Lyndsey Lewellen

Proofread by Ellen McGinty

Chapter Illustrations by Mikayla Drewry

To the mediocre girls,
The ones who are good but never good enough. Pretty but never pretty enough. Smart but never smart enough.
Christ loves you and died for you. He perfectly created you with a light and a voice, and in Him, you are enough. Use your voice and be bold.

To my parents,
You never laughed when I told you I wanted to be a writer. You never doubted even when I did. You never gave up even when I felt like it. This book is here because of you. Thank you.

Chapter One

Gas stations were the hunting grounds of old ladies. And I'd been trapped.

Despite her thinning hair, the woman sported a beehive that poofed nearly six inches off her head—a style that would have earned her a second look from any man if we lived in the 1960s. Although she probably gathered quite a few second glances now. Just those of a more gaping, "what is on your head" variety.

She peered at me through her thick bifocals, and I knew then that I was in trouble. She held tight, one hand on the edge of the bathroom door, the other on the doorframe, sufficiently blocking me from my goal: to pee and get back on the road.

Then came the smile, the catlike gleam in her eye, and the question I hated most.

I'd already seen and heard it before. Too many times before. The snooping brightness in their faces fading to disappointment when you told them that no, you weren't doing anything brilliant with your life. You were only a college dropout living in your parents' basement.

But the worst part of the conversation always came next.

The pat on the hand. The pitying look. The "Well, you're young. You can do whatever you want."

I stalked out to my brother's waiting car nearly ten minutes later, a scowl plastered to my face.

Stupid advice. Because what if you had no idea what you wanted to do? But they never had an answer for that.

I yanked open the car door and plunked down in the passenger's seat, slamming the door shut behind me.

Theo, my brother, raised an eyebrow at me from the driver's seat.

"I don't want to talk about it."

But, like always, he knew. "Cornered again? Next time, tell them you help your brother chase dead people." Theo beamed. "You create the ghosts, and I find them!"

I snorted. "And telling people I'm a killer is better than telling them I'm unemployed?"

"They'll be doing everything they can to run away from you instead of pestering you with their 'never-before-heard' advice."

I turned toward the passenger-side window so he didn't see my smirk. Maybe it wouldn't be such a bad idea. It'd at least save me from having to explain my current situation again and again.

I rolled down the window and let the breeze sweep in off Lake Erie, carrying with it the crashing lull of waves against the rocks further down the road. Golden sun shone high above, its glowing rays reflecting off the surface of the lake until it looked like diamonds sparkled on each crest of the waves.

I drew in a deep breath of the lakeside air and let my fingers dangle outside the car window. Mimi had always talked about the magic of Thisbe Harbor. Hopefully, some of that magic would rub off on me this weekend. As much as I loved my parents, I didn't want to live in their basement forever.

The car's engine hummed as my brother slowed. He flicked on his turn signal, then swung the car into the parking lot in front of a drab gray aluminum building. A sign, which was once white but was now so covered in mildew you could barely read it, pronounced the place Compass Cove Marina.

Docks stretched behind it, boats bobbing up and down with the gentle rise of the waves. And despite the fact that every other board seemed to be missing from the gangways and several of the railings were cracked in half, I somehow could overlook it for the glittering expanse beyond.

The moment my brother stopped the car, I hopped out and let the fresh air sweep through my blond coiled curls. It felt so good to be back.

"Listen to me!" The high-pitched, demanding voice was startingly familiar.

I whirled around. My aunt, clad in her signature too-tight white pants and baby-blue blouse, stalked up to a burly man in worn overalls and a white long-sleeved shirt and began gesticulating wildly.

So much for my relaxing beach weekend.

"Did you know she was coming?" Theo climbed out of the driver's seat and gaped at me.

I shook my head and swallowed back a groan. Our grandfather had tricked us.

Two days ago, Papa Sawyer had called and begged my parents, brother, and me to make the two-hour trip to Thisbe Harbor this weekend for the Smallmouth Bass Festival. He'd promised to take care of all the arrangements if we'd come for a short visit. Considering this month was also the twelfth anniversary of Mimi's passing, we couldn't say no. Besides, it was long past time to visit Thisbe Harbor. And after being laid off from my third job this year... Well, I could use a relaxing weekend away.

With my brother home from college on summer break, we'd taken off for sunnier days. At least, the days had seemed sunnier until ten minutes ago. Dad had called and ordered us to race to the marina where he and Mom were supposed to be picking up the keys to our rental. And now, as two men on either side of the walkway lifted a banner proclaiming in all-bold, all-capital letters "WELCOME TO THE SMALLMOUTH BASS FESTIVAL. FOOD! FAMILY! FUN!", I knew why.

For years, the whole family had vacationed together here in Thisbe Harbor, my aunt and uncle our best friends. We'd kickstart summer with two weeks of family vacation before Theo and I spent the next two weeks with our grandparents.

The laughter and smiles and memories were imprinted on my heart forever. Then Mimi died in a freak car accident, and the family fell apart. A year later, when Mom won the town's best of home award over Aunt Penelope, my aunt hurled vitriol at my mother and walked out of our lives forever.

Now that very aunt leaned forward and jabbed a finger against the burly man's chest. A flush tinged his cheeks, but he didn't back down. He balled his fists at his sides and glowered at my aunt, who hadn't stopped her tirade.

They stood to the left of the marina office building, three or four boats down the dock. A few people wearing bright yellow volunteer shirts glanced their way as they shuffled past, arms laden with colorful boxes of what I presumed were decorations.

In the parking lot behind us, a few food trucks worked on setting up their stations for the next day, and in the green space on the right side of the office building, small businesses set up tents and tables to sell their wares. But while at least a dozen people were about, I didn't see my mother anywhere.

Tightness wormed its way through my chest. "Where's—?"

"You're here!" Dad appeared behind us, his face already flushed and perspiration beading on his forehead. He dragged a hand through his thinning, brown-and-gray hair and puffed to a stop. "I have her distracted for now, but it won't last long if Penelope keeps it up like this. Your mother's bound to hear her."

"What is she doing here?" Theo asked.

"I need you to calm your aunt down long enough for me to find your grandfather, get the house key, and drive your mother away."

Theo's face twisted in horror, and I couldn't help grimace myself. Clearly, our grandfather had had a secret agenda when arranging this trip.

"Please?" Dad whispered.

Before I knew what I was doing, I found myself nodding in response to the desperation in his voice.

"I always can count on you, Bumble Bea." Dad squeezed my hand and hurried back toward the marina building.

"You're a conniving liar and a thief!" Aunt Penny shrieked.

I glanced toward my brother, horror building in my chest. "What did I just do?"

He raised his hands and took a step back. "I did not sign up for anything."

"I can't talk to her myself!" I whimpered and shot another frown at my huffing aunt.

"I demand you give it to me," Aunt Penny snapped, face turning tomato red.

"Over my dead body." The marina man sneered.

Aunt Penny raised a well-manicured fist toward the man. "We'll see about that."

"Do something!" I squeaked and shoved my brother forward.

He tripped over the edge of the pavement as I raised my voice. "Hey, Aunt—" Her name choked in my throat. Dare I call her Penny like in the good times? Or Penelope because we hadn't spoken in years? I decided to press my luck. "Aunt Penny!"

With a speed I didn't expect from such a big man, the marina worker snagged Aunt Penny's fist and, in an attempt to redirect her, shoved her arm back to her side. Unfortunately, my aunt's clothing choice was more for style than for convenience. She stumbled backward in her stilettos, and one caught on a loose gangplank.

An otherworldly screech emitted from my aunt's lips, and her arms pinwheeled. Her wide-eyed gaze caught mine for a second before she fell.

And what a fall it was.

Aunt Penny shouted curses and threats all the way down, using language I'd never heard in my life. Her designer sunglasses flew off her face, and her stilettos soared high into the air.

Lake water sprayed, a small wave sweeping over the docks then sliding through the cracks in the boards back into the cove.

Three seconds of silence reigned before Aunt Penny spluttered to the surface, hair matted to her face and her baby-blue blouse clinging to her skin.

Her scream cracked whatever semblance of peace had settled over the lake in those three seconds. She flailed her arms in the air and bobbed up and down in the water, coughing and choking. Considering the marina was only around three feet deep, I knew the entire thing was an act. But all the world was Aunt Penny's stage, so flames forbid that she actually act like an adult for once.

Aunt Penny's threats echoed across the water.

The door to the office flew open and yellow-clad volunteers raced out. My mom ran at the head.

I closed my eyes and tilted my face toward the sun, counting silently to twenty. Because ten seconds wasn't enough to compose myself for what was to come.

"It's okay!" Theo raised his arms and strode over to head off our mother. "Just a slight mishap, but we've got it covered. No need to be alarmed. You can go back to your decorating and setting up." He planted himself in front of Mother, grabbed her shoulders, and redirected her back toward the office building.

Mom tugged against Theo's grip and tried to peer behind him. "Theseus? What are you—"

"Bea and I came to help set up. A volunteer slipped and popped into the lake is all. We've got it handled."

I wanted to facepalm. Theo never could pull off a good lie. Aunt Penny was clearly visible behind him, quiet for once as she narrowed her gaze at the volunteers to gauge their reactions to her dramatics.

Theo walked my mother back toward the still-open doors. "I'll let you know if we need anything."

"What about clothes?" Mom tried to twist around and get a better look, but Theo kept a firm arm around her shoulders. "Do they need an extra—"

"Between Beatrice and me, we have all the clothes in the world they could need."

Seeing their fearless leader turning back, the rest of the volunteers shuffled after my brother and mom, but not after sending several curious looks in the direction of my aunt and the marina man. I dragged a hand through my hair and blew out the breath I'd been holding. Disaster one—averted, for now. Perhaps Theo wasn't as bad a liar as I thought.

Rather than attempt any sort of rescue, the marina man smirked, turned his back on my aunt, and strolled away to the aluminum building.

"I'm going to sue you for harassment!" Aunt Penny screamed, miraculously standing on lake bottom to make her threat. "I'm going to take everything you've got!"

I prayed that Mom was safe enough inside not to recognize my aunt's voice, and hurried onto the docks where she still sat in the water. "Are you okay? My brother and I saw you fall in." I forced the words out, even though I could see she was perfectly fine. Better to placate than aggravate in this situation. When Aunt Penny was in a mood like this, who knew how she'd react to anything but platitudes.

"Fall?" She scowled up at me. "You think I fell?" She stabbed a finger toward the marina building. "That—that man pushed me!"

It took everything in me not to snort.

"I've probably got a concussion." She pressed the back of her hand to her forehead, then after a glance in my direction, she waved her hand toward the sky. "Or catch my death of cold. I'm soaked."

The air outside was anything but "death catching." The sun beat down on the back of my neck, and the golden rays almost seemed to buzz in the air with heat waves of energy.

I held out a hand. "Can I help you get out?"

Aunt Penny huffed without any mutters of gratitude and grasped my hand. I clasped my fingers around her wrist and started to pull. Only to realize that she hung like a dead body, limp and unhelpful.

Thankfully, Theo hurried up beside me. He wrinkled his nose at our aunt and said, "Dad was inside, so I passed her off to him."

"Help me," I wheezed to my brother and anchored my other hand around my aunt's wrist as well.

I could see the "Do I have to?" question in my brother's face, but he laid across the dock on his stomach then reached down and grabbed under my aunt's other arm. On the count of three, we hauled her onto the dock.

She collapsed the moment we released her and gasped for air as if she'd been underwater for minutes rather than standing on the bottom hurling insults. What she thought she was accomplishing at this display of dramatics was beyond me.

I bit back a sigh and sat back on my heels. "I have some clothes in the car you can use to change." Not that she'd like my style of baggy t-shirts and jeans, but it'd be better than laying there soaked.

Aunt Penny squinted up at me. "You look familiar."

Of course she wouldn't remember me. I'd grown up in the ten years since we'd last seen each other. "It's Beatrice." I forced my hand forward, but she only blinked once. Twice. Not an ounce of recognition in her gaze. Ouch. I'd thought we'd been close before the contest blow up, but apparently I was all-too forgettable. "Helene's daughter?" I offered.

Her mouth dropped open, and she threw a quick glance up and down my figure. "B-Beatrice? Beatrice Sawyer?"

She continued to stare at me. I couldn't help smoothing down my frizzy curls, and it took everything in me not to push my glasses up my nose—I'd always thought it a bit bulbous compared to her thin Greek nose. Not that I really cared what she thought about me. But when someone was inspecting your every inch, it was hard not to feel self-conscious.

The slightest grin tugged up my aunt's lips, and my eyebrows rose. It'd been so long since I'd seen *her* much less seen her smile. Perhaps she had changed after all these years.

"What are you doing here?" Theo asked.

Aunt Penny shoved to her feet and tugged her blouse to smooth out the wrinkles. When she faced me again, her friendly expression shuttered behind a visage of coolness.

"One thing your mother never understood, kids. You have to work hard for what you want. There are no handouts." She scowled and stared at the building behind us. "Which is why this marina will be mine. Whether that man realizes it or not."

Chapter Two

Aunt Penny threw back her shoulders and marched toward the parking lot. I exchanged a look with my brother.

"Let's be thankful Mom didn't hear that," he muttered.

I nodded and blew out a breath. Apparently my aunt hadn't changed like I'd hoped. Was that what she thought of my mother? That she didn't work hard? Sure, we weren't nearly as rich as Aunt Penny and Uncle Rubin, but that's because my mom had chosen to leave her well-paying corporate job to stay at home and raise us kids. I didn't know where or who I'd be today if my mom hadn't made that sacrifice.

"What now?" Theo asked. "We headed her off once, but the whole weekend?"

I picked myself up from off the dock and glanced around. Lake Erie glittered in the warm sunlight, and a handful of boats bobbed as the waves splashed against the docks. It'd been so long since I'd come back to Thisbe Harbor—my childhood second home.

For the first time, it hit me how empty the marina was. In summers' past, there wouldn't have been a docked boat in sight on a Friday afternoon, but today . . . I swallowed hard. Mimi would be devastated to see her beloved Thisbe Harbor near empty and her family always on the precipice of slinging verbal blows. But without her, the magic she'd insisted resided in Thisbe Harbor was waning, and our family was drifting further and further apart.

"Beatrice?" Theo's voice pulled me out of my thoughts.

"We should find Papa," I said. A sudden chill sent goosebumps skittering up my arms, and I wrapped them around myself. "And find out what he wants from us."

I led the way toward the office building. Two men carried a folded white tent on their shoulders, and I ducked underneath it to reach the double glass doors leading inside. I pushed the door open, and a silver bell tinkled overhead.

Wood paneling straight from the seventies lined the walls, and carpet the color of goose poop covered the flooring. Wooden frames boasting black-and-white photos covered every inch of the wall, and a glass case that doubled as the reception desk took over nearly half the space. A woman sat behind the desk, typing away on a laptop. Model boats of all shapes, sizes, and colors crammed into the glass case alongside gaudy sunglasses, tubes of sunscreen, and dozens of shells. On top of the glass case resided several spinning display cases of key chains, cheap rings, and postcards.

At the back of the room, behind the reception desk, a closed door was marked with a plaque announcing "Owner." To my right, an open gray door led to a room brimming with boxes, tables, chairs, extra folding tents, and volunteers. The workers sorted through the boxes, dragging out strings of multicolored pennants, bright tablecloths, and little knickknacks for decorating.

In the middle of them all stood a woman bellowing orders. She wore a yellow visor with "Volunteer Coordinator" printed in bold black letters on the brim. White linen pants, strappy brown sandals, and the loudest orange, yellow, and black flowered flowing shirt completed her ensemble. She pointed to several boxes on the opposite side of the room and a collection of gold bangles jingled on her wrist.

I grinned at my brother and headed farther into the room. As kids, Cindy had often taken us for rides in her family's speedboat and enabled any and every crazy idea that we'd come up with. She'd stuck by our side through Mimi's passing and still texted me every once in a while to "check in" as she liked to call it—although it was more of an opportunity for her to pass on the latest gossip she'd learned in town.

"No, not that way," Cindy said in her signature Southern and British accent—a combination she'd once proudly told me she'd invented herself. "Bring that over here so I can see it." She paused as a different volunteer stepped up to ask her a question.

I waited until the volunteer moved away before hurrying forward and flinging my arms around the woman. She gave a startled squeak, but true to her nature, gave me a fierce hug in return before stepping back, adjusting her wire-rimmed glasses and giving me a once-over.

"Beatrice Ophelia Sawyer!" She yanked me into another hug, and I couldn't help relaxing. Her familiar scent of sunscreen and coconut enveloped me again, and I inhaled the smell.

It brought back a memory of my grandmother I'd long forgotten—her slim figure hunched over a double broiler, stirring melted yellowish soy wax. Mimi had winked at me and had slid a small glass jar of fragrance oils toward me. "For our dear friend," she'd said.

I'd lifted the jar to my nose and blinked in surprise at the all-too recognizable fragrance. "Cindy?"

"Her husband." Mimi had removed the melted wax from the stove and had set it on the counter to cool. "Scent is one of the strongest ways to bring our memories back to life."

I'd never met Cindy's husband, since he'd died before I was born, but I'd never forgotten that the perfume Cindy always wore was her way of bringing her husband with her wherever she went.

"Welcome back to Thisbe Harbor, my dear," Cindy whispered in my ear. "I've so missed you." She pulled away to give Theo the same welcome and ruffled his hair. "Shame on both of you for not visiting more often."

I flushed and ducked my head, remembering that I hadn't even texted her back last time she'd checked in.

"But no matter." She clapped her hands, sending her bracelets clinking again. "You're here now, and that's what counts. Your grandfather has been looking forward to this weekend for quite some time now."

My smile faded at the reminder of my grandfather's plot to bring my aunt and mother here together. I opened my mouth to question her about it when a booming voice interrupted me.

"Excuses!" The voice thundered from the main room.

Cindy's face darkened. Several of the volunteers moved toward the open doorway, and I let my curiosity drag me forward with them.

The marina man from earlier slammed his hand down on the glass case, and the receptionist standing behind it shrank back. She stumbled and landed in the rolling chair, making it look like the man was towering over her. He jabbed a meaty finger at her. "You're a waste of air, and if I didn't have to, you wouldn't be here."

"I-I'm sorry, I don't—"

"One more mistake, Maeve, and I'll make sure you regret it." He stalked around the side of the desk and slammed the office door shut behind him.

As soon as the ringing of the door's slam quieted, the receptionist dropped into her chair and rubbed her hands over her face. Her glasses clattered onto the desk in front of her, and her shoulders shuddered.

"I've got this." Cindy barged through the crowd of volunteers. She clapped her hands twice. "Back to work, everyone. This festival isn't going to decorate itself."

The volunteers peeled themselves away from the spectacle, and I followed Cindy through the door. My grandmother's best friend marched right around the glass case and wrapped an arm around the receptionist's shaking shoulders.

I inched forward and fished a wad of tissues from my purse. Then I pushed them over to her. "They're unused." I hoped.

The receptionist jumped, sending her rolling chair back a foot and Cindy scurrying out of its way. Swiping the back of her hand across her eyes, she straightened and forced a smile as if the puffiness of her face and tight lines pinching her cheeks didn't exist. "Welcome to Compass Cove Marina. What can I help you with today?"

"Oh, she's with me." Cindy patted the woman's shoulder. "Maeve, this is Beatrice. Sawyer's granddaughter."

"Are you okay?" I nudged the tissues a bit closer.

Maeve studied them only a moment longer before taking one. Tears filled her eyes again and she sank back. Cindy dragged the chair under her.

"He didn't used to be like that, you know?" Maeve choked out. "He used to be kind. Attentive. I thought he cared for me."

Cindy gave a small, "Hmph," then masked her indignation with a cough.

"But he's bullied me for too long. Threatened everything for too long." Maeve crushed her tissue in her fist and glared at the glass case in front of her. "And if he thinks he can take anything else away from me, then he'd better watch out."

"Apparently no one likes this guy very much." I startled at the sound of my brother's voice so close behind me. I hadn't even realized he'd followed us.

Maeve's glare turned into a snarl. She snatched a purse off the floor and pushed to her feet. "When you've wronged as many people as he has, no one much cares if you live or die." She flung her purse strap over one shoulder and nodded toward Cindy. "I'm heading home. If Owens complains about it, tell him to take a dunk in the lake."

The moment the doors swung shut behind her, I raised an eyebrow at Cindy. "And Papa claimed this would be a weekend to relax and reset."

She lifted a shoulder in a shrug, sighed, and shook her head.

"Where is he, by the way?" Theo asked. "Considering Mom's not in there, I assume either Dad whisked her away or she got roped into setting something up outside."

"I believe they all went back to the house he rented." Cindy reached across the glass case and squeezed my shoulder. "I promised your grandfather I wouldn't say anything more than I already have but . . . brace yourselves."

Chapter Three

With Cindy's words ringing warning bells in my mind, I led my brother out the front doors and rammed straight into a walking pile of bones. Or, at least, it was a man who felt like a walking pile of bones. He yelped and reeled backward. The manila envelope he'd held soared through the air in a flutter of papers and scattered across the walkway and nearby grass.

"I'm so sorry!" I squeaked and leaped forward to grab the man's elbow and steady him. "I wasn't—"

He swatted my hand. "Unhand me, fool!"

I jerked back and gaped at him.

"Look what you've done." He scowled at me before squatting and sweeping the papers back together. "Kids these days. Don't know how to respect anyone, much less their elders."

"I'm sorry." I shot my brother a wide-eyed look. He held his phone in one hand, recording the entire thing. I swallowed back a groan. He was sure to show it to all his college friends. As if I wasn't already known as klutzy. "I should have looked before—"

"You absolutely should have looked! You should have held the door open for me. Kids in my days respected those of hoary head." He continued his ranting about "kids in my day," but I caught my brother's muffled snicker.

I glanced toward him, and he mouthed, "Those of hoary head?"

My lips twitched, but I knelt to help pick up the man's papers. Whatever I thought about his disgruntled manner, I had been the cause of his distress, so the least I could do was help him.

I'd barely touched the corner of one sheet, though, when a screech echoed in the still air. I jerked my head up in time to the see the man's wiry form leaping toward me. He slammed into my shoulder and sent both of us tumbling into the grass.

"Thief!" he hollered and pinned my arms at my sides. "Burglar!"

I stared up at his tomato-colored face, completely speechless. This was it. I was never going to be nice again. Not if it meant getting tackled by crazy old men.

"Are you insane?" Theo appeared above us and grabbed the man under his armpits. "You can't treat my sister that way."

The man bucked and writhed in my brother's grip. "Help! Help me!" He flung his head back, and Theo dropped him to avoid being bashed in the face. The moment he was free, our attacker lunged for me again.

I squeaked and held up my hands. What was wrong with this guy? I'd only tried to help.

"What's happening—hey!" Another volunteer raced around me, his dreadlocks swinging over his back, and intercepted the crazy man. "Vincent, what are you doing?"

I froze at the sound of the voice. Because although the squeaky, cracking voice from our preteen years was no longer audible in the deep baritone, I knew that voice. I'd never let myself forget. I lowered my hands and stared into the dark eyes of my childhood best friend, Julian.

His tightly woven dreadlocks were longer than I'd remembered, and the muscles on his arms were much more developed, but it was him—the boy who'd always hung out with my brother and me every summer. The boy who I'd always got in trouble with my mischievous plans.

My mouth went dry. After all these years, he was still here.

"Beatrice?" Cindy's voice came from behind me, and she bustled into view. She gasped when she saw me on the ground and swung her glare toward Vincent. "Did you lay a hand on her? What is wrong with you? That is not how you treat a guest of the town."

A pang shot through me at her words. Thisbe Harbor used to be mine as much as Cindy's. Yet now, I was simply a guest of the town.

I couldn't help sneaking another glance at Julian. My breath caught at his intense stare. He'd changed so much, yet he was still so familiar. I could still hear his laughter ringing in my mind as we swung our legs over the side of the docks and licked our rapidly melting ice cream cones.

"What's going on here?" Another man hustled to our growing group and stopped next to Julian. In contrast to the rest of the volunteers, he wore a navy blue t-shirt with a white stenciled police badge on the left breast and "Festival Security" written beneath.

I studied his short hair and broad shoulders. He also seemed so familiar.

"It's her fault!" Vincent shrieked and stabbed a finger toward me. "She tried to steal my papers after ripping them from my hands."

My jaw dropped. I'd done no such thing. What was this man's problem?

Theo stepped forward, hands balling into fists at his sides. "She was trying to be neighborly and help you pick them up!"

The security guard slid in between my brother and Vincent and held up his hands, palms out. "I suggest we all take a moment to calm down." He shot a pointed glare over his shoulder at Vincent, and at that moment, it clicked.

The security guard and Julian shared the same dark skin, same nose, and same brown eyes. I'd only met Julian's twin brother a handful of times throughout the summers I'd stayed in Thisbe. While Julian had no problem slipping away from his chores to adventure with me, Joel was a rule follower through and through and often missed out on the fun. And the subsequent punishments, but that was beside the point.

I prayed Lake Erie might wash up onto shore and swallow me up. Joel had never been my biggest fan. And after I'd abandoned his brother when he'd needed me most, I was sure I was on Joel's list of top ten most hated. Any chance I had of convincing everyone of my innocence was gone.

"Did anyone see what happened?" Joel asked. He flicked a glance toward me and my brother, then over at Vincent. "Other than these three."

"I saw the whole thing." Cindy marched forward and planted herself next to Joel. "She ran into Vinny when leaving the marina, and he dropped his papers. When she went to help him pick them up, he bowled her over and began screaming like a madman." She rounded on Vincent again. "Sophie would be ashamed by your attitude. Treating young ladies like that."

The older man pursed his lips, and the wrinkles around the corners of his mouth tightened. Something in him seemed to crumple at Cindy's words—a tremor rippling through him that dropped his shoulders and added decades of pain to his gaze.

Emotion twisted in my chest. While I couldn't excuse his behavior, this man had been through something, bearing an agony that weighed down his soul.

"It was just a misunderstanding," I found myself saying. "No harm done. Right, sir?" I offered him a small smile, then bent down and lifted the paper that sat in the grass at my feet. The paper was now wrinkled and marked with a shoe print of dirt. At the top of the page in all-capital black letters read, "Proposal for Legacy Lagoons."

Vincent snatched the page from my hand and held it close to his chest. He swallowed hard. "Right. I-I overreacted. No harm done."

A moment of silence overtook the crowd, then Cindy clapped her hands. "All right, people, we've a festival to prepare. Let's move on out." She turned and gave me a quick once-over.

"I'm all right," I assured her, although a sudden exhaustion swept through me at the words. Unfortunately, after Cindy's warning earlier, I'd wager a guess that the afternoon's chaos was just beginning.

She tilted her head and studied me for a long moment. "Make time for tea this weekend, yeah?"

A lump formed in the back of my throat. Before she'd passed, Mimi had spoken those words countless times to me, always knowing when I'd needed a moment to speak, to have someone listen to my worries, my fears—no matter how small.

I sucked in a deep breath and straightened my shoulders. There must be something in the air at Thisbe Harbor because we'd been here no more than thirty minutes and I was a sentimental mess. I needed to get it together. "Tea sounds great."

"I'll text you my festival schedule and we'll find a time." She winked at me, then strode back into the marina building.

With Cindy gone, my gaze landed on my childhood best friend once again. Julian smiled, the corners of his eyes crinkling with the gesture, and he shoved his hands in his pockets. He opened his mouth to speak, but before he could, Theo barged in front of him and grabbed my arm.

"No harm done? Really?" My brother shook his phone in front of my face. "I have video footage of the guy tackling you!"

I shook my head and started forward, Theo keeping pace with me. "It wasn't that big of a deal. He didn't hurt me, and I didn't want to cause a scene." I met Julian's gaze and shrugged.

"Cause a scene?" He gaped. "Beatrice, you—"

"Could we get coffee this weekend?" Julian asked as I paused by him.

Theo flicked him a glance, then tried to tug me forward. "She's already got a boyfriend."

I wanted to smack him upside the head. It was no wonder I'd never had a boyfriend. Theo thought it hilarious to pretend that he was my boyfriend to ward off any "unsavory characters" as he liked to call anyone who deigned look in my direction.

But Julian only snorted and crossed his arms. "It's certainly not you."

This brought my brother to a halt, and I grinned at the surprise that overtook his features. He slowly turned and opened his mouth for what was sure to be a sarcastic comment.

I interrupted. "It's Julian. Remember him? From summers with Mimi and Papa?"

"Oh, man!" Theo clapped Julian on the back and pulled him in for a quick hug. "It's been so long since we've seen you. How are you doing?"

"I'm doing all right. It's good to see you guys. Sawyer said you were coming."

My cheeks colored at the statement. He'd known we would be here. Which meant he'd known I hadn't reached out.

Julian shoved his hands into his pockets and rocked back on his heels. "I, uh, was hoping I might run into you. It's been awhile, eh?"

"I—" My mouth was so dry I couldn't force any words out."

"She'd love to get coffee!" Theo bumped my arm. "In fact, she could use a ride back to our rental. My car's a little small, you know, so if you don't mind taking a bit of a detour, that'd be great."

My jaw dropped, and my face blazed. He didn't have a subtle bone in his body. His car wasn't small enough that it couldn't fit two people. And Julian would certainly know that.

But before I could protest, Theo whispered, "Have fun with your Benedick," then hightailed it to his car and out of my arm's reach.

I clenched my hands into fists and rolled my eyes up to the sky. Ever since Dad had revealed that I'd been named after Shakespeare's Beatrice in *Much Ado About Nothing*, Theo had never failed to irritate me about "finding my own Benedick in life." Usually I tried to shoot back some quip about his Hippolyta since he'd been named after Theseus in *A Midsummer Night's Dream*, but he shrugged it off much better than I did. Not that I usually cared that much, but how many times would I have to be embarrassed in front of Julian today?

I swallowed and forced myself to look at him. "Sorry about that. He's... He's..." A jerk, a nut, a liar, a mischievous little twit.

"Some things never change, eh?" He forced a chuckle, then rubbed the back of his neck. "But I, uh, guess you need a ride?"

My left eye started twitching—curse my annoying tic. It always happened when I was embarrassed. But it'd been nearly a decade of always regretting never making that phone call. Would he ever forgive me? What would have happened if we had kept in touch?

"Yeah. A ride would be great." I swallowed and brushed a foot through the grass.

"Cool."

I lifted my gaze, and we stared at each other. I longed to apologize, to explain why I hadn't called, to beg him to be my friend again. But with a crowd of people working to put the festival together around us, it didn't feel right. I didn't want him to see my apology as fake—forced because we'd stumbled upon each other.

The moment passed, and Julian started toward the parking lot. "Car's this way."

Forcing myself forward, I racked my brain for something to talk about. I mentally kicked myself for overthinking the situation. I should've apologized right away. What must he think of me? "So, uh, why are you still here?" The minute the question left my mouth, I regretted it. Of all the dumb things to ask. "I'm sorry. That sounded so rude. I didn't mean—"

Julian's lips turned upward in a smile, and he laughed. "No, you're fine. I actually ask myself the same question every day. I'm working on my Masters in Music over at Cleveland U so I can teach at the collegiate level, but grad school is expensive. Performance musicians don't make a lot of money in a place like this, but I find myself unable to leave. The water, the fresh air, the people here. I don't know."

One of the quotes Dad often spoke to me after I dropped out of college came to mind. "To thine own self be true."

Julian tilted his head, his grin widening. "What?"

"Sorry, Dad's a Shakespeare nut—I don't know if you remember that or not. I'm a college dropout, and when everyone else scolded me for it, he always shared that quote. I couldn't force myself to be a nurse if it wasn't my calling. I needed to be true to myself and follow my passion." Not that I knew what that passion was. And since nurses were always in high demand, and I was on my third layoff of the year . . . perhaps I should reconsider the nursing career.

"Don't apologize." He vigorously shook his head. "You're doing what you love. Not many people can claim that, and you should be proud of it."

"I—" That was the thing. I wasn't doing what I loved. I didn't even know what I loved. But he was probably already disappointed in me enough. How could I tell him that I was jobless on top of everything else? I licked my lips and straightened my shoulders. I'd hidden enough from him. "I'm not doing what I love. I'm currently jobless, homeless—unless you count living in my parents' basement—and completely everything-less." A bit dramatic, maybe, but it's what I was feeling.

The corner of his mouth tilted upward in a half smile. "But you're not friendless. Yeah?"

I could only stare at him in response, my heart drumming so loud in my ears that it even drowned out the sound of Lake Erie. Could he really forgive me so easily?

Before I could say anything, Julian stopped in front of a beat-up '90s Saturn with peeling gray paint and a half punched in side door.

He affectionately patted the car's hood. "Welcome to my sweet ride. She's not much, but she's fully mine. Don't mind the noise. I just had her in the shop and she works fine, but she likes to pretend that she's on death's door."

I couldn't help but watch him confidently stride to the driver's seat. Most people I knew would be embarrassed to have a car like this, but Julian just seemed happy to have a ride to get him to and fro. A good attitude to have.

He caught me watching, a small glint in his eye as if we were sharing some sort of secret.

Warmth spread through me. That gaze. I ducked my head, sucked in a deep breath, then climbed into the passenger seat. The car started with a rumble and shakily backed out of the parking lot. I bounced up and down in my seat as we started down the road.

"So," he practically shouted over the engine, "that coffee?"

"I'll be here until Monday," I admitted.

"I'm playing at different points over the festivities, but I could do tomorrow morning early or after lunch, say, three o'clock?"

"Three sounds good." I swallowed hard.

Conversation faded between us, but although it should have felt incredibly awkward, it didn't. It felt normal. Somehow, it felt right to be here with him.

We turned into the rental house's neighborhood, and he slowed as we approached the house. A car engine revved behind us, and a black

Cadillac Escalade roared around us. The huge SUV raced down the street then screeched to a stop right in front of my rental's driveway.

My heart dropped into my stomach, and I tightened the grip on the car door until my knuckles turned white. I knew even before she stepped out who owned that car.

Chapter Four

Julian maneuvered his car alongside the curb out front in time for us to see my still-damp aunt climb out of the SUV. She pushed her Louis Vuitton sunglasses into her blond hair, which she'd pulled into a messy bun.

"Oh no," I whispered. This was what Cindy had warned me about. Papa hadn't just gotten us together this weekend—he'd booked the same place for us to stay.

I swallowed hard and climbed out of the car, Julian not far behind me. My mother would not take this well. There'd be no way to avoid them interacting now.

Aunt Penny rounded her SUV and paused at the base of the driveway, a pout on her lips. She spotted me and crossed her arms. "Suitcase is in the back. Be a dear and carry it in for me, won't you? I'm in desperate need of a shower." Aunt Penny lifted an arm to her nose, sniffed, and shuddered. "Who knew the lake smelled so awful."

I stiffened. Leave it to Aunt Penny to pretend like I was only a servant girl.

"Penelope!" Papa's voice, filled with joy and a tinge of laughter, boomed from behind me. I glanced over a shoulder, and his grin widened when he met my gaze. "Beatrice. Both my girls here." He wheeled down the front ramp of the house and slowed as he neared me to spread his arms wide. "Welcome back to Thisbe Harbor."

I forced a smile, but my chest tightened at the welcome. I hated how I couldn't feel fully happy about seeing him. But after the way he'd tricked us to come here . . . I crossed the lawn, wrapped my arms around his neck, then kissed his forehead.

"My Beatrice." He squeezed my arms, and my cheek brushed against his tear-stained one.

A pang squeezed my heart. He hadn't meant to deceive us. He'd only wanted to see his family again—his whole family. And he'd been so desperate that he'd done the only thing he could think of to accomplish that.

"What are you doing?" A tight, high-pitched voice trilled from the porch.

Papa went rigid in my embrace, and I pulled back to see Mom standing at the top of the porch, arms crossed and lips pursed.

"You can't park there."

The brief ghost of a smile that had upturned my aunt's lips at the sight of Papa vanished. She slowly crossed her arms and mimicked my mother's stance, whether intentionally or not I didn't know, but I knew from experience it would only flame the fuel of my mother's fury.

"What do you mean, 'I can't park here?' There's no sign telling me I can't."

"How is anyone else supposed to get out?" Mom stomped down the ramp. "I was going to go to the grocery store, and your big honkin' semitruck of a vehicle is blocking the road!"

Aunt Penny's jaw dropped, and anger seethed in her gaze. "You're just jealous you're still driving a 2010 minivan."

"That has nothing to do with this!" Mom's cheeks colored, and she balled her hands into fists at her side. "No one can get out of the driveway because you're in the way. Like you always are!"

Papa reached up and tightened his fingers around mine. All laughter had drained from his eyes and the wrinkles on his face had deepened in sadness. My lungs squeezed at the transformation. I hated knowing how much pain the family split had put him through over the years. If Mimi were here, she'd be crushed to know what had happened to the close family bond she'd cultivated and encouraged.

I chewed on my lower lip, knowing full well he wanted me to head off the argument but not having the courage to barge in. Not when fists could fly at any second.

Thankfully, Dad hurried out the front door, hands raised. "Ladies, please." He used his high school English teacher voice, the sound thundering over insult after flung insult.

Mom shuffled back a step and sucked in a ragged breath. Her gaze still flashed venom, but she pressed her lips together once again.

"This is a time to honor your mother." Dad strode down to put an arm over my mom's shoulders. "Let's keep it that way." He stared at my mother for a beat, then glanced over to my aunt. "It's good to see you again, Penelope. Will Rob be joining us this weekend?"

"Not this weekend." She sniffed and swiveled back to her car, but not before throwing over her shoulder, "He is defending a high-profile client in LA. He'll make enough that maybe we can afford to cruise Europe for a month." Aunt Penny paused at the trunk of her car and waved a foot under the bumper. The car beeped once, and the trunk mechanically rose into the air. My aunt flashed Mom a triumphant sneer. "Don't you wish you could go on one?"

Dad tightened his grip on Mom's shoulder and turned her toward the house. "Let's finish up the grocery list." But despite his calm manner, a blush tinged his cheeks. He'd retired early from teaching due to the high stress causing health complications. But even on his teacher's salary, there would've been no way he and mom could ever have afforded a month-long European cruise.

I crouched next to my grandfather, never letting go of his soft wrinkled hand. "We need to talk." After that display of temper, I needed him to understand that while I'd do everything in my power to keep the family from fighting and severing further, fixing our family's mess wouldn't be resolved in one weekend.

Aunt Penny breezed past us, blowing a kiss at her father. "I'll give you a proper hug once I'm washed up, okay, Dad? Don't want to impart this smell on you."

"Of course, dear." He watched as she sauntered into the house and shut the door.

A breeze rippled through the bright green oak tree planted in front of the house. Birds twittered one to another, and a dog barked from somewhere in the neighborhood. Peaceful. That's what Thisbe was—or would be, if my family wasn't here.

I sucked in a deep breath and prepared myself for the conversation to come. "Papa—"

He held up a hand and slowly maneuvered his wheelchair around to face me. "I don't pretend to understand this whole rift they have going on, but it must stop. I need you to help them see reason. This can't keep going." His voice broke, and he ducked his head. I held my breath, somehow sensing that he wasn't done.

After a long moment, he tilted his head back up, tears shining on his cheeks and his jaw trembling. "It's been twelve years since your Mimi passed. This family is all I have." He swiped at his eyes, smearing trails of tears across his cheeks. "Your Mimi and I always dreamed of having a family who was close. Who loved each other and supported each other through all of life's ups and downs. She died thinking that's what we had. But we don't. Not anymore."

He wasn't wrong. This wasn't supposed to be how family was. Wasn't how I'd ever imagined our family to be.

But we were broken. Hurt had run too deep for a single weekend to simply brush away.

"I'm not God, Papa." I crouched in front of his wheelchair and clasped his hands. "I can't work miracles."

"We shouldn't need a miracle." He huffed.

We shouldn't. But we did.

"Promise me, Beatrice." He crushed my fingers in his grip. "Just this once. Just this weekend. Someone needs to believe in this family again."

I swallowed hard. Believing in my Aunt Penny was something I'd stopped doing ten years ago. But what choice did I have? I couldn't disappoint my grandfather. Not when he was already suffering so much. "I promise." Giving it a try couldn't be that hard, right?

Chapter Five

"What do you mean, 'she's gone?'" Mom's shrill voice shattered the remnants of sleep still drifting through my mind.

Peeking open an eye, I winced at the bright sun spilling through my open window. After a dinner of silent glares and Papa's strained attempts at conversation, I'd opened the bedroom window to fall asleep to the sound of crashing waves.

Even with the soothing repetitions, it'd taken me till well after midnight to fall asleep—not that my brother's loud snoring helped anything. It'd been years since Theo and I had to share a room, but with Papa and Aunt Penny joining us in the rental house, we hadn't gotten a choice.

Theo cocooned in a heap of blankets near the door, face plastered into his pillow and soft snores brushing through his blond curls spread haphazard around him. How he could breath, I had no idea, but I couldn't help a snicker at his burrowed form. A goofball even in his sleep.

"Doesn't she realize we have to leave in an hour?" Several thumps from somewhere in the house followed the protestation.

I groped on the side table for my glasses and shoved them up the bridge of my nose. A quick run of my fingers through my hair, and I mentally deemed myself presentable enough to see what was going on. After tiptoeing over my brother, I squeezed out the door into the hall.

"And where's that husband of hers? He should be here to keep her in line." A pan clattered in the kitchen, and I followed the noise, the carpet absorbing my footsteps.

I paused and peered around the corner of the wall. I was pretty sure Mom was referring to my aunt up and disappearing this morning, but just in case Aunt Penny was around, I didn't want her to see me freshly rolled out of bed.

Mom padded around the kitchen in her fluffy white slippers, hair already brushed and makeup on despite the fact she still wore her pajamas. Apparently she didn't want Aunt Penny to see her morning bedhead either. Dad leaned against the island counter, a sixteen-ounce mug of coffee in one hand and a powdered-sugar donut in the other.

Mom rarely made donuts since Mimi's passing. We all associated them too much with her. Not that they were difficult to make or anything special, but every summer and every holiday we visited my grandparents, Mimi always fried up multiple tubes of store-brand biscuit dough in crazy shapes and sizes, then coated them in a thick dusting of powdered sugar. She'd serve them piled nearly a foot tall on a fancy China platter, and we'd devour them within minutes.

It'd been years since I'd eaten them, and when Mom plopped another circle of dough into the fryer, the scents of butter and sugar tugged me from my hiding place.

"Sign me up for a dozen." I sidled over and gave my dad a hug.

He smiled and kissed the top of my head with his powdered-sugar coated lips. "Morning, Bumble Bea."

"Have you seen your aunt?" Mom tossed a frown over her shoulder before focusing back on her task.

I shuffled forward to look at the golden brown circles floating in the bubbling oil. I inhaled the smell. If I could capture that in a candle, I'd be a millionaire.

"We leave in an hour, and she's nowhere to be found."

"Where are we supposed to be going?" I asked.

"Dad rented a boat for us. He wants to take a trip around Kelley's Island before the festival kicks off." Mom snorted and muttered, almost to herself, "And where's that husband of hers? His 'big' case too big for him to handle spending time with family?"

"Now, Helene," Dad murmured in a voice that both soothed and warned.

"It's just like her to abandon us when Dad needs her most." Mom's voice trailed off before she added in a whisper, "Couldn't find her anywhere after Mama passed."

Dad set his coffee down and brushed his powdery hands on his plaid pajama pants before walking over and embracing my mom from behind. He whispered, "Everyone grieves differently. That doesn't mean it hurts less."

Mom picked up the straining spoon and used it to lift the perfectly fried rings of dough out of the fryer. Resting them on a paper-towel covered plate, she then slipped from my father's arms and stiffly grabbed the paper bag filled with powdered sugar. Her silence lent more power to her sadness than words would ever convey. And while I didn't know all the details, I did know that Aunt Penny had hurt my mother. Deeply.

Unease settled in my stomach. How could I keep my promise to Papa? No amount of begging would ever get Mom to even speak kindly to Aunt Penny let alone reconcile. Not with the pain that touched so many of her recent memories with her sister.

"Beatrice?" Dad slid an arm around my shoulder and turned me away from Mom. Voice low, he asked, "Could you drive to the marina and see if it's possible to reschedule our tour? To either this afternoon or tomorrow morning. I think it'd be best if we had a little more time."

The paper bag crunched behind us as Mom coated the donuts in a healthy dose of sugar. My stomach growled at the sound, and I inwardly sighed at the thought of missing out on fresh donuts. But no matter how hungry I was, giving Mom a measure of peace was more important.

I nodded and gave my dad a quick side hug. "Don't eat them all." Then I hurried back down the hall. If I moved fast enough, I might still be in time to snag one fresh out of the fryer. I burst through the bedroom door at top speed. Unfortunately, I forgot my brother sleeping in front of the door.

I rammed into him and tripped.

He yelped and flipped over, flinging his blankets off. My feet and flailing arms tangled in the woven threads, and I sucked in a sharp breath as I fell. Theo's half-lidded gaze met mine a second before I hit the ground next to him.

We both stared at the ceiling for a long moment, then I rolled onto my elbows and shot Theo a sheepish grin. "Can I borrow your car?"

He grumbled something I'm sure wasn't kind, rolled over, and buried his face in his pillow.

"I'm sorry." I crawled over to my suitcase and dragged it out from underneath the bed. "I forgot you were there. But I really do need the car. Dad wants me to reschedule the boat tour."

He lifted his head and growled, "Can't you call?" then faceplanted once again.

"Considering how Aunt Penny treated the marina owner yesterday, I think going in person would be best." I pulled an oversized cream t-shirt and jean shorts from my suitcase and tossed them onto the bed. "I can use all my charms to convince them to let us change the time."

"What charms?"

I rolled my eyes and threw my pillow at him. It bounced off his head and tumbled onto the floor. "We both know you won't let me drive your precious car, so you'd better get up so we don't miss out on the donuts."

"Donuts?" It was incredible what one word could do for a college-aged boy—and yes, my brother was a boy, not a man, in my opinion. Theo popped back up. "Mom made donuts?"

"Mimi's special ones. And they're still warm."

He flung his covers the rest of the way off and dove for his suitcase. After grabbing the first outfit he came across, he hightailed it to the bathroom. I grinned and shut the door behind me. Sometimes it worked in my favor to know my brother so well.

Ten minutes later, I maneuvered into the passenger seat of my brother's car, two steaming paper bags of donuts in hand—Dad's "thank-you" gift to us. Theo started up the car, and the moment we backed onto the road and started forward, he held out his hand.

I tucked one bag between my legs and handed the other to him before digging in. The smell of the sweet buttery pastry and melting sugar wafted from the bag, and my stomach growled in delight. I shoved half of one donut into my mouth, chewed, and moaned. It'd been years since I'd tasted something this good.

"So what happened to Aunt Penny?" Theo asked between a mouthful of dough.

"She's not in the house apparently." I licked the powder off my fingers then plunged my hand into the paper bag for my second donut. "And since we have no idea when she'll show up again, Dad wants the boat tour delayed."

"Boat tour?"

"Papa's idea."

He snorted, powdered sugar puffing from his lips and scattering through the air like snowflakes. Some must've caught in his throat because he gripped the steering wheel and wheezed. The car jerked side to side and I pounded on his back until he waved me away.

"What was that about?" I asked.

Theo coughed again then managed, "I think getting us all onto a boat out in the middle of nowhere sounds more like 'And Then There Were None,' not a happy family reunion."

"We have to try. For him."

Despite my fervent proclamation, I agreed with my brother. Spending this weekend with family, praying for a miracle, would only hurt my grandfather further when it ended the exact way it had begun—or worse. Theo and I descended into silence, both finishing our goodie bags and licking our fingers clean until we reached the marina.

White tents scattered across the lawn, packed in tight rows until the docks. Colorful banners and tablecloths drifted in the morning breeze. Even the dinky, faded white marina building seemed brighter thanks to the huge yellow and blue banner proclaiming the festival's name that graced the building's front. Yet, despite the color, an eerie silence descended on the marina. Not a single boat put-putted away from its docking, and not a single tourist roamed the aisles of vendors.

"It's kind of creepy," Theo murmured, apparently sharing the same thought. Then his eyes brightened. "Maybe it's haunted."

I groaned and swatted his arm. "It's not haunted!"

"I dunno, I could see it." He parked the car and leaned back in his seat. "Imagine it now. A mist crawling over the lake at dusk, shadows harboring secret ghouls under the decks. A creak here, a whisper there." He spoke in a low, almost reverent tone that sent goosebumps up my arms.

For being in school to study Forensic Investigation, my brother had quite the obsession with the paranormal. I would've thought his classes would teach him that ghosts were not only unproven but they were also impossible to prove. If anything, however, his obsession seemed to be stronger than ever.

"Okay, that's enough." I unlocked my car door and popped out into the warmth and sunshine. "There are no ghosts." Rubbing the goosebumps from my arms, I hurried toward the marina office building. Waves lapped gently against the docks, creating an almost mesmerizing, rhythmic song that could have carried away all my stress.

But before the tension could dissipate from my shoulders, I spotted the red sign announcing the office was CLOSED. A groan built in my chest, but I picked up my pace as if getting there faster would somehow change the sign. Alas, it did not. I reached the double glass doors and stared at the red letters.

"Why are you closed?" I leaned my back against the doors. To my surprise, they opened. Arms flailing, I tumbled through the crack and landed on my butt on the cool white tile flooring.

Even through the now-closed doors, I could hear Theo's hoots of laughter. I crossed my arms and glared through the glass at him as he bent over, smacked his knee, and snickered.

"So funny," I grumbled and pushed myself to my feet. A scuffle came from behind me. I swallowed any angry retorts directed at my brother and prepared an apology for busting into the closed building. But when I turned, all words fled from my lips.

"Beatrice, that was—" Theo pushed through the doors, but his laughter turned to a gasp. "Is that a body?"

Chapter Six

My aunt's gaze met mine, and her eyes widened. She was hunched in the doorway of the marina owner's office, arms wrapped around a body slumped against her chest. The man's head lolled forward. Dark blood crusted over jagged scratches on the man's cheeks, and blotchy red marks ringed his neck.

He was dead.

And he was cradled in my aunt's arms.

I screamed—a shriek my drama-and-literature-loving father would have deemed worthy of a Shakespearean stage.

Aunt Penny's eyes widened, and she jerked back, the body slipping from her grasp and thudding back on the floor. My stomach rolled, and I screamed again.

My aunt was a murderer.

"It's not what you think!" She held out her hands and started forward. "I can explain."

I shrank back against my brother, grateful the receptionist's desk and display case stood between us and my aunt. For now, at least.

Theseus slapped his phone into my hand. "Call the police." His teeth were clenched and jaw trembling from the exertion to stay calm. All his training from school was kicking in as inspected our aunt and the body she was dragging. At this moment, I couldn't have been prouder to have a Forensics Investigator in training as a brother because I was useless.

"Wait, I didn't do anything," Aunt Penny choked out. Tears trickled down her cheeks, but whether she was genuine or trying to manipulate us, I couldn't be sure. "I-I found him like this."

Theseus met my gaze. "Call the police."

"You have to believe me!"

I swiped to emergency calls on my brother's phone and started dialing 911.

Aunt Penny snarled. She vaulted over the glass case, somehow landing perfectly on her killer heels, then she straight-armed me, sending me stumbling back into my brother. Theo's phone sailed from my grasp and skittered across the floor.

"Don't let her get away!" Theo shoved me away from him, sending me off-balance again, and I fell to my knees.

My brother barreled through the front doors after her, hollering for help the entire time. I snatched my brother's phone, leaped to my feet, and burst through the doors after them.

For sporting her signature stiletto heels, my aunt could run. She pounded down the marina docks toward who knows where, her arms pumping at her sides. I slowed to a stop and watched my brother hightail it after her. At this point, there was no way I could catch up.

Sirens wailed in the distance, faint at first, but growing louder with each passing moment. Within seconds, police cars, an ambulance, and two fire trucks swerved into the parking lot and emergency responders poured from the vehicles. My brother gave a last burst of speed, then leaped forward in a spectacular move that would rival any flying squirrel. He slammed into my aunt's back, knocking them both to the ground.

Suddenly, it felt like the docks were swarming. Police ran toward my brother and struggling aunt, shouting orders at each other. But how had they known to come? My brother's phone warmed in my palm. I hadn't called them.

Aunt Penny kicked and clawed at my skinny brother's hold. "I didn't do it. Let me go!"

I started toward them, anger boiling in the pit of my stomach. How dare she treat my brother in that way when she—Hands grabbed me from behind and pulled me against a muscled chest. Scents of cedar and soap and something minty overwhelmed my senses, calming the churning of my stomach for a moment.

"Let the police handle it." I could almost feel the hum of Julian's deep voice in my own chest, the lyrical sound slowing the racing of my heart. I squeezed my eyes shut and dragged in a shaking breath right before the chaos exploded further.

Theo must've told the police about the body as a group of paramedics rushed into the marina , two officers accompanying them. The thought of what they'd find inside brought back the all-too-real images of my aunt cradling the body.

Acid roiled up my throat. I turned, forgetting about Julian standing behind me until it was too late.

I threw up my donuts.

He staggered back, a surprised cry bursting from him.

Tears flooded my eyes, and I choked back another heave. My humiliation was complete. First, I'd caught my aunt in the act of covering up her murder, then this. Julian would never want to see me again now. A sob tore from my throat, and I slowly started to back away, apologies sticking in my throat.

"It's okay." Fingers pushed up my glasses and swept the tears from under my eyes. "You're safe, Beatrice."

I heaved in another sob, did my best to swallow it back, and ended up making a noise more akin to a gray whale than anything. Julian's lips twitched. I met his twinkling gaze, and we both dissolved into awkward laughter. Julian's deep laugh eased some of the panic twisting my insides, and I managed to suck in an actual breath.

His smile tightened a bit as he focused back on the scene around us. But then he looked back at me and moved forward to lightly touch my arm. "It's going to be okay."

The reek of acid and donuts crawled up my nose. Vomit splattered the front of Julian's black t-shirt, and the smell covered any hint of his delicious cologne.

"I'm so sorry," I groaned.

"Beatrice?" My brother's voice caught my attention.

He rounded the circle of officers and medics, face flushed from his tussle. Light scratches reddened his cheek and neck, but the minute he was close enough, I wrapped my arms around him and pressed my face against his neck. He winced but squeezed me tightly back when I tried to move away.

"You okay?" he whispered in my ear.

I shook my head and held him tighter, my heart picking up speed again and my lungs seeming to twist with every breath I tried to take. How could anyone be okay after witnessing *that*? What were we going to tell Mom, Dad, and Papa?

Papa. The thought slapped me in the face.

I'd promised my grandfather that I'd do all in my power to bring the family back together. But how could I keep that promise now?

"Has someone examined you?" Theo interrupted my thoughts.

"What?" I tilted my head and frowned up at him. Why would anyone need to examine me?

"You could be going into shock." He pulled back enough to scowl at Julian. "Why haven't you called a medic?"

"I don't need a medic. I need . . ." I needed the last ten minutes to not have happened. I needed my aunt to not be a murderer. But I'd seen Aunt Penny with the body. I'd seen her panic when we caught her. I'd seen her threaten the marina man the day before.

Theo wrapped an arm around my shoulders and tugged me against his side. I leaned into him, my body trembling like I'd stepped barefoot in the snow.

"Witnesses say you were the first on the scene here?" A burly police officer strode to our little group, and I found myself looking into the eyes of Joel. He sighed when he realized who we were and pressed two fingers in the space between his eyebrows. "I should've known that the two 'teenagers' breaking into the marina were you."

"What do you mean breaking in?" Theo wrinkled his nose. "The doors were open."

"We got a call that two teens were breaking into the marina and sneaking around. Then I arrive to find you tackling your aunt and a body inside, so does anyone want to explain what happened?"

Well, that answered how the police arrived so quickly.

"You're police?" I asked, although why I was surprised, I didn't know. Joel never did want to take part in our summer shenanigans.

"Chief Joel Laurent of the Thisbe Harbor Police," he said.

Great. Not only was he a police officer, but he was the chief of police. Always nice to know the chief of police hated your guts.

"Beatrice! Theseus!" Mom's voice rose above the crowd, and I spun to see her shove through the front and bolt toward me. My jaw dropped, but before I could say anything, she jerked me into her arms and pressed a tear-streaked cheek against mine. "You're safe. Oh, baby girl, you're safe."

"Helene!" Aunt Penny shrieked. "Make them let me go. I didn't do this!"

Mom and I both stiffened and slowly turned. I swallowed hard and finally took in the crowd of people around us. Two police officers held Aunt Penny by her upper arms, another one forcing her hands behind her back to be cuffed, and four paramedics ushered an empty gurney from the building behind us. The black coroner's car turned into the parking lot and pulled into the spot next to the ambulance.

"What?" Mom sucked in a breath, the color in her cheeks slowly fading to a ghostly white.

I wrapped my arms around myself and dug my nails into the skin of my biceps to feel something. But the dull pain didn't bring any answers. What did you tell your mother when you'd seen her sister trying to carry away a dead body?

"What's going on?" Mom demanded, taking a step toward her sister.

"Please, just give them space. Let them do their job." I repeated what Julian had told me earlier, no other words of comfort coming to mind. Joel—the chief of police—shifted a little outside of our circle, but I knew his attention had never left us.

My nails bit deeper into my skin, and I grit my teeth. Anything we said or did in front of him could be used against us in a court of law. I'd remembered Theo sharing that much from his classes.

"What is going on?" Papa's bellow rose above the cacophony of the crowd.

I grabbed my mother's hand. "You can't let him see. You have to stop—" But my warning came too late.

Papa wheeled through the front of the crowd, Dad trying to push through after him. The moment Papa spotted Aunt Penny, he froze.

"No, no, no." I raced over to him. "Papa, please, you should go."

"Penny?" Papa's hoarse voice raked over my heart and snatched the breath from my lungs.

His gaze flicked toward the coroner's car, then back to my handcuffed aunt, and he gripped the sides of the wheelchair with whitened knuckles. "What is happening?" He shoved his hands over his wheels, launching his wheelchair forward. "Unhand her! Let her go!"

"Papa, please." I grabbed the handles of his wheelchair and forced him back. "You can't. You have to let the police work."

Mom scurried over, eyes already rimmed red, but determination in the set of her shoulders. "Go ahead." She waved me toward Joel, who still stood not too far away. "Do what you need to do. We'll take care of him."

I ground my teeth and watched her hustle to Papa, bending down to kiss his cheek and whisper something in his ear. This wasn't how the weekend was supposed to go. We were supposed to be having a relaxing vacation. Not watching Aunt Penny be carted away by the police.

Julian shuffled over and rested a hesitant hand on my shoulder. "It'll work out. Joel, he's a good cop."

I bit my lip. Even after all these years of silence, after all these years since I'd seen him, he hadn't changed. He was still the kindest, most loyal person I knew.

"Are you ready to continue?" a voice asked behind us.

I turned, wrapping my arms around myself, and nodded at the chief of police. Talking to him was inevitable. But before I could say anything, Theo shifted and pulled something from his pocket. He handed a small business card over to the chief.

Chief Joel took one look at it, then raised an eyebrow. "Forensic Investigator in training? I assume you handed this to me for a reason?"

"Let go of my daughter!" Papa's strained voice somehow rose above the gossiping crowd, and my lungs squeezed with the agony laced in it.

Theo opened his mouth to start his explanation, but the sudden urge to defend my aunt overwhelmed me. Mimi had always said that family was worth fighting for. And while I couldn't help but feel like my aunt deserved to go to jail, especially for the way she treated Mom and pretty much everyone else, she was still family. If I didn't defend my family, who would?

"Aunt Penny isn't a murderer," I blurted.

My brother shot me a silencing glare, but I couldn't stop myself. Not anymore. The entire story poured from my lips, from Aunt Penny's argument with the marina owner to finding her cradling his body.

When I finished, Chief Joel blew out a breath. He opened his mouth once, paused, then turned to my brother. "Do you have anything else to add?"

"I think she covered it." Theo crossed his arms. "And then some." He pursed his lips at me, and I could feel his annoyance that I hadn't consulted him on anything I'd said. Not that he'd want me to hide anything from the police, but he probably wanted to tell the story. After all, he'd pulled his Forensic Investigator card—as if a Forensic Investigator in training held any clout with the police.

Joel tapped his pencil on his notepad. "You said your aunt threatened the marina owner?"

"He said something about 'over his dead body' and she replied with 'we'll see about that,'" Theo said. "We both—well, Beatrice and I both—heard it."

I shivered at the implication. Aunt Penny had threatened the marina owner, and now he was dead. I rubbed my hands up and down my arms. She couldn't have killed him. She was family.

To his credit, Joel didn't bat an eye. He simply wrote something in his notebook and glanced back up at us. "I'll have some more questions later. For the rest of your family as well. However"—he glanced toward where paramedics were helping my parents load Papa into their car—"I don't want to distress your grandfather further. I'll be by his room this afternoon."

After explaining that we were renting a house for the weekend, Theo wrote down the address in Joel's notebook. The chief promised to stop by later, then moved on to another cluster of potential witnesses further down the docks.

I chewed on my lower lip, my heart thudding so hard against my chest it hurt. All I wanted to do was curl up next to Papa as I used to do as a little girl during a thunderstorm. No matter the time of night, he and Mimi always made room for me when the first lightning bolt flashed across the sky and thunder shook the house. And somehow, being next to them always made things less scary.

"Hey." Theo squeezed my hand. "It'll be all right."

A pall swept over the marina, and the ambulance pulled from the parking lot, sirens quiet and lights off.

I shivered, the silence somehow a roar in my ears. Nothing was all right. And I wasn't sure it ever would be again.

Chapter Seven

"This is not good."

I startled and frowned at Julian. I hadn't thought I'd spoken aloud, but why wouldn't he agree with me? How would he feel if his family—I realized that he wasn't looking at me, but past me.

I twisted around and followed his gaze to the sleek, vintage black Mustang pulling into the lot where the ambulance had just been.

Julian groaned. "Where's Joel?"

"Who is that?" Theo asked.

A squat, balding man dressed in a black suit and tie slid out of the front seat. Red already splotched his cheeks, and he pumped his arms at his sides as he rounded the front of the car. When he finally saw the crowd, every eye on him, he paused, and his eyebrows rose. What had he expected to see? It wasn't like this town saw a murder every day.

"That's Mayor Gilberth," Julian muttered. "Joel's boss."

"How long has he been mayor?" I asked.

"You know this town. The less that's changed, the better." Julian blew out a breath. "It's why it's in the state it's in." He chewed on his lower lip, then dragged a hand through his hair.

"Joel's the youngest police chief hired in the Lake Erie region. The job doesn't pay much, but Joel loves the people and this town. He didn't want to be yet another young person that gave up on it. But when the mayor hired him, he acted like he was doing Joel this big service. Said he was taking a big risk on Joel being so young, but he was willing to do so since he was a 'local boy.' He's been breathing down Joel's neck about everything ever since."

Mayor Gilberth swallowed, pushed back his shoulders, and stalked into the crowd. He clapped his hands and forced a smile. "Nothing to see here, folks. Please return to your homes until the beginning of the festival."

Joel looked up from where he was interviewing another couple on the docks. His face tightened when he met the gaze of the mayor, but after a few quick words to the couple, he tucked his notebook back into his pocket and jogged over. The mayor grabbed Joel's upper arm and steered him toward the side of the marina office, away from prying eyes, his fake smile never wavering.

I wrinkled my nose. What a way to treat the chief of police. If the mayor was going to so publicly display his distaste toward the police, how could he expect anyone else to respect them and follow the law? I already didn't like the man.

"First the drugs, now this?" The mayor hissed to Joel as they passed. "I hired you to take care of problems in Thisbe. But ever since you started, there have been..." His voice faded as they rounded the corner of the office building.

The crowd shifted when they disappeared, and I could tell I wasn't the only one that wanted to hide by the corner and listen in. But something the mayor had said echoed in my mind.

"Drugs?" I faced Julian again. "What'd that mean?"

Julian's shoulders drooped. "Thisbe isn't the town you remember. Someone's been peddling powdered cocaine. Joel's already uncovered three drop points this month and crime has skyrocketed. A big-city station like Cleveland or Columbus probably wouldn't think anything of it, but Thisbe Harbor's police can barely be called a force. It's mostly made up of volunteers who have other things to do with their time, but the mayor won't hear of asking bigger cities for help."

I stared at Julian. It wasn't unusual to hear of drug busts back home in Columbus. But to hear of them in sleepy Thisbe Harbor? I couldn't imagine any of the residents I knew and loved during those childhood summers allowing drugs in the town.

"Businesses have shut down and the townsfolk are giving up." Julian motioned to the festival banners above us. "This was us giving this town one more shot."

"But why the name? I mean, Smallmouth Bass?" Theo scratched his head. "It's not exactly appealing."

"Rumor has it the mayor went on a fishing trip and got the 'brilliant idea' there. But I don't know if that's true or not. Either way, he's claiming this as the town's salvation and taking all the credit for it."

"What will happen now?" Theo asked. "The festival is a crime scene."

"That's not how this works!" Joel's voice rose.

I bit my lip, then shuffled a dozen paces toward the side of the office building. It wasn't eavesdropping if they were the ones talking loudly and I just so happened to be standing nearby, right?

Theo's eyes nearly bugged out of his face, and he motioned for me to rejoin him and Julian. But I shook my head. The mayor and Joel's conversation didn't seem to be going well. And whatever they said would impact my aunt—my family.

"We need this festival. We've been advertising for months, and the turnout is supposed to be the biggest we've seen in a while. If this festival doesn't move forward . . ." The mayor growled. "I won't let anything get in the way of this."

"This is a murder investigation, Mr. Mayor. Someone has died," Joel said. "And it's my job to figure out who did it and why. I can't do that if—"

"You already know who did it and why. Penelope was no friend of Owens. Everyone in town knows that. Do you know how many complaints I've received of the two of them bickering in public? You've got your murderer, Laurent. Case closed. The festival goes on."

My heart thudded in my chest. Was the mayor saying what I think he was saying? He wasn't even going to give my aunt a fair chance? Not that she wasn't suspicious, even I heard her threaten the marina owner, but this wasn't fair. Other people hated him too.

"Sir, with all due respect, that—"

"No. Not another word or I'll have your job. We need this festival, and that is that."

I leaned forward in an attempt to hear Joel's response. Was he really going to let this guy bully him into not investigating? What kind of mayor did that? Having a murderer running around town was not worth some stupid festival. Smallmouth bass. Who even cared about smallmouth bass anyway?

The mayor marched around the corner of the building right to where I was standing. I startled and jumped back. His gaze narrowed, and his plump cheeks reddened. He crossed his arms over his chest.

I reached over and straightened one of the streamers draped around the bush next to me. "Just finishing up these decorations?" I gave a forced laugh. But something told me he didn't appreciate my excuse.

"Are you a festival volunteer?" he snapped.

"No, but I—"

Joel strode into view and paused at the corner of the building. He glanced at me, then the mayor, and his eyes widened. He hurried over and pasted a gruff expression on his face. "Miss, I told you yesterday that the festival doesn't open until this afternoon. That was posted online where you would've seen the event." He motioned toward the mayor. "Sorry, Mr. Mayor. This *tourist* was here yesterday trying to get early access to the boat tours. I told her yesterday that she'd have to wait in line along with everyone else."

The mayor's anger dissipated, and he gave me a slimy sneer. "Oh, a tourist?" He scrutinized me as if calculating how much money this festival could fleece out of me. Too bad for him, I had hardly anything to my name. "Well, yes. The police chief is right. Festival starts at one sharp with a kick-off speech by yours truly. Boat tour sign-ups open after that. See you at the festival."

Joel gave me a hard look, and panic swirled in me. Was I supposed to say something else? Did he need me to really sell this cover? I slipped back in front of the mayor and forced my own too-bright grin. "Are you sure you can't give me early access? As the mayor and everything, surely you"—Joel facepalmed behind us. Okay, so wrong move. But it was too late to back out now—"can do something for me?"

The mayor's lips twisted into the slightest of snarls before his professionalism slid back into place. "I'm sorry, but there's nothing I can do for you. If you'll excuse me, I have a great many things to prepare before the kickoff. I hope you enjoy the festival."

Before I could decide if I needed to say anything else, he hurried off. Joel sighed and started past me.

"Joel." I grabbed his arm, and he jolted to a stop. "What he said . . ." How did I admit that yes, I was eavesdropping and didn't like what I'd heard?

"Pro tip." Joel shook off my arm. "Stay out of his way, and don't let him know who you are."

Chapter Eight

We had to do something. *I* had to do something. They were going to blame my aunt for everything to save this stupid festival. And then what would that do to my grandfather?

I'd heard of more than one elderly person passing from a failed heart due to shock. Would it happen to Papa too? I'd never thought of my grandfather as elderly before. Theo had inherited his penchant for pranks and humor from Papa after all. But seeing the paramedics help him into my parent's car...he'd never seemed so old, so hunched.

Had my aunt even thought of Papa? Or was she once again so caught up in herself that nothing else mattered?

I straightened my shoulders and pursed my lips. If Aunt Penny was named a killer, it would destroy my grandfather. It would destroy my whole family. And I wasn't about to let my family go down without a fight.

"We need to prove her innocence." It took everything in me not to choke on the words as I wasn't sure I actually believed them. But that didn't matter. This was for Papa.

Theo scowled. "What are you talking about?"

"She didn't do this." I spoke the words with as much confidence as I could muster, although my insides were quaking. How could I convince everyone that my aunt was innocent when I wasn't even sure myself? "So we need to find out who did."

"You can't." Theo hissed the words. "Obstructing an investigation is against the law."

I snorted and shot back, "Says the one who whipped out his forensics card at the first sign of a police officer."

"I'm on the same team as them."

"Great. So if being on the same team as them means you get a pass for whatever, I'm on the same team too." I crossed my arms and nodded toward the parking lot. "After Joel's done, we need to get back to the house and put our heads together."

Theo opened his mouth to make what I was sure would be another protest, so I forged ahead. I explained everything I'd overheard from Joel and the mayor. "They're going to railroad her into accepting the blame. We have to do this for Papa's sake."

Theo muttered something under his breath, but he didn't complain further.

"Did you say you were more than happy to join the cause for Papa's sake?" I patted his shoulder. "So glad to see you come to reason."

Julian cleared his throat, and Theo and I pulled back from each other. I'd been so wrapped up in our conversation that I'd forgotten Julian could also hear our every word. He shoved his hands into his pockets and rocked back on his heels. "Do you think . . ." A frown flickered across his face, his eyebrows drawing together for a brief moment before he straightened his shoulders and faced me. "I'd like to help. If you'd let me."

My jaw nearly dropped. He wanted to help my crazy family? After I'd ghosted him?

"I know this town. Have lived here all my life." Julian waved a hand toward the crowd still milling around us. "People trust me."

Theo cocked his head and a slow, mischievous grin tugged at his lips. "It'll be just like old times." He nudged me and wiggled his shoulders. "What do you say, sis?"

Something twisted in my stomach. An image of Julian standing on my grandparents' doorstep, hand raised to knock on the door, flashed through my mind. The wide, white-toothed smile that spread across his face when I invited him to play. He'd come over nearly every day, every summer we spent in Thisbe. And then, I'd abandoned him.

The corner of my left eye twitched, and Theo's gaze narrowed. Curse my inheriting Dad's annoying tic. But I couldn't help the confusion that curled through me.

Julian swallowed hard and rocked back on his heels. "I mean, I don't want to impose. If you—"

"No!" I reached out and brushed my fingers over his arm. He jerked, and the knot in my chest tightened further. "I didn't—I was just—if you . . ." I dragged a hand through my hair.

Ugh, why was I acting like such a schoolgirl? I needed to get it together. I had a family to save. Julian's knowledge of the town and of those in the town would be invaluable for an investigation. "I'd love for you to join us. We could use your expertise." And now I sounded more formal than my dad on the first day of school.

"Great. I'll just"—he paused and glanced down at his shirt—"go home and change first."

My cheeks burned hotter than the Lake Erie sun. In the chaos of everything, I'd forgotten my earlier "greeting" to Julian.

Theo clapped me on the back. "My sister always was unforgettable."

"I'll meet you in half an hour?" Julian asked.

I chewed on my lower lip. Even though the investigation was for Papa's sake, we needed to make sure he was okay first. "Make it an hour?"

He nodded. "How about I call before I head over? Number still the same?"

I stiffened and studied his dark eyes for a long moment. Admit that yes, I still had his contact information after all this time, or pretend that my number had changed and the possibility of our contact lost with it? "It's the same," I whispered.

"I'll see you later then." And he jogged away.

Mom was baking again. Scents of apples and cloves swarmed around me as we stepped through the front door of the BnB.

Theo raised an eyebrow. As kids, Mom could always be found in the kitchen baking treats for us or next door neighbors or a friend at church whose meal train she'd signed up for. But ever since she'd gone back to work nearly eight years ago, she hadn't darkened the door of a kitchen except when she was stressed. Looking back on it, maybe she baked so much when we were younger because she needed the stress-relief from us.

"Welcome." Mom walked down the hall, her usually heavy footsteps padded by the thick wool socks she wore. "Your papa is down the hall resting so please stay as quiet as possible. The only way the paramedics allowed him back here is if he promised to lay down in a quiet area."

I immediately walked over and hugged her tight, her usual smells of vanilla and lavender intermingled with cinnamon and sugar. Pulling back slightly, I studied Mom's face. Tense creases surrounded her eyes and mouth, and even though she'd hugged me as warmly as always, I could feel the tightness of her muscles and see the pain in her gaze.

"Apple crisp is in the oven. It'll be ready in an hour." She smoothed a hand over my frizzy curls. "You doing okay?"

I shrugged one shoulder. Since dropping out of college, I'd been so intent on finding out who I was and what I was meant to do. Life held so many options, so many possibilities, and I was overwhelmed. Still was.

But that was no excuse. I'd been blind for too long to the division burdening my family.

I hugged my mom again and breathed in her bakery smell. If only Mimi were here to capture the scent in one of her signature candles.

"I think the question is: are *you* all right?" I asked. Aunt Penny was her sister after all.

She pinched the bridge of her nose, her telltale sign that she was trying not to cry. "Well, I can't say this is how I expected the weekend to go."

"So what's the plan?" my brother asked.

"Well, I'm hoping Rubin—your Uncle Rob—will be able to give us some sort of update," Mom said. "I gave him a call as soon as we got Dad settled in, and he promised to contact the police station while on his way to the airport to come here."

"Interrogations can take a while." Theo wrinkled his nose and leaned against the wall. "Especially with someone like Aunt Penny."

Mom sucked in a sharp breath and wrapped her arms around herself.

I glared at Theo and hissed, "Not helpful."

"Right. Sorry," he muttered.

Silence blanketed the hallway, but not with the comfortable, warm sensation blankets usually provide. This one felt itchy, scratching over my skin but unable to be thrown off.

"Do you think he'll see me?" I finally asked.

"I think he'd like nothing more." Mom nodded. "I'll bring in some dessert once it's ready."

I shuffled down the hallway to my grandfather's room. The sky-blue hallway walls decorated with fake seashells and white-framed pictures of Lake Erie mocked the somber mood that held the household in its grip. A sign hanging from the door to my grandfather's bedroom proclaimed: "Life is better at the beach."

If only the beach could solve all my family's problems.

I lightly knocked on the door and slipped inside after hearing my grandfather's murmur to come in.

He lay in bed, his wheelchair parked nearby, head tilted against his propped-up pillows and eyes closed. A gray pallor tinged his face and cheeks. I gripped the doorknob tighter.

"Papa?" I whispered.

"Why can't they get along?" His voice cracked, and he tugged the comforter further under his chin. "Why can't they love each other like they used to?"

I crept across the room and lowered myself onto the bed next to him. The white-painted iron bed creaked under my added weight, but I ignored the simultaneous flash of panic and annoyance that coursed through me. Instead, I lifted Papa's hand and kissed his wrinkled knuckles. The blue veins under his skin seemed even more pronounced than usual, and I shivered at how frail it made him appear.

"I'm sorry, Papa."

The morning sunlight beaming through the sheer gauzy curtains highlighted the tears that now trickled down his worn cheek. I wound my fingers through my grandfather's and tightened my grip on his hand.

"We're going to find out who did this," I promised.

"What?" Papa tilted his head toward me, focusing on mine for the first time.

"We're going to figure this out. Me, Theo, and Julian." I pressed my lips to his hand again. "We're going to clear her name."

Hope flashed in his face, and he squeezed my hand back. "She didn't do this. My Penny would never."

Words stuck in my throat. I wanted to reassure him, to tell him I agreed. But the truth was, my aunt wasn't the sweet lady my grandfather remembered. She was ruthless and cold when it came to getting what she wanted. And based on the conversation Theo and I overheard on the docks, she wanted something from the marina owner. Wanted something badly.

The light dimmed in my grandfather's eyes. But my thoughts didn't matter. Right now, Papa needed something—he needed hope—to cling to.

"She didn't do it," I said, although it felt like a lie. "And I'm going to prove it."

Chapter Nine

A bell tinkled overhead as we stepped into Dine on a Dime, the local sandwich shop boasting "Best Cuban Sandwich" and "Come for the Smells, Stay for the Food" in neon signs across the front window. Mom wasn't too happy about Theo and I disappearing for lunch, but if I was going to keep my promise to Papa, we needed to start investigating. I only hoped Julian could give us a place to start.

Waitresses bustled around the red, orange, and yellow room, offering mugs of hot coffee and depositing overladen trays. I couldn't help squinting against the too-bright, garish retro coloring of the room—red chairs, orange-and-white-striped ceiling and walls, and yellow tables. And to top it all off, vomit green carpet under my feet.

Julian grinned at my obvious distaste. This place hadn't been updated since the 1970s and it really showed. Papa had always loved taking my brother and me to the mom-and-pop stores and hole-in-the-wall restaurants as kids, but I didn't remember them being quite this retro.

Theo coughed. "Well, one thing's for sure. I certainly wouldn't be staying for the smells."

"Come on, you used to love it here." Julian laughed and elbowed Theo in the side. "You couldn't forget their Reubens, could you? You would eat one almost every day!"

A waitress dressed in a screaming orange skirt and top complete with a cherry red apron strode up to us. She smacked gum between her lips then lifted her clipboard. "Table for three?"

Julian wrapped an arm around my shoulders, sending a wave of heat prickling over my skin and butterflies swirling in my stomach. "Yes, ma'am."

The waitress turned and motioned us forward with long, manicured red nails. "This way." We'd barely taken two steps forward when she flung over her shoulder, "Who's the girl?" Her gum popped again. "Can't recall seeing you with her before."

A knot pinched in my chest. Had he come here with other girls before? Was he actually dating someone? All of a sudden, I couldn't remember if he'd said he was single.

Not that I cared. Definitely didn't care.

I tried to be as nonchalant as possible as I shrugged off Julian's arm. No need to make this look any worse than it already did. "Um, we're not—"

"Come on, Sue Helen, you remember Beatrice and Theo, right?" Julian called to her over the noise. "Sawyer's grandkids?"

The waitress paused in front of an empty barstool and chairs and raised her manicured hand to her lips. "So you're related to that crazy woman? The one who killed Mr. Owens?"

"What?" I blinked. I'd forgotten how quickly news traveled in small towns.

Sue Helen slapped two menus onto the table then stilled. "Wait a minute. I do remember ya." She pointed a finger at my brother. "You're the kid who always came in for a Reuben with extra salty fries and a vanilla shake. Then you'd dip your fries in your milkshake and make a melted mess all over my floor. My shoes were always sticky when ya visited."

The memory clicked in my mind. This really was the "sammich shop" I'd forever craved? Every summer I'd return home and rave to my parents about their food and shakes. Mom called the place a time warp, but I'd never understood. Until now. They probably hadn't updated since Mom was a child.

Funny how a place can appear so different when seeing it through jaded eyes.

I turned my attention back to the waitress. Sue Helen rambled on, apparently unconcerned that I hadn't answered her first question, "Pretty involved, if you ask me."

"I'm sorry." I shook myself and slid onto the nearest chair. "What was that?"

"Heard your aunt was found with the body. Sounds like she's pretty involved in the murder then, eh?" She leaned against the table, eyes gleaming, waiting for any juicy tidbit of gossip to pass around.

Exactly why we came here. Except I expected to be the one interrogating.

I crossed my arms on the table and gave her my best innocent look. "Have you heard anything about the situation?"

The waitress straightened, lips slightly curled. "Maeve came in this morning afterward. A mess, that one. Said the marina would be closed for a few days without pay and everyone knows she can't afford that."

"What do you mean?"

"Everyone in this town can use a little cash, honey. Some of us just need it more than others."

"Did she say anything about the cause of death?" Theo asked, and I could almost see his investigator senses tingling.

The waitress snorted and planted her hands on her hips. "As if that police chief would say anything to anyone." She paused and shot a sheepish glance at Julian. "No offense to your brother, of course."

"Sue!" someone bellowed from the back.

The waitress wrinkled her nose and stuck out her tongue near the direction of the kitchen. "Ya'd think if ya owned the place, ya could do whatcha want. But Harold's always yellin' at me for gossipin' instead of waitressin'." She pulled a pencil and pad of paper from the front pocket of her apron. "What can I get you? And be quick. Harold don't like waitin'."

Theo and I both ordered a Reuben sandwich with a chocolate milkshake while Julian opted for the daily special. The waitress clicked her pen three times and scribbled our order on her notepad. After we all agreed to extra salty fries and coleslaw, she was off.

"Strangulation." Theo rubbed his hands together.

"What are you talking about?" I asked.

"The red burn marks on his neck and the scratches on his cheek. The man was strangulated. With a small rope of some sort."

I blinked at my brother. It always shocked me what hidden details my brother picked up on and what obvious things he missed.

He puffed out his chest. "Investigator training, you know. We have to notice everything."

"Then maybe forensics isn't the field for you." I snorted. "Remember the year Dad hid your Easter basket right next to your bed and it took you till morning the next day to find it?"

"That was back when I was young. I've—"

"Or when we were trying to leave yesterday and you couldn't find your shoes. Even though they were on the mat right in front of the door." I pressed a hand to my chest in mock pride. "You've grown up so much, my dear brother."

"I don't remember asking your opinion." He pointedly turned to Julian. "Am I right?"

Julian frowned then shrugged. "I mean, when you said you were an investigator in training, you kind of invited—"

"Not about that!" My brother huffed. "About the strangulation."

"Oh. Joel doesn't tell me anything—work policy and all that."

"Aunt Penny didn't have any rope on her, though." I straightened my shoulders and leaned forward. "So it couldn't have been her."

"I said 'a rope of some sort,'" Theo reminded me with a self-important straightening of his shoulders. "She wore a headband, if I remember. And carried that purse with the thin little straps. Great strangulation devices. Especially that kind of purse. You could twist it around the victim's neck and put a little distance between yourself and—"

I groaned and slapped my hand to my forehead. "Theo." What a conversation to be having in public. Giving everyone ideas how to knock off someone they didn't like.

"Remind me not to ever make you two mad," Julian muttered.

"So Aunt Penny isn't in the clear. I get it. But who else are our suspects?" I asked. "Cause we're operating under the assumption Aunt Penny didn't do it."

"But is that really a good assumption?" Theo broke in. "After all—"

I glared at him. "Do you want to be part of this investigation or not?"

"I'm just saying, if we want to be true—"

"We have to do this. I sure don't want my claim to fame to be that my aunt went to jail for murder. Especially not when I also have a brother who likes to spout off facts about how anything can be used as a murder weapon."

"Well, you're not wrong." He swiped a spoon from his napkin-rolled utensils. "This, for example—"

Julian burst out laughing, drowning away any gory details my brother was sure to have shared. At the interruption, Theo frowned, his eyebrows drawing together in genuine confusion.

"Thank you." I rolled my eyes toward my brother. "Otherwise, we would've been stuck here for the next century hearing all the uses of a spoon in murder. Can we get back on track, please? Who would want the marina owner dead?"

Chapter Ten

"Daily special?" A waitress that wasn't Sue Helen appeared at the side of our table.

I jumped, and my chair started to topple sideways. I scrabbled for the edge of the table, managing to grab it just in time to right myself. My cheeks blazed. Real smooth, Beatrice.

The waitress chuckled, then raised an eyebrow. "Sorry. Didn't mean to scare you."

"That's me." Julian raised a hand. "Then the two Reubens go to them." He pointed to me and Theo.

A five inch tall sandwich slid in front of me, the small dish of coleslaw barely visible under a pile of fries. I popped a fry into my mouth and relished the salty goodness. You never could go wrong with French fries.

The moment the waitress left, Theo shot not-so-subtle looks around the room. Most of the restaurant-goers were focused on their food or in conversation with those at their table.

"Who are our suspects?" Theo ticked off on his fingers. "Means, motive, opportunity. That's what we need to figure out. We know the means—strangulation—which we've already discussed nearly anyone can do."

"Now we need to figure out who could and why," Julian finished.

I bit into my sandwich, and dressing dribbled down my chin. What we needed to know was who stood to benefit from Mr. Owens's death. But how was I to know when I didn't even know Mr. Owens? When I didn't know anyone in town, really.

I chewed thoughtfully and swiped a napkin across my chin. What did I know about Mr. Owens? That he was a jerk and no one seemed to like him. The two times I'd seen the guy, he was yelling at someone.

The image of an irate receptionist, grabbing her purse and swinging it over her shoulder, came to mind. My aunt hadn't been the only one to argue with Owens the day before.

Owens had said something about a mistake to his receptionist. And if she made any more, he'd make her regret it. Maeve had seemed crushed at first, but by the time she'd left . . . What was it she said?

"When you've wronged as many people as he has, no one much cares if you live or die." Her words echoed in my mind.

"You're deep in thought," Julian murmured next to me.

I swallowed, then asked, "How much do either of you know about Maeve?"

"She seemed pretty ticked at Owens," Theo said.

I nodded. "Owens said something about her making a mistake. And if it happened again, he'd make her regret it." I recalled the waitress's words from earlier. "She was short on cash, and if he was threatening her job, well, people get desperate when it comes to money."

"She's always been nice to me." Julian shrugged. "Quiet, closed off. I can't say I know much about her, and I don't often see her around town."

Not much to go on, but it was a start.

"What about that old guy? The one who attacked you." Theo waved his phone in the air. "I have footage that proves he has a temper and he isn't afraid to hurt people."

"Vincent?" Julian raised an eyebrow. "I've seen him around the marina a few times."

"Arguing with Owens?" Theo asked.

"Just kind of skulking around. Muttering to himself. He seems like a loner."

Theo frowned and crossed his arms over his chest. "We brought you in on this investigation because you were supposed to know people. Know this town. So far, you've given us a whole lotta nothing."

A flush deepened the color of Julian's cheeks. "Okay, so maybe I'm a bit of a loner myself, but college is expensive and there's not much around here. Joel is letting me stay in his apartment for free until I get my feet under me."

I tilted my head. Julian avoided my gaze and twisted his fingers in his napkin. He appeared so put together, so confident. Other than his beater car and this confession, I never would've guessed that he was in the same place of life as I was—struggling.

I picked up a fry and threw it at him. Not the most mature, but how else was I supposed to break the awkward silence?

The fry hit him square in the forehead, and he startled. I grinned at him, and my smile only widened when he grinned back. His eyes sparkled, and something fluttered in my chest. I'd missed our friendship. Missed him.

Theo cleared his throat. "Hello, third wheel here." He snorted.

Oh if the world were rid of brothers.

I glared at him and sucked down the rest of my milkshake to cool my face.

"I think we need to back up a bit," Theo said in his superior I-know-more-than-you-do voice. "We're getting too much in the weeds of the investigation, and we just started."

"Oh ye of wise investigator knowledge." I gave a mock half bow in my chair. "Lead us in the paths of true investigating and guide us with your mighty powers."

Theo pretended to flick his hair over his shoulder. "I'm glad you finally recognize my prowess." His grin faded. "But seriously. I think we need to back up. We need to find out more about Owens. We don't even know the guy, yet we're trying to point fingers. Means, motive, and opportunity, remember? We can't figure out the motive if we don't know who Owens was."

"Other than the fact that he was a jerk?" I asked.

"There are plenty of jerks in the world. But only the extra jerks are killed."

The extra jerks?

"There's gotta be some other motive." Theo raised his hands. "That's all I'm saying."

I slowly nodded and tapped my fingers against the table. When we'd confronted Aunt Penny after her tirade against Owens, she had said something that I hadn't connected until now. She wanted the marina. And her threat to do whatever it took to get it from Owens was her motive. But why did she want the marina, and if this place was struggling as much as everyone said, why wouldn't Owens sell? While my aunt wasn't the most pleasant person to be around, she wasn't a cheapskate. She would've offered Owens more than a fair deal. Why didn't he take it?

"How long until the festival kickoff?" I asked.

Julian slid his phone from his back pocket. I had to stop myself from leaning over and reading the screen like I would if he were my brother. Mom always said I was too nosy, and I suppose my enjoyment of snooping other people's phone screens proved that.

"Half an hour," Julian said and pocketed his phone again. "Do you want to go?"

"I think we should talk to Aunt Penny." I explained my questions to them and said, "She might be able to give us some insight into who might've wanted to do away with Owens."

"That's a good idea. It's a place to start, at least." Julian paused. "But I don't think I should go with you. If I'm there, Joel will know we're butting into his investigation. But if it's just you two . . . well, you're her family."

"If I go, she might think we're ganging up on her. You know, both of us against her," Theo said quickly. "I'll head back and convince Papa to come to the festival. It'd be good for him to get out of the house and do something fun. Right?"

I narrowed my gaze at him. He just didn't want to talk to Aunt Penny, and he knew I knew that. But he was right. It would do Papa good to go to the festival, and if anyone could convince him, it'd be Theo.

"Beans & Leaves is supposed to have a food truck at the festival. We can meet there and grab coffee or tea?" Julian said. "It'll be a little black truck with what looks like a cross between Buckeye nuts and marijuana leaves on the side. I don't know who thought of their logo, but they make a good cup of coffee."

Theo laughed. "You sure they don't add anything extra to it?"

After we'd paid for our meals, we split ways, and I headed the five blocks downtown to the police station. The single-story, brown brick building stood by the road, a hundred or so feet away from the tracks.

The police station used to be an old train station, and while trains still occasionally passed through, they never stopped here anymore. White letters marked the side of the building: Thisbe Harbor Police Station, and under that, a bronze plaque read: "This Property Has Been Placed on the National Register of Historic Places by the United States Department of the Interior."

Sweat dampened the armpits of my t-shirt by the time I walked up to the steps. I yanked open the door and closed my eyes in sweet relief at the blast of air conditioning that shot down my sticky neck.

Wood panels lined the atrium's walls, and wooden benches sat along the wall closest to the door for those who needed to wait for assistance. Opposite the front door, a desk area was built into the wall, a glass partition protecting the staff behind it from any unseemly criminals. This place was definitely built to be functional rather than pretty.

An older woman with white curly hair pushed her spectacles further up her nose. "Can I help you, dear?"

The front door opened and closed again, and a chuckle came from behind me. "Beatrice Sawyer. I should've guessed."

"Back so soon, Chief?" the older lady asked.

"Left my volunteer shirt in the back," Joel explained. He came to stand in front of me and crossed his arms. "What can I do for you, Miss Sawyer?"

"I'd like to talk to my aunt," I said. Then added, "Please?"

"About?"

"My family. And why she would do this to us. Especially Papa."

He dropped his arms to his sides. "Well, I'm not one to keep family away from family."

"Chief." The older lady pointed to the clock on the wall. "Your appointment with the mayor is in five minutes."

Distaste flashed across Joel's face, but he quickly replaced it with his usual expressionless mask. "I know. But being a few minutes late won't kill the man. Especially not for this." Without further comment, Joel led me to the back of the station where a row of three solid oak doors lined the hall.

A police officer stood guard by one of the doors, and he nodded at us as Joel stopped in front of the first room and knocked. "Ma'am, this is Chief Joel. Beatrice has requested to see you, if you're willing to allow me to admit her?"

"You're the one with the key, so I don't know why you're asking me," Aunt Penny snapped. "Just let her in."

Joel nearly took a step back in surprise. I covered my mouth to hide a smirk. Despite his tough cop act, even Joel couldn't help but startle at Aunt Penny's determination to strike fear in the hearts of all.

"Well then," Joel muttered, "sounds like you'll have a lot of fun. You have ten minutes."

Aunt Penny sat on the edge of a cot, legs swinging over the side. Despite the calm, cold expression on her face, she looked like she'd been on the run for a week rather than sitting in a jail cell overnight.

Someone must've brought her a change of clothes because she now wore a pair of skinny jeans and a wrinkled olive t-shirt. I don't even remember the last time I'd seen my aunt in a normal t-shirt rather than a blouse or dress shirt and suit coat. Her manicured nails were bitten to the quick, and her usually perfectly in place brown hair frizzed out from a sad attempt at a bun.

She pursed her lips, crossed her legs, then clasped her hands over her knee—the perfect picture of a frazzled model. "Helene send you to gloat?"

"What?" I wrinkled my nose. Did she really think that poorly of my mother? "No. Why would she do that?"

Aunt Penny sniffed at my lack of response and turned her face toward the wall. But not before I thought I detected the faintest shimmer in her eyes. She swallowed and muttered, "I would've expected her to be thrilled to see me in here."

"She misses you," I blurted, not sure what made me say the words. Now that I had, though, I realized they were true. Mom missed her older sister, and that's why it hurt so much for them to fight.

Aunt Penny sucked in a sharp breath, and for a moment, I thought her hardened exterior would crack. But she shook her head and tightened her grip on her knee. "How's Dad?"

"He's..." Devastated. Heartbroken. How could you be so selfish? All ran through my mind as potential answers. But I couldn't let my own frustration ruin this chance to speak with her. Licking my lips, I answered, "He still believes in you."

Aunt Penny's eyes widened for a fraction of a second and her face blanched.

"Why are you in here, Aunt Penny?" I asked. "What happened? Why were you threatening him yesterday?"

"I wasn't threatening him." She crossed her arms. "Is that what you told the police? No wonder I'm stuck in here!"

I ground my teeth. Of course she'd blame me. Because she could never do anything wrong. But getting angry wouldn't solve anything. "Please, Aunt Penny. I want to understand. I want to believe you."

She stared at me for a long moment, and I tried to infuse a plea into my gaze. I did want to help her. I did want to believe in her. She was my aunt, and I wanted the old days with her back again.

A knock shattered the silence. "Miss Sawyer, I'm sorry to cut this short, but I have to leave for the festival now."

I could've screamed. I'd been so close. So close to reconnecting with her again. But a glance back at Aunt Penny, and I knew she wouldn't speak now. She stared at the floor, shoulders hunched.

Joel opened the door and motioned for me to come out.

I sucked in a deep breath and said, "If you need anything, Aunt Penny, we're just a phone call away. Okay?"

She didn't answer, and Joel shut the door behind me.

Chapter Eleven

Not even Joel's genuine apology and offer to drive me to the festival could dampen my frustration. I opted to walk, knowing I needed the time to clear my head and figure out my next steps.

What would have happened if Aunt Penny had been given enough of an opportunity to speak? After all these years, could Papa's dream have finally come true?

I slowed my walk and leaned up against the ivy-covered wall of the nearest brick building—yet another forever-closed downtown shop. My heart raced in my chest, but I didn't know if it was from the walk or from the hope now rising within me.

Maybe, in a weird twist of fate, Aunt Penny's being accused of murder would be what our family needed to pull back together. If I could clear her name, that might prove to her and mom that family was worth fighting for.

I thrust off the wall and headed further downtown. The closer to the opposite side of the town I got, the busier the road and sidewalks became. Tourists milled about, and cars parked every which way by the sidewalk and in any open grassy area. A ferris wheel had been erected by the waterway, and children hooted with laughter as they waited their turn. Dozens of food trucks lined the marina parking lot, and several boats putted about in the sparkling harbor.

The spark of hope in my chest flared a bit brighter. While I didn't appreciate the mayor's crass manner, he was right about one thing—Thisbe Harbor was also worth fighting for. It was home.

I startled at the thought. Home was the bustling metropolis of Columbus. Where you were one person in a thousand struggling to find your place in the world. But I couldn't stop the feeling of peace, despite the chaos of life, that surrounded me when I stepped into Thisbe Harbor. This was my safe haven as a child. Could it perhaps be the same now that I was an adult?

And Julian lived here.

I pushed the thought aside. Now wasn't the time. First things first, I had a murder to solve. A family to save.

I joined the throng of people crossing the threshold of dying town to bustling festival. The Smallmouth Bass Festival banner gently rocked in the breeze and welcomed all.

"Beatrice!"

I paused at the sound of my name and turned in a full circle. Julian stood by the white pole supporting one side of the banner and waved his arms above his head. I grinned and hurried over to him.

"What happened to meeting at the coffee truck?" I asked.

"There's a lot more people here than I thought. I didn't want you to have trouble finding it," he said.

I fell into step next to him, and we wove around white tents and swarms of kids and adults to a black food truck near the front doors of the marina office building. Bright white, swirling letters announced the truck as Beans & Leaves, and what indeed looked like overlarge Buckeye nuts nestled among marijuana leaves was painted beneath.

The aroma of freshly baked cinnamon buns iced with homemade cream cheese icing and vanilla bean scones settled around me like a cozy blanket. Behind the counter, one barista pulled a shot of espresso and steamed some milk while another handed two cups out the window to a waiting customer.

Julian lightly rested a hand on my back and waved his other arm toward the counter. "Order what you want. My treat."

I clucked my tongue. "You realize my dad always taught me that when a boy offered to pay for something, I should buy the most expensive thing, right?"

"Good thing I brought my credit card then." He winked and pulled his wallet from his back pocket.

We slid into line, and I studied the chalkboard menu displayed near the window. Dozens of flavors of coffee and tea were written in curly letters across the board. A coffee truck with flavored coffee in Thisbe Harbor? Despite the run-down appearance of the rest of the town, Thisbe must be moving up in the world to have a place like this. For as long as I could remember, Papa hated that the only coffee you could buy around town was the burnt dregs at Dine on a Dime or gas station coffee that tasted strangely like aluminum.

"Oh, Jules! You're back in town?" The barista pulling espresso shots stepped up to the window and flipped her brunette curls over her shoulders. Her black t-shirt plunged into a deep V-neck, and her apron hung low enough to allow any and all to see her display, especially as she leaned over the counter to bat her eyes at Julian.

I pursed my lips. My fingers twitched to tug up her apron then lecture her on decency. After watching my cousin on my dad's side barista for nearly three years, I knew how hard they worked behind the counter, and there's no way I wanted sweat in my latte.

Julian's jaw clenched ever so slightly, but then he gave her a smile that was too friendly, in my opinion. "Hey, uh, good to see you."

Miss Sweaty Latte tucked a stray hair behind her ear. "Oh, you always were so sweet. How long are you here for?"

I looked between him and this barista. Apparently there was a history between them that I had no idea about. Either that or this lady wished there was some history between them.

"Um, I'm here off and on. Been working a lot before school starts back up." Julian shifted uncomfortably, then glanced up at the menu and back at me. "Know what you want?"

I wanted to gag, but I said, "I'll have a large iced matcha latte with extra cinnamon on top and one of those cinnamon buns." According to the menu board, they crafted all sorts of matcha deliciousness—matcha with raspberry syrup, matcha with almond extract, and on and on. But in my opinion, if a coffee shop couldn't make a delicious basic matcha and cinnamon bun, then they weren't worth my money. Time to put Beans & Leaves to the test.

The barista scoffed and wrinkled her nose. "I'm sorry, but Julian here was in front of you." She beamed at him again. "What can I get you, Jules?"

"Um, she's actually with me." Julian pulled one hand from his pocket and rubbed the back of his neck.

"Oh." Her syrupy look turned sour, and for some reason, I felt thrilled knowing that the reason was me. "You said a matcha latte?"

"With extra cinnamon. And a cinnamon bun."

"And I'll have a salted caramel cappuccino with almond milk," Julian said.

"Bun on the house?" The barista winked, and this time, I couldn't help rolling my eyes.

"No thanks. Can't have dairy."

Her smile dropped for the second time, and it was everything I could do not to pump my fist in triumph. Not that I knew Julian was dairy-free until now, but it was oddly satisfying to see her desperation crushed. Was that wrong of me? Probably. But there was a reason I was never in with the popular girls in high school. Desperate and flirty weren't my thing.

"Right." She focused on the cash register, rang up the order, and let Julian pay without another word.

Once we'd been served our drinks and my cinnamon bun, Julian led me around the side of the truck, tucked a bit away from the crowd. I took a sip of my latte. The milk and matcha melded together smoothly, no chunks or grainy bits from the powdered matcha detectable. And the added cinnamon contrasted with the earthy taste of the matcha perfectly. Julian was right. This place could make a good matcha. I took another sip. Perhaps even better than my go-to coffee shop at home.

If I was honest, I was a little surprised Julian's number one fan hadn't tried to sabotage my drink.

"What do you think?" Julian asked.

A devilish grin upturned my lips. "Are you sure you don't want one of those . . . 'on the house cinnamon buns?'"

I'd never seen him blush so hard before, and I couldn't help giving a little cackle.

"That's not what I was asking," he said.

"It's good." I wiggled my eyebrows. "But not as good as—"

"Okay, okay!" He swatted at me, and I jumped out of the way with a little squeak. "You're so funny." He shook his head. "How did your talk with Penny go?"

My laughter faded, and I sighed. "It was complicated." I shared everything my aunt had said and Joel's interruption before Aunt Penny could say anything very useful.

"Complicated is the right word," Julian said. "What are you going to do now?"

Something moved behind Julian, and I shifted my stance to get a better look. Yellow crime scene tape blockaded the front doors of the marina office building, but a stout man in a tan suit paused in front of the doors. He glanced both ways, then shoved his hands in his pockets and hurried around the side of the building. Was that the mayor?

"Beatrice?" Julian lightly touched my arm. "Are you okay?"

"Is there a back door to the office building?"

"Yeah. Why?"

"Is anyone supposed to be in the building?" I started past him.

"No, Joel convinced the mayor to at least let him close that off as a crime scene. Where are you going?"

I ran along the back of the food trucks lining the front of the marina building. Thankfully, the crowd kept the truck owners busy enough that no one seemed to be paying any attention. Even if that man was the mayor, I didn't think he was supposed to be messing with Joel's crime scene. Not that I could think of a motive for him—he'd been furious with Joel at the potentiality of canceling the festival. He wouldn't murder someone and put his festival at risk . . . Unless he wanted the crime scene to be contaminated by the festival goers.

It'd be the perfect cover. Pretend to want to save your town, when in reality, you only want to hide your murderous tracks.

"Are you crazy?" Julian grabbed my arm and pulled me to a stop. "We can't go in there!"

"We have to find out what's going on," I said.

"There are better ways to find out about Owens than breaking and entering. Joel will have our heads if he catches us."

"No, it's not about that." I motioned toward the building. "Your mayor just snuck around the side. I think we should see what he's doing."

His eyes widened, and he lowered his head toward mine. "Mayor Gilberth? Are you sure?"

"He walks like a penguin. I'd recognize it anywhere. Besides, who else would wear a suit to the festival?"

Julian glanced at his phone. "His talk is in thirty minutes, though."

"Plenty of time for him to sneak around. Now, are you coming or not?"

He sucked in a breath and rubbed a hand over his forehead. "Why do I let you talk me into these things?"

Chapter Twelve

B ecause you're a good friend.

The words stuck in my throat.

Something pinched in my chest, and I swallowed hard. He'd always been a good friend. And then I'd left. Never calling, never texting, for all those years.

Sucking in a deep breath, I mentally prepared my apology. But what could I say? That I'd been so engrossed in myself I'd shut out everyone? Shut him out until I felt too afraid to call?

After we'd stopped coming every summer to Thisbe, life had become a whirlwind—high school, Mimi's passing, college, dropping out of college, feeling like a failure. Papa had told me when Julian's mother had passed, and I'd wanted to call. I'd stared at my phone for over an hour trying to convince myself, but I never could make myself press the button. It'd been too long, I'd failed too much, and I didn't know what to say. What could a person who'd failed at so much tell someone who was grieving? I had no hope for myself much less any hope to offer someone else.

"Are we going?" Julian's voice broke through my spiral of thoughts.

I startled out of my thoughts. Now wasn't the time to wax long with an apology. But it needed to happen. I owed him an explanation.

It wasn't fair to him to pretend things were just like they used to be. He deserved a better friend than that.

I shook my head and focused on the task at hand. I'd talk to him after this craziness blew over.

We crept along the side of the building. Heat radiated from the aluminum, and sweat trickled down the back of my neck. If I'd known it'd be this hot—and that I'd be chasing criminals and getting nervously sweaty—I'd have changed into a tank top. But too late now.

When we rounded the corner to the back, I paused. A concrete block had been wedged in between the back door, holding it open.

"It's our lucky day," Julian murmured. "Let me go first."

He tiptoed forward and stilled by the crack in the door. I held my breath, straining to hear anything from inside, but after several quiet moments, Julian motioned me forward. He opened the door just enough for me to slip inside, then followed.

Still, muggy air swarmed around me, and I could almost feel the moisture beading on my skin. With no one working inside, they must have shut the AC off to conserve electricity. Three doors stood in the short hallway, one to either side of us, and one straight ahead. A rustling, followed by a slamming drawer, came from the door to our right. The beam of a flashlight swept underneath the door, and heavy footsteps scurried across the room.

"Where is it?" a voice muttered inside.

Julian tapped me on the shoulder, and when he had my attention, he made a texting motion with his hands, then a gun symbol with his fingers. He wanted to call his brother? Joel would never forgive us if he found us snooping in here.

I shook my head.

Julian frowned, then leaned forward and whispered, "What's the plan?"

"We need to figure out what he's searching for," I whispered back. "Then we have concrete evidence for Joel."

"Isn't breaking and entering evidence enough that something's going on?"

Another drawer slammed inside the office. I ignored Julian's concern and stretched out on the floor. The acrid, smoky scent of cigarette smoke permeated the carpet, nearly overpowered by the thick smell of too many chemical-infused carpet fresheners. I gagged and held my breath as I rested my cheek on the floor. Thankfully, the puke-colored carpet was so worn and matted, I had a clear view under the door.

Two massive filing cabinets lined the wall directly opposite me, and a desk littered with papers and books stood to the right. Light peeked in from the grime-covered window and illuminated the mayor's polished shoes in front of the filing cabinets.

He knelt, yanked the bottom drawer open, and shuffled through the folders. "Contracts. Contracts. Contracts. This is chaos in here," he grumbled. "How did the man expect to find anything?" He shoved the drawer shut again and struggled to his feet. "It has to be here somewhere!"

The mayor crossed to the desk, and I lost sight of him. I tried to adjust my position, sweeping my feet around so I could switch the side I was laying on. But I forgot Julian standing behind me.

My legs smacked into the back of his knees. He stumbled forward and thumped against the wall to catch himself. I cringed.

"Who's there?" the mayor called out.

Footsteps thudded across the floor.

I scrambled to my feet right as the door swung open.

The mayor stood in the doorway, a manila envelope clutched to his chest and his eyes wide. When his gaze landed on me, he growled. "You. What are you doing here?"

I shot Julian a panicked look. My plan hadn't accounted for getting caught and actually talking to the mayor, much less being recognized. But my friend's face was like a deer facing down death in the headlights of a car. I was on my own.

"Isn't this a crime scene?" I blurted and wrapped my arms around myself.

The mayor flicked a glance toward the envelope in his hands, then straightened his shoulders. "Yes. Which means you two need to leave immediately. This isn't a place to be messing around."

"Aw, we just thought we'd take a peek. I mean, I've never seen a real crime scene before. And to think a murder happened in here!" I infused giddiness into my voice and forced a preppy girl giggle. "Could we have a souvenir too?"

"A what?" The mayor pulled back and frowned.

"A souvenir." I motioned toward the envelope. "Isn't that what you have?"

He spluttered for a moment, his cheeks turning eggplant. "Souvenir. Young lady, you think this is a souvenir? I don't need to take souvenirs from a crime scene. I am the mayor!"

I shrugged. "Sure. But I don't know why else you'd take something from a *crime* scene."

His cheeks turned more of a prune color. Maybe I'd gone a bit far . . . I slowly took a step backward.

The back door banged open.

"Police!" A voice shouted. "Put your hands in the air."

I yelped and flung my hands into the air. Julian groaned behind me. We'd both recognized that voice. Our situation had just gotten worse.

Joel stood in the doorway, gun raised. He glanced from me to Julian to the mayor. His eyebrows drew together, and he slowly straightened and lowered his gun.

The mayor strode forward. "I'm so glad you've arrived. These young—well, I don't have a nice word for them right now, but these young people broke in here and thought they could gallivant around your crime scene."

My jaw dropped. "Excuse me, we did—"

"I, of course"—the mayor straightened—"came in to secure the scene and to ensure these two didn't do anything worse than they already did." He shot us a glare.

"We did nothing of the sort!" I huffed. "You were the one who broke in, and we followed you. And I can prove it. You're the one holding the envelope that you found in Owens's office and were going to take."

"This?" The mayor waved the envelope in my face, then threw his head back and barked a laugh. "The things young people come up with these days to get out of trouble." He handed the envelope over to Joel. "She was standing in the doorway with this when I got here. I demanded she give it back, and I planted myself in the office door to keep them from getting by again."

If my jaw could've fallen off my face to the floor in shock, it would have. That was a bald-faced lie! And I'd given him fodder for it. What an idiot I was.

"You don't believe that, do you?" I gaped at Joel.

"You wouldn't take the word of these two teenagers over your own mayor and employer's, right, Joel?" The mayor gave the police chief an expectant look.

Teenagers? I didn't know whether to be offended or not.

Joel ran a hand over his face, then took the envelope from the mayor. "Thank you, Mr. Mayor, for your assistance. I believe you have your talk in a few minutes? I can take care of these two."

The mayor adjusted his tie and sneered. "Tampering with a crime scene is a third-degree felony here in Ohio. And you'll find our police chief not a man to be trifled with. Good day now." He squeezed past Joel and hurried out the back door.

As soon as the door shut behind us, Julian flung up his hands. "You can't seriously believe that lying, no-good, manipulative—"

"Julian," Joel growled. "He's my boss."

"That doesn't mean he is above the law! We followed him in here. He was the one tampering with a crime scene."

Joel sighed and shuffled through the pages inside the manila envelope. "But he's right. It's your word against his. And in this town, his holds more clout. I can't do anything without solid evidence."

I pretended to lean against the wall and eased to the side to put myself in view of the papers. On the top of the first sheet, in all-black capital letters, was "Proposal for Legacy Lagoons."

"Dust for fingerprints then," I said. "You'll find his all over the place and ours nowhere to be found."

"And he'll say you only had time to grab the envelope off Owens's desk." Joel shook his head. "I'm sorry." He blew out a breath and dragged a hand through his hair. "I'm not going to arrest you as he so blatantly implied, but stay away from him. If something like this happens again, he may tie my hands."

Julian crossed his arms. "He's hiding something, Joel. Hiding something and using you for it. I don't like this."

"It's not your problem to fix." Joel leveled his gaze onto his brother. "You can't afford to get on his bad side. If you get arrested, they'll kick you out of school, and you're so close to finishing. I can handle myself. Stay out of this."

Chapter Thirteen

Kids shrieking in delight, the chatter of hundreds of conversations, and the clanging whoosh of carnival rides rang in my ears. Joel had dismissed us with one more admonition to stay as far away from the mayor as we could. And I planned on following that advice. Sort of.

Scents of caramel apples, funnel cakes, and buttered popcorn filled the air. A quintessential summer festival. I inhaled deeply and could almost savor the tastes on my tongue. Mimi's voice echoed in my mind, "Sweet aromas can help us hold our favorite memories, our favorite moments, a little bit tighter."

Julian strolled next to me, and I studied his sun-kissed dark cheeks, the easy way he stood next to me, his body angled slightly toward mine like he wanted to be here, next to me.

Despite the craziness of this weekend and as much as I wished some things hadn't happened, other things I never wanted to forget.

"What's going on in that mind of yours?" Julian nudged my arm. "You look like your thoughts are going a mile a minute."

A flush colored my cheeks, and I ducked my head. I couldn't admit what I was thinking. Not with thoughts like sun-kissed cheeks. Julian and I were friends. Just friends. And maybe not even that if I didn't explain my high school stupidity soon. Or maybe once he heard my dumb excuse—because now that I was older and wiser, I knew high-school Beatrice's reason for abandoning her best friend was stupid—he might walk away anyway.

My phone buzzed, saving me from answering. A quick check revealed a text from Theo: "Couldn't convince Pops to leave the house. Uncle Rubin is supposed to call with an update."

I straightened. Uncle Rubin was calling. Perhaps fate was finally smiling down at me. Here was a second chance to find out about Aunt Penny and the marina.

"I need to go home." I waved my phone. "I have an idea on how to get some answers."

Julian raised an eyebrow, knowing I was avoiding his previous question. But he nodded. "Then let's get you home."

Theo was waiting on the porch when we pulled up. The minute I said goodbye to Julian and stepped out of his car, my brother hurried over to me.

"Uncle Rubin's on the phone."

"It's about time. Any word on when he can actually get here?"

"Well, the minute he heard, he handed off his case to an associate and booked a flight. Which has been canceled three times so far. He's still waiting on when the next flight will be scheduled." Theo led the way into the BnB and down the hall to the small dining room. Dad and Papa already squeezed around the four-person, white-washed circular table. Dad lifted a hand in a wave from where he sat in front of his phone, my uncle on a video call. I could've cut the awkward tension with my candle-wick trimmers.

Mom bustled into the room behind us, plates of shortbread cookies and fruit balanced in her arms. She shoved the plates into my hands. "Rubin just heard from the police station and has an update for us. He said he didn't mind if we ate while he talked. Dad needs to keep up his strength."

I settled the treats onto the middle of the table, then took my seat as Mom returned with mugs of coffee and one of tea for me.

She sat next to me and waved a hand over the table. "Anyone hungry?"

"Smells delicious." Papa's voice cracked. He cleared his throat and watched the slumped form of my uncle on the phone screen.

Mom's lips twitched, and she blinked rapidly to hold back tears. I remembered her words to my father yesterday morning. How upset she'd been when their family had fallen apart. How alone she'd felt when Aunt Penny hadn't been there to rally with her.

But she didn't need to be alone now.

I lifted my shoulders, plastered a smile on my face, and leaned over to wave at my uncle. "It's nice to see you, Uncle Rob. Did the police let you talk to Aunt Penny? How's she doing?"

He lifted his wan gaze toward me and blinked once, twice.

"I'm sure it's all a misunderstanding and she'll be released soon, right?" I didn't let the upbeat tone of my voice or my smile slip.

"I—I..." He buried his face in his hands, and his entire body began to tremble. "This is all my fault," he croaked.

It was my turn to blink, dumbfounded at his response. Before her marriage, Aunt Penny and I had been inseparable. I had spent many nights sleeping over at her apartment, watching movies and painting our nails and eating enough candy and popcorn to sour my stomach. When Aunt Penny met Uncle Rob, their romance seemed one from the books to my little-girl perspective. He'd swept her away, and I'd never forgotten their loving first dance and tender kisses at their wedding. To a flower girl dressed in a full-skirted gown fit for a princess, their wedding was a fairytale.

Their wedding was also the only time I'd ever seen him cry. The moment the double doors had opened to admit my aunt in her tulle ballgown, he'd broken down in adoration.

Shortly after their wedding, Mimi had died, the family had imploded, and I never got to know the man that had captured my aunt's heart. And as the years passed and the vitriol sharpened between my mom and aunt, I found myself not even wanting to give my uncle a chance. After all, it'd been after their marriage that things had fallen apart. That my aunt had become a person I didn't even recognize.

"Why would this be your fault?" Theo broke the silence, his voice muffled by the cookie he'd shoved into his mouth. "She's the one who—"

"What Theo means"—I glared at him. Leave it to my big-mouth brother to not even think of being sensitive in the situation—"is we're not even sure what happened ourselves. Theo and I saw Aunt Penny arguing with the marina owner, but we don't know why."

Okay, so maybe I was also being a *little* insensitive, but at least my questions made more sense in context and they'd get us somewhere.

"It's my fault," he whispered again.

I wanted to say that we already knew that based on his previous statement, but instead, I clasped my hands in my lap and waited for him to continue.

"She was only trying to help." He lifted his head and drew in a deep breath. "To help me."

"What did you need help with?" Mom moved to stand behind us.

My uncle fished a tissue from his pocket and gave a long blow that was not unlike a foghorn. Theo startled at the sound, and cookie crumbs dropped from his mouth as he gasped. I swallowed hard to keep from laughing. Apparently my suit-wearing lawyer uncle wasn't the pretentious, dainty man I'd come to think of him.

"Penny loves that town," Uncle Rob started. "And over the years we've visited, I've come to love it too. The slower pace of life compared to Columbus, the fresh air, the charming shops." He sighed and rubbed his dark-circled eyes. "I've wanted to leave the practice for a few years now. Get away from the constant barrage of cases and the need to always be on the clock. We've been looking for opportunities up here to use our skills to rejuvenate the town. To make it a little more of the haven we see it as."

"But what's the marina have to do with that?" I asked.

"It's no secret the town is lacking tourists, which means it's lacking in funds. With the wealthier clientele going to Huron or Sandusky or even Cleveland, Thisbe Harbor needs something to draw them here instead. An incentive, of sorts, to choose Thisbe. We thought the marina could be that opportunity." He spread his hands out. "Think of it. A yacht club right on the lake. White buildings, white-sand beaches, a luxury restaurant. Those are the things the wealthy tourists want to see. And the more wealthy tourists we can bring in, the more money other shop owners receive to fix up their own businesses. It's also a nice piece of real estate for Penny and I to build our own place on."

I had to force myself to close my mouth. Aunt Penny and Uncle Rob were planning on helping the town? She and Uncle Rob must've been trying to negotiate some sort of deal with Mr. Owens. A deal that they both believed might bring some life back into the town. A deal that he wouldn't take. No wonder she'd sounded so frustrated.

Why couldn't she just tell me when I'd visited her at the station? I would've understood. It would've made things so much easier to know.

But maybe I wouldn't have believed her. I ground my teeth at the whisper of truth that unfurled from the back of my mind. Maybe I would've let my frustrations, my prejudices of our past block any understanding of what she was trying to say. Maybe that's what we'd all done over the past several years. Stopped listening and let our own angry voices cloud out any reason.

"Why didn't she tell us?" Mom murmured. "We could've helped."

Papa cleared his throat and spread out his arms. "Well, doesn't this clear her? She was trying to help the town, not harm it. She couldn't be a murderer."

Uncle Rob half grimaced, half smiled. "The police won't see it that way. They'll see it as more of a motive. Owens was our roadblock. And with him out of the way . . ."

"But she didn't do it." Papa's shoulders slumped.

"Why was she there that morning?" Theo asked. "We'd witnessed an argument between her and Owens the evening before. Why did she go back?"

"We'd decided to take out a small loan. Up our offer one more time to see if he'd take it."

"And she walked in on a murder instead." My brother bit his bottom lip and leaned back in his chair. "The official time of death won't be announced until the medical examiner and coroner give the go-ahead. But if Joel is still holding her, the body had to have been warm enough for the time of death to be around the time of Aunt Penny's entrance. Which means she could've seen the killer."

"She would've told the police," Uncle Rob said. "If she'd seen anything, she would've told them."

I sat back in my chair. Knowing the time of death might help Aunt Penny's cause, but there was something else that was bothering me. "How much did you offer?" I asked.

"Beatrice!" Mom and Dad both shot me an exasperated look.

"You don't ask such things," Mom hissed.

I held up my hands in defense. "I'm assuming Uncle Rob and Aunt Penny offered a reasonable amount. And if it's true that all the businesses out here are struggling, why didn't Owens take it?"

"If he'd taken our offer, he could've settled somewhere very nice for a very long time." Uncle Rob rubbed the five o'clock shadow under his chin. "You have a good point."

Talking to Uncle Rob wasn't so bad after all. Aunt Penny had married a pretty reasonable guy, and they were trying to start their dream jobs and build their dream house on what my uncle termed "a nice piece of real estate." I could only ever daydream about living right next to the lake much less owning an entire marina and yacht club.

Wait a minute. Real estate. The contract we'd seen. Wasn't "Legacy Lagoons" the same name on the contract the crazy older gentleman had? Could Owens have balked on my aunt and uncle's offer because he expected a better offer from this other guy?

"He led your aunt on for a while," Uncle Rob continued. "Said he wanted out of the business and was more than happy to sell. This was back when we were still getting our finances in order. When we were ready to buy, he balked. Asked for more time. And the longer this dragged on, well, Penny didn't take the delays very well."

"Has anyone heard of Legacy Lagoons?" I asked.

Uncle Rob slowly shook his head. Mom and Dad looked equally confused, but Papa nodded.

"That was the marina's former name," Papa said. "Back when Sophie and . . . Oh, what was her husband's name?"

"Vincent?" I asked.

He snapped his fingers and pointed at me. "Yes. That's right!"

I bit my lip and glanced toward my brother. We had just found our third suspect.

Chapter Fourteen

Theo and I excused ourselves from the table and retreated to our shared room. The moment I shut the door, Theo rounded on me.

"You know something. I could practically see the lightbulb go off above your head."

I filled him in on Julian and my's adventure in the marina office. He wrinkled his nose when I finished and plopped down on my bed.

"Why would the mayor have those contracts? Was that what he was looking for or just what he was holding when you interrupted?"

"My questions exactly," I said. "And Joel seems to find him suspicious as well."

"But this Legacy Lagoons. Isn't Vincent the guy who attacked you?"

"Yes. And he was carrying that proposal inside. When I helped pick up the papers, I saw the title of the document."

"So that brings up another question: Why did this Vincent get rid of the marina in the first place and why's he want it back?"

I sat on the bed next to my brother and pulled my phone from my back pocket. Our knowing nothing about Owens was becoming more and more of a problem. It was time to do what we could to solve that. I swiped to the search bar and typed in Mr. Harry Owens of Thisbe Harbor, Ohio. I probably could've dropped the Mister, but years of being told to "respect your elders with their proper title" made it a habit. Hundreds of results popped onto the screen.

An article of Mr. Owens standing in front of the Compass Cove Marina sign with two thumbs up and a sneer on his face graced the cover of the first news article. Dated for earlier this summer, the article announced the marina's reopening after the winter season had come to an end. It described the marina's hours, their new stock of sunscreen and souvenirs sold inside the office, and also included a "now hiring" blurb. Nothing new.

Over the next five minutes, I scrolled through article after article regarding the marina without gleaning any new information about its owner. I chewed on my lower lip and stared at my phone, trying to will it to provide me with what I needed.

Harry Owens didn't have a single social media platform available except for an unused page for Compass Cove Marina. On the page, he'd made two posts—updating the profile picture and cover photo to both be of him.

"You'd think the guy would've advertised more," I muttered. "At least something about when he bought the place."

"Research Legacy Lagoons. Maybe that Vincent had something?"

I tried scrolling back to the search bar, but my phone registered the movement as tapping the blue like button on the profile photo's post. Three names popped onto my screen. Two I didn't recognize, but the third dropped my jaw.

Maeve Owens.

That couldn't be the Maeve I knew. But I clicked on her name and stared at the profile picture on the screen in front of me. The same tired, frazzle-haired woman I'd met yesterday smiled at me.

While her brown hair hung in loose waves around her shoulders and she sported a cute white blouse, the same tight lines pinched the corners of her eyes and mouth. In the photo, she crouched next to a small boy—no more than four or five—her arms wrapped tightly around him. The boy's pale, wan face split into the biggest beaming grin I'd ever seen, and his small, bony arms wrapped around Maeve's neck. Her son?

I scrolled down her short profile until I was blocked by her privacy settings. Only three other pictures were available to me since we weren't friends—a photo of her driving a boat, hair whipping behind her, and two other pictures with the same little boy.

"Are you seeing this?" I whispered.

My brother studied the picture, then wrinkled his nose. "I don't get it."

"This is Maeve." I shook the phone in his face. "The receptionist?"

Maeve Owens. Could she really be married to that crotchety marina owner?

The way he'd threatened her—his own wife—with a lawsuit for something she wasn't even doing. The memory of her cowering away from him burned into my mind. What bruises, internal or external, did she hide from onlookers?

If they were married, it certainly wasn't a happy marriage. Could she hate him enough to kill him?

A pit opened up in my stomach. How long had Maeve endured her husband's abuse? How long had she silently called for help until she felt she had to take things into her own hands?

I pressed my fingers to my temples. I needed to stop jumping to conclusions. Joel would know that Maeve and Harry Owens were married. In TV shows and books, spouses were always the top suspect.

Unless there was a stray aunt of mine who just so happened to be hanging around the body that day, of course. Joel could've glossed over Maeve as a suspect because Aunt Penny made an easier target. And had a motive. And the opportunity.

"I still don't get it." My brother shattered my spiral.

I blinked and stared at him for a long moment. "What?"

"I don't get it. What's the receptionist got to do with this right now?"

"Her last name. Owens. Maeve Owens. She's the marina owner's wife."

Theo's eyes slowly widened. "The wife?" I nodded and he sucked in a breath. "Why isn't Joel investigating her? Wives are statistically—"

"She must have an alibi," I interrupted before he could wax eloquent on his investigation knowledge. "Or, at least, lied about an alibi."

"So we've got two really good suspects. But no idea how to find them."

I bit my bottom lip, then straightened, an idea forming in my mind. I tapped out a quick text to my grandfather's gossip-loving friend.

"We may not, but I think I know who would."

Once again, the nostalgic smell of corn dogs, salted pretzels, and kettle corn filled the air. The putter of boat engines and the soft splash of waves on the docks added a subtle, more gentle current to the cacophony of noises around the festival. For having an odd name—and no sign of smallmouth bass anywhere about—the festival sure seemed to be busy. But, I supposed, who didn't love fair food and rides?

Cindy had promised to meet me at the volunteer shed, but had only guaranteed a handful of minutes before her volunteer coordinator duties would likely whisk her away again. I wove in and out of crowds and between food booths to the back of the festival, near the end of the docks.

A shed, no larger than a postage stamp, sat at the end of the dirt pathway. Cindy stood in the doorway, pointing at someone, then gesticulating wildly at them. Even from where I stood a few yards away, I could hear the jangle of her bracelets. The yellow-shirted volunteer scurried off to obey Cindy's orders, and I hurried forward.

Cindy beamed at me and swept open her arms. "My dear." I allowed her to envelope me in a tight hug. "What a day it's been for you. This is just devastating. Sawyer and I have been texting back and forth all day, but of course, the crazy old man won't let me come see him. Insists I'm needed here." She blew out a breath, but my mind hitched on the words "texting."

I didn't even know my grandfather texted, much less going back and forth with Cindy. This was an interesting development.

"Come, come. As I mentioned, we probably only have a few minutes before we'll be interrupted, but it's plenty of time for a cuppa tea, yes? The water just needs warmed a bit more." She wrapped an arm around my shoulders and led me inside the shed.

A desk crowded with pens and papers and clipboards took up the vast majority of the room, with two wooden chairs filling the rest of the space. Cindy scooted around the side of the desk, then produced an electric kettle from underneath it. She plugged it in, then poured several water bottles worth of water into the kettle before popping the switch on. The lights in the shed flickered once, twice, but held steady as the kettle hummed to life.

I lowered myself onto the wooden chair opposite my host and watched her pour two cups of steaming tea, the dark liquid swirling around the rim.

"My apologies, but I don't have cream or sugar. I hope you don't mind plain black tea?"

I preferred a splash of cream to add a bit of richness to black teas, but I told her I didn't mind at all. She handed me a cup of swirling tan liquid, then lifted her own to her lips. I curled both my hands around the warm teacup and inhaled the delicate scents of bergamot and lavender. My throat tightened at the smell. It reminded me of my grandmother. Lavender Earl Grey was always her favorite tea, and her house so often smelled of it.

"How are you holding up?" Cindy's dark eyes bore into me as if seeking the inner workings of my soul. But somehow, it didn't send the same uncomfortable shiver through me as when others did the same. Somehow, hers felt calming, almost a gentle probe to find my true feelings.

She stirred her tea like we had all the time in the world.

"I'm . . ." To lie, or not to lie. That was the question. If I told her how I was really feeling, I'd never have enough time to get to the questions I really wanted to ask her. But if I lied, well, I was tired of being okay. Tired of saying I was, when I wasn't. I had no job to speak of, no idea what I wanted to do next with my life, my aunt was accused of murder, my family was falling apart, and I didn't know what to do next with Julian.

Cindy took another sip of her tea, pursed her lips as she swallowed, then said, "We were never made to be strong all the time, Beatrice. Your grandmother taught me that. After my husband's death, she reminded me of that every day as I cried and cried in her arms."

I twisted my fingers in the bottom of my t-shirt and studied the concrete, dirt-covered floor. "There's so much, Cindy. And I don't know what to do. By all counts, I'm a failure. I have no job, no idea what to do next. I'm a washup living in my parents' basement with no future."

"Well," Cindy leaned across the desk to squeeze my arm, "that's the first step. Admitting you need help. And the second step is asking for help."

"That's the thing." I looked up at her, desperation thumping in time with my heartbeat. "I don't even know what help to ask for."

"You have many friends. Your brother, Julian, me. Your parents and your grandfather. We all love you dearly, my girl, and we want to help you."

A knock on the door interrupted our conversation. Cindy waved at whoever stood behind me.

"Oh, I'm so glad to see you!" She rose and rounded the desk to start for the door.

I grabbed her wrist, inwardly scolding myself. I'd selfishly taken all of our time to talk about me, rather than to discuss the important reason I'd come here. "One more question, please. And then I'll leave you to your job."

Cindy tilted her head at me. "Yes?"

"I need to speak with Maeve, if at all possible." As Owens's wife, perhaps she'd also know about Vincent's marina proposal, and I could kill two birds with one stone.

"Well, you're in luck." Cindy motioned behind me, and I twisted in my chair to see a dark-brown haired woman standing in the doorway. "This is Wren, Maeve's sister."

Chapter Fifteen

The woman stepped into the cramped space and flicked a glance over me, her eyebrows pulling together and wrinkling her forehead. Cindy swept over to her and gave her a tight hug.

"How is Maeve doing?" Cindy asked. "I'm so glad she has you."

Wren's shoulders drooped. "I worry for her. That's why I'm here. I know you've helped her before." She glanced at me again before focusing back on Cindy. "I don't know what to do."

"Is Maeve here?" I asked. I hated the note of desperation tingeing my tone. I didn't want to bother Maeve—not if she really was struggling. But what if it was more guilt she was struggling with? Guilt that she'd finally succumbed to the anger building inside her at her husband and lashed out at him. This could be my only chance to find out.

"I'd hoped the festival would take her mind off things," Wren admitted. "But it seems to have only made it worse, considering it all happened here." She sighed and rubbed a hand over her face. "I don't know why I thought this was a good idea."

Cindy wrapped an arm around Wren's shoulders. "Because you're a good sister and you're trying to help. How about a cup of tea? I just boiled some water."

Wren bit her lip and looked back at the door.

"Where's Maeve at?" Cindy asked gently. "Beatrice here can go keep her company. She's Sawyer's granddaughter. A very sweet girl, here to visit her grandfather."

"I left her on the docks. She wanted to watch the waves."

I set my teacup on the desk and pushed to my feet. "I'll keep her company while you talk with Cindy." Before Wren could argue, I scurried out of the building and back into the edges of the festival.

Boats bobbed out of the docks to my right, and tourists gathered in lines, awaiting their own tours of the lake front. I sucked in a breath of the fresh lake water air. However suspicious the mayor seemed and however much I disliked him, I couldn't fault him for this idea. If the town could hold out for a little longer, the Smallmouth Bass Festival could be what saved them.

I stepped onto the docks and skirted around several groups of people. After walking several piers down, I spotted her.

Maeve sat at the very end of the docks, legs swung over the side, face turned toward the water. I slowed as I approached and cleared my throat to make sure she heard me.

She glanced over her shoulder. Exhaustion lined her face and darkened the circles under her eyes. She squinted against the cloudy light and raised a hand to peer at me.

"Hi, my name is Beatrice Sawyer." I gave a little wave. "We met yesterday at the Compass Cove Marina."

"I remember you," she croaked. "What are you doing here?"

I shuffled forward a few steps. "Can I talk with you?"

"About the murder?"

I pursed my lips. I hadn't prepared for that question. Although that was why I wanted to talk to her, yes, I didn't expect her to be so blunt about it. Was this the behavior of a murderer? It seemed so cold, yet if her husband was abusive, as I suspected, perhaps it was hard to feel much of anything.

I held my breath as she continued to stare at me, not seeing me but something in her mind. Finally, after a long moment, she blew out a breath, shook her head, and patted the seat next to her. My heart leaped into my throat, and every muscle in my body tensed. She was just going to let me in? No questions asked?

I lowered myself to the dock next to her, peeled off my shoes, and let my feet dangle over the side like she had. I licked my lips and considered my next words carefully. As insistent as I'd been about talking to Maeve, this didn't feel right. Questioning her about such a sensitive topic. Asking for an alibi—it felt like I might as well accuse her of murder.

Smoothing a hand over my thigh, I cleared my throat and said, "I'm sorry. With what happened."

Maeve massaged her knees, knuckles white with each press of her hands. Her jaw clenched and unclenched for several seconds before she finally answered, "You know I hated him."

"I also know you were married." I winced at my directness. I should've made Theo do this. He was the investigator in training. Although his bluntness was often worse than mine. Julian would've been the one to excel at interrogating. His sweet expressions and compassionate words would loosen the tongue of the hardest criminal. At least, if that criminal were me.

Maeve squinted her puffy eyes at me. "You think I killed him."

A flush warmed my cheeks, but before I could form a response, she huffed a dry laugh.

"I suppose I can't blame you. You were there that day. You saw what kind of man he was."

"Why did you work there?" I asked. "With him."

"My son is in the hospital. Has been off and on for years." She sucked in a shuddering breath. "Poor guy's fighting for his life and I'm stuck in a—" She broke off and covered her face with her hands.

"I worked at the marina because I had no other choice. Harry gave me no other choice." She laughed bitterly. "We separated five years ago, right after Isaac was born. It was shortly after that the doctor's found his heart condition. I worked three jobs to pay for the care he needed."

My lungs tightened. Mr. Owens had to have known their son was struggling for his life. Yet it sounded like he'd done nothing to help. My disgust for him only grew.

"What happened?" I murmured.

She exhaled and ducked her head. "I lost almost everything. Gave it up to drown my feelings in drink. And I almost lost Isaac too. But that was the slap in my face I needed." She rubbed her hands up and down her thighs. "But try getting a job in a small town with having alcoholic on your record. I didn't have a choice but to work for Harry. Not that he ever did anything to help.

"He cut my pay a month ago. Said we weren't getting enough business and he was doing his best. Now the hospital is sending debt collectors after me. Apparently the meager payments I'm making aren't enough to their liking. My landlord is hounding me for the next payment. My phone company just shut down my account. All while Harry sits in his little mansion and on his little marina throne."

She sniffed and wiped her nose on the back of her hand. "Even if my little guy wakes up from his surgery, he'll be so disappointed in me. I've got nothing for him."

"No, he wouldn't." I scooted closer to her and rubbed a hand over her back. "You've worked so hard to make sure he has the care he needs. I'm sure he's proud to call you Mama."

At the name, tears poured down her face and a sob tore from her throat. I wrapped my arms around her and pulled her close.

"He's just a little guy." She sobbed. "He doesn't deserve anything that's happening to him."

I stayed silent, rocking slightly back and forth until her tears slowed and her cries quieted. After several more moments, she leaned back and wiped her face.

"I'm sorry," she choked out. "Crying like that in front of a complete stranger."

"No, you have nothing to be sorry for." I sat back to give her a little more space.

The barest of smiles lifted her lips, and she wiped her nose on the bottom of her t-shirt. "Thank you." She swallowed hard. "Now, you said you had questions?"

I didn't know if I could rule Maeve out completely. Not without verifying her alibi. But everything in me wanted to believe that she was innocent. And even if she wasn't, perhaps she'd still give me the truth about Vincent.

"Do you know of a Vincent? He would've been talking with your—with Owens about the marina. On Friday right after you walked out, actually."

"Vincent Crawford?" She blew out a breath. "He and Owens argued that day." She held up a hand before I could comment. "I only knew because I went back to give Cindy a key to lock up. The two of them were in the office screaming at each other. Which wasn't irregular."

"Did Vincent want to purchase the marina?" I asked.

"Ever since he lost it to him." Maeve shrugged. "It wasn't anything new. It's why no one batted an eye at them arguing again."

"Lost it to him?" It was all I could do not to gape at her. She acted like everyone knew this information, yet neither my grandfather nor Cindy had bothered to tell me?

"Gambling." Maeve blew out a breath. "One of the many secret lives my husband hid from me was his penchant for gambling." Her gaze darkened, and she curled her lip. "And one of his favorites was taking what was dearest from people."

"Vincent owned the marina before your husband?" I asked.

"His wife did. Sophie poured her heart and soul into the marina. Grew it into what it used to be—a happy, bustling place. After she died . . . Well, Vincent struggled. And my husband was more than happy to take advantage of that."

"And now Vincent wants the marina back."

"Has wanted it back for years. But Owens wouldn't sell to him. Refused."

I frowned at that. If Owens wouldn't sell to Vincent, why would Vincent have a proposal prepared? A proposal that our mayor then had in his hand after breaking into the marina office.

"What is it?" Maeve asked.

"Are you ready?" Another voice, this one a deeper version of Maeve's, asked above us.

I jumped and twisted to see Wren standing over us.

She frowned down at me. "What were you two talking about? Maeve, were you crying?"

"It's nothing." Maeve climbed to her feet and slipped her shoes back on. "Beatrice was just keeping me company."

Wren's frown only deepened, and she wrapped a protective arm over her shoulders. Maeve squeezed her sister's hand and eased out from under her. She shot me an apologetic glance.

"We're heading to the lawyer's office today. He called and said he has a few things to review with me."

"Hopefully you have a marina to sell in your future," Wren muttered. "It's the least that godforsaken husband could do for you."

I slowly rose to my feet, and I couldn't help my eyebrows rising. "You get the marina?"

"I don't know." Maeve flushed and lightly elbowed her sister. "Come on, we're going to be late." She started back up the docks.

Wren took a step after her, then paused and turned back. She waited until Maeve was several paces away before growling, "Leave my sister alone. She's had enough to handle without people like you plaguing her with questions." She added under her breath, "This town's always spreading gossip."

Wren stomped after her sister. I hated the thoughts now swirling in my mind. Maeve had seemed so innocent. So earnest in her explanation of her awful husband and what he'd done to her. How she'd overcome the odds and was now trying to provide for her son.

But I couldn't help hearing Wren's words repeated over and over. Maeve could sell the marina, and if my aunt and uncle were to purchase it, the money would be more than enough to cover the cost of Maeve's son's care and help them start over. Theo had said over and over that money was one of the leading motives for crime.

Add to that an abusive husband and a sick child... Maeve would solve two problems with her husband's murder. Rather than erase herself from my suspect list, Maeve had just shot to the top.

Chapter Sixteen

An ache throbbed against my temple, dragging me from a sleep I didn't want to end. After a quick goodbye to Cindy, I'd returned to the BnB and filled Theo in on my conversation with Maeve. But instead of investigating more like I'd wanted too, Mom had roped us all into a movie that had dragged on and on in an attempt to take our minds off the day's events.

The movie hadn't helped.

I'd replayed my conversation with Maeve over and over again, trying to find some clue that would give me some answers. Instead, I'd finally fallen in bed after midnight and tossed and turned the rest of the night.

I rubbed my eyes and buried my face in my pillow. But it was no use trying to go back to sleep. My brain was awake, so I was awake.

Blowing out a breath, I grabbed my glasses from the side table, tucked my phone into the pocket of my pj shorts, and traipsed out of my room to the kitchen. A cup of tea and a walk would do my head wonders. Theo still snored, face in his pillow, as I quietly closed the door behind myself.

Neither Mom nor Dad stood in the kitchen, and not a sound could be heard throughout the house. Odd for either of my parents to sleep past 7:30, even on vacation.

I filled a kettle with water and set it on the electric stove before prepping a mug with a satchel of Earl Grey. The moment the water boiled, I poured it over top the satchel and inhaled the warm scents of bergamot mixed with a hint of lavender. I could bathe in the wonderful scent.

"Beatrice?" Papa's voice called softly behind me.

He sat at the entrance to the kitchen, gripping the arms of his wheelchair with white-knuckled fingers. Dark circles shadowed his cheeks, giving him an almost haunted look.

The fog of exhaustion fled from my mind, and I hurried to him. "You shouldn't be up. Where's Mom? Does she know you—"

He shook his head and waved away my concern. "I'm fine. But I have something for you, and I want to give it to you now."

Ooookay. With my aunt in prison, this didn't exactly seem like the time to be giving gifts. But I followed as he wheeled around and rolled back down the hall to his room.

"It's from your grandmother," he said over his shoulder, and my heartbeat picked up at the words. When she'd died, Papa had gifted Mom, Aunt Penny, and I small trinkets to remember her by. I'd received a thin gold necklace with a stunning opal and matching earrings along with a small book Mimi had been putting together with her favorite memories of my brother and me. Both the jewelry and the notebook had become some of my most prized possessions.

But to give another gift—so many years after her passing?

"When your grandmother died, I felt so lost. It was all so sudden, and I couldn't bear to see her in everything around me. So I packed up her things and shoved them into storage." He opened his bedroom door and ushered me inside. "Over the past year, Cindy has been helping me through what feels like a final goodbye. Sorting through your grandmother's things. Deciding what to keep, what to donate, and what she would want her family to have."

A small packing box sat in the middle of Papa's bed, the flaps folded down, and my name written on the side in Mimi's fancy script. I took a step forward, and my lungs constricted. Mimi's handwriting. It'd been so long since I'd seen it.

"I found this box," Papa whispered, "for you."

Tears clogged the back of my throat, and I was frozen to the carpet. For months after Mimi's death, I had prayed for one more phone call or one more letter from her. One more chance to tell her how much I loved her.

And now, twelve years later, God was answering that prayer.

I took one step, then another, and another, until I finally stood at the edge of the bed. My hands trembled, but I fumbled with the box's flaps and managed to open it. Nestled on top of multicolored confetti was a small amber jar, a golden lid twisted on top. A photo of Mimi and a younger Beatrice smiled up at me, and underneath our goofy grins were the words: Beatrice—bringer of joy.

A candle.

Mimi's last gift to me, her last words to me.

I lifted the candle from its wrapping and held it to my chest for a long moment, a sob rattling deep within me. Memories of stirring melted candle wax, measuring fragrance oils, and playing "make that scent" came flooding back to me. I cherished every memory with my grandmother, but there was something about candlemaking that felt so us. It was something only she and I loved to do together. It was something that felt almost sacred—a time when I knew I could always have my grandmother to myself.

We'd held so many deep conversations over a pot of wax, yet I couldn't help but feel like we should've had the opportunity for so many more.

I sucked in a shuddering breath and slowly unscrewed the lid from the top of the candle. The soy wax had yellowed and frosted with age, but the light scents of sage, lemon pound cake, and bergamot tickled my nose.

Tears—now combined with a generous amount of snot—trickled down my face again. Mimi had known the power of memories. It was why she'd made candles in the first place. To help others hold onto something precious to them.

And now, I had my own tangible Mimi memory to hold onto, to smell, to remember.

The thought planted a seedling of an idea.

"Papa?" I set the candle on the bed, then faced my grandfather and gave him a shaky smile. "Thank you." I dropped to my knees by his wheelchair and wrapped him in a tight hug.

My grandfather kissed the side of my head then squeezed me back. "She was so proud of you, Beatrice. And I am too."

His words should've given me a measure of pride, of peace, but instead, my mouth went dry. He shouldn't have been proud of me. I'd spent the entire day yesterday looking into the murder, trying to clear his daughter's name, but I'd found nothing but more questions. Even with my new clues regarding Maeve, I had no evidence, and Joel would require evidence to free my aunt.

"Papa," I croaked, pulling back just enough to meet his gaze. He cocked his head and smiled as he waited for me to continue. "I have to tell you"—I swallowed again. My throat felt like sandpaper—"I don't know if I'll be able to clear Aunt Penny's name. I-I'm working on it, but I don't know." I didn't know what I was doing. I'd never solved a murder before.

Papa's entire body sagged, the lines creasing his face deepening. In the thirty seconds it'd taken me to say those words, he'd aged a decade.

"Papa," I whispered. "I'm trying. I really am. But—"

He straightened and reached over and gripped both my hands in his. Wrinkles and sunspots marked quavering hands. But despite the tremble, his hold on me was firm.

"Thank you for believing in this family," he said. "Thank you for not giving up when everyone else has. Your Mimi was right when she made that candle—my Beatrice is a blessing and a bringer of joy."

"I'll figure this out." I swallowed hard. I knew his words weren't meant to pressure me, but the panic that had threaded through me this morning only tightened its hold. For the first time in years, I had an inkling of an idea of something I could do. Something I wanted to do. But if my aunt was booked for murder, any small business I might start would be lost to the "girl whose aunt killed a man" rather than given a chance to spark. "I promise."

"Beatrice, that's not—This isn't on your shoulders. I never meant—"

I rested my hands on his shoulders. "I want to do this, Papa. For you. For Mom. For Aunt Penny. For me. But if I'm going to, I need your help."

"Whatever I can do for you," he murmured, "I'm here."

Despite his protests, I tucked my grandfather back in bed, then returned to the kitchen. I set Mimi's candle next to the sink and traced a finger over the dusty gold lid.

A candle company. Specializing in bringing one's memories and nostalgia to life through scent.

I stared out the kitchen window above the sink. My still-warm tea puffed fragrant steam toward me, but the scent couldn't carry me into dreamland now.

Out the window, a two-minute walk away, the street dead-ended, and Lake Erie shone over the barrier. Waves rolled toward the cliff and crashed against the rocks below, sending a glittering spray into the air. The trees near the window swayed in the gentlest of breezes that I could almost feel on my own skin.

My first candle, after I solved this case, would be of this town. Of Mimi's town.

My mind went back to summers spent in Thisbe. Skin always red and pruny from days spent on the beach competing with my brother as to who could swim the farthest, who could run in the sand the fastest, and who could build the biggest sand castle. Thisbe seemed to contain a kind of magic in those days. Mimi had always told us that the sea heard our pleas, and if we gave it a token of something that meant a lot to us, it would grant our greatest desires.

Countless pieces of my jewelry and little trinkets I'd found on the beach had ended up in the ocean waves as I begged for the days to stretch a little longer, the weeks to never end. Of course, such a thing could only be accomplished by God, but I'd never stopped hoping and never stopped believing in that magic.

A bit of magic that I could use right about now.

The sun's warmth tickled my cheeks the moment I stepped outside, and the salty scent of the air carried my headache away. I sucked in a deep breath and shuffled across the summer heat-dried grass to the edge of the street. The light breeze coming off the waves wrapped around me, and I closed my eyes to focus.

What could I give the sea? And what did I even want to ask?

So far I had three good suspects—Maeve, Vincent, and the mayor—but not enough evidence or answers to convince the police of anything. I only had questions. Questions I didn't know how to get the answers to.

I sighed and walked along the edge of the road toward the barrier. Aunt Penny certainly had lots of evidence stacked up against her.

"But she didn't do it," I reminded myself. No matter what evidence Joel collected and presented, I had to cling to that.

I blew out a breath and sat down on the barrier, swinging my legs over the side. Not the safest thing to do, maybe, but none of the thoughts swirling in my mind felt safe.

Start my own small business and solve my aunt's murder. Two things I had no idea how to do. Two things I, somehow, without any idea of them only two days ago, desperately wanted to accomplish.

"You look like you're deep in thought." Dad's always-calm voice hummed behind me. He strolled down the street toward me, already dressed in his typical button-up shirt, sweater vest, and khaki pants and cradling a coffee mug between his hands. The tense muscles in my shoulders relaxed. There was something about Dad's presence that exuded calm.

He came up next to me, and over his shoulder, I could see Mom slipping into the front door of the BnB. I burrowed against Dad's side, and he wrapped an arm around my shoulders.

Gently squeezing my shoulder, he focused out on the waves sweeping toward the cliff below us. "You know what the great playwright said, 'Give sorrow words; the grief that does not speak knits up the over wrought heart and bids it break.'"

A soft smile lifted my lips. Dad always knew when something was bothering me. But to confide in him or not to confide in him. That was my question. I doubted he'd approve of my sticking my nose into a police investigation for the sake of Aunt Penny, but I also knew he held to Papa's philosophy regarding family—Dad would do anything for Theo, Mom, and me. In regard to my thoughts of a small business . . . well, I wasn't ready to share those yet.

"I know you're worried about your aunt. About your mom and grandfather too," Dad murmured. "But this isn't all on your shoulders, my sweet girl."

I wrapped both of my arms around my father's waist and hugged him tight. As aloof as my father often seemed to others, he was surprisingly good at reading people. Especially me. Ever since I'd started talking, Dad had known what I needed, even when others couldn't understand my childish babble. We understood each other.

I'd never forget my senior year of high school, desperate to figure out what I wanted to do, all of my other friends having known years prior which school they wanted to attend and which career they'd wanted to pursue.

Dad had slipped into my room, somehow knowing I needed him despite my silent tears, and held me in his lap like he'd done countless times when I was a child. We'd rocked back and forth until my sobs calmed, then he'd kissed my forehead and brushed back my sweaty, tear-soaked hair and whispered, "Choose what you want to do, not what you think you should do. I'm already proud of you, sweetie."

If only I'd known what I wanted to choose to do. Here it was almost six years later, and I was just getting an idea.

I lifted my head and studied my father. "Have you ever wanted to do something—not because you knew what you were doing or because someone told you to—but because it felt right?"

Dad smiled down at me, and my heart squeezed in my chest. He'd given me that same smile at my high school graduation, when I'd dropped out of college, and when I'd moved back in with him and mom having no idea what was next. He really was proud and supportive of me, even if I wasn't of myself. "Your caring heart is one of the things I love most about you, Beatrice Ophelia. But remember: It's not your responsibility to save everyone."

I gave my dad a tight squeeze. Perhaps I couldn't save everyone. But I could at least try to save my aunt. "Thank you, Daddy. I love you."

And I now knew what I was going to ask the sea.

Chapter Seventeen

Armed with the backing and encouragement of both my father and grandfather—and Mimi in a way—I marched back to the BnB. Mom fried eggs in the kitchen, and the scent of buttery toast accompanied her. Theo sat at the table, still in his pajamas, shoveling dry sugary cereal into his mouth. His eyes were glued to his phone, which sat next to his cereal bowl.

"Lomk a dis." He shoved his phone toward me, chewed, swallowed, then repeated, "Look at this. Remember that old house down the way? The one with the tower that we swore was haunted?"

The photo on his phone screen was of an old Victorian brick house. A sagging porch with dozens of missing boards and a caved-in roof wrapped around the front and one side of the house, while a tower meant for a princess—or a ghost, as my brother thought—composed the other side. Stately windows invited in plenty of sunlight, as well as plenty of wildlife thanks to the numerous broken glass panes. Ivy crawled up the entirety of the tower and wove its way through several of the shattered windows.

But despite the ramshackle appearance, the sun shone brightly behind the house amidst a sky the color of the Mediterranean Sea. Over the side of the cliff several yards from the house, Lake Erie sparkled like polished glass. I'd loved the house ever since I'd spotted it as a little girl. It had such a castle-like quality to it, how could I not have fallen in love?

Fixed up, it would be a dream. But who was I kidding? I didn't have the money to purchase the place much less fix it up.

"The town's auctioning it off. The owners haven't paid property taxes in years, so the bank foreclosed on it and is trying to dump it on someone." He rubbed his hands together. "Think they'd let me in for a looksee? There's gotta be a ghost haunting that place."

I rolled my eyes. "They're not going to let you inside. That's a lawsuit waiting to happen if you fall through a floorboard."

"I'd sign something promising not to sue." He shook the phone. "Just look at it. I can smell the ghost through the phone."

I scowled and shoved my brother. "Stop that. You can't smell ghosts!"

"Have I ever been wrong?"

"Considering you've never seen a ghost, yes, you're always wrong." I snorted.

"Remember the abandoned house—"

"That was so creepy I peed my pants? Yeah, no thanks." As kids, my brother had had an obsession with eerie abandoned houses and warehouses. And, of course, being the older sister who was forced to babysit her little brother, I was often dragged on his adventures. He always claimed he could sense ghosts, and he'd pretend to hunt for them everywhere we'd visit.

For his senior trip in high school, he'd convinced my parents to take us to Salem, MA, the city best known for its execution of witches in 1692. Every night we'd wandered the streets, our ghost tour guide holding only a lantern to illuminate the dark paths before us. Theo had never been more excited in his life, and I'd never been so petrified.

As we'd circled the grounds of the witches' graveyard, our tour guide had woven tales of the gruesome tortures the witches had endured and the spells they'd cast to ensure that the knowledge they possessed was passed down only to those who were worthy. At the scariest points of the stories, actors dressed as the ghosts of the alleged witches had jumped out with a shriek that still sent shivers down my spine every time I thought of it.

Needless to say, Salem was not a place that I planned on visiting again. No matter how tasty their matcha chocolate lattes might be—which Theo bribed me with every morning of our trip after I swore never to go on another ghost tour again.

"Come on. It's worth an ask, right?"

My phone rang in my room, saving me from having to answer. I dashed for to my room in time to see Cindy's name flashing on the screen. I frowned as I swiped to answer.

"Is everything okay?" I asked.

"I hope you don't mind me calling, dear." Cindy's voice boomed over the phone. I winced and held it slightly away from my ear. She always had a voice that could carry across any room. Apparently she didn't realize that she didn't also have to use that voice when on the phone. "Your grandfather gave me your number because I left my phone book at home."

I swallowed back a chuckle. Of course she'd still use a phone book rather than input everyone's numbers into her contact list.

"But this was an emergency," she continued.

My smile disappeared. "Emergency? What happened? Are you okay?"

"It's not about me, dear, it's this festival. I've had five volunteers call this morning and say they can't work their shifts. Five! I told them I don't know what they expect me to do at such late notice, but they very rudely said that was my problem not theirs. Which, I suppose it is as the volunteer coordinator, but the way I was raised, when you volunteer for something, you go, rain or shine." She humphed, and I could imagine the scowl on her face. Then she cleared her throat. "My apologies, I let my temper get carried away with me there, but when people don't keep their promises, well, it makes me upset."

"I'm sorry that happened. But what do you need from me?"

"I'm so glad you asked. I was talking with your grandfather about it this morning, and he recommended giving you and Theo a call. He knew you'd be darlings and help me out. Won't you?"

"The mayor . . ." I took a deep breath. "He kind of kicked me out. He won't let me back in."

"I've already cleared you with Joel. I've conveyed just how desperate our situation is, and he's promised it won't be an issue."

I chewed on my lower lip. Joel may be more than happy to look the other way, but I couldn't say the same for the mayor. "What exactly do you need us to do?" I asked.

"Nothing too difficult. I need you to help out at the baked goods booster tent. All donations are going to fund a new playset at the park, which heaven knows we need. That old one is so rusted it's unusable. I need two people to man the register and one to restock as needed."

"Well, Theo and I could help, but that's only two people. I don't know if Mom—"

"We are absolutely not bothering your dear mother. She has enough to think about right now. I already have my third person, and I think you'll be thrilled. He will be a little late, but he'll be there."

"Cindy." I closed my eyes and counted to ten. I knew exactly who she'd called.

"My dear, true love always finds its way home."

I tightened my grip on my phone. Julian and I were tentative friends, at best. We still hadn't talked through what had happened all those summers ago when I'd been a jerk and stopped talking to him. And until that happened, I couldn't expect anything more. Not that I was wanting anything more. I had a business to start and that'd take a lot of time and thought. I didn't have time for a relationship.

But I couldn't help picturing Julian's bright smile and teasing wink. His fresh minty, soapy smell. If I had a candle of him . . .

My cheeks flamed at the thought.

"Beatrice Ophelia," Cindy huffed, apparently not liking my silence, "how do you expect Romeo to get down on one knee if you keep running away?"

I massaged the tight lines between my eyebrows. A tension headache knifed through my skull. "He isn't Romeo," I said as slowly and carefully as I could, "and I'm not running away. I'm simply—"

"Oh, I'm getting another call from one of my volunteers," Cindy said. "They'd better not be canceling too. See you in fifteen?"

I opened my mouth to reply, but the call had already disconnected.

I facepalmed then gave a silent scream. I loved Cindy, I really did, but why did she always have to make things so awkward? Is this how she talked to Julian too? Did he think I was using Cindy to force myself upon him? I could only imagine how she described me to him if she called him Romeo to me.

Blowing out a breath, I sank down on the edge of my bed.

The door to the bedroom squeaked, and Theo poked his head around the side. His gaze swept up and down me before he stepped into the room and closed the door. "You look like a ghost soul-sucked you."

"I feel like one." I flopped back on my bed and let my phone fall to the floor.

He sat down crisscross-applesauce on the floor and picked at the carpet fibers. "Want to talk about it?"

"No." But Theo didn't move. He knew I'd eventually spill my guts. I always did.

But this time, I truly didn't feel like talking. He'd only tease me about Julian too. I sat back up, dragged a hand through my tangled curls, and blew out a breath. "We're volunteering at the festival today. Papa voluntold us for Cindy. She wants us there in fifteen minutes."

He wrinkled his nose. "Volunteering? At the festival? What about the mayor?"

"Cindy promised she'd take care of it. She sounded desperate."

Theo snorted. "You and I both know that Cindy can sound like whatever she wants at whatever moment she wants to get someone to do something."

"It apparently worked on Joel if he's letting me back in."

"Well"—he pushed to his feet—"I'm always up for more fair food. Lead the way, dear sister."

I grabbed his arm. "Keep an eye out too. And not just for food. Food courts are the best place to hear gossip."

"Juicy secrets and juicy hamburgers." He winked at me. "My favorite."

Chapter Eighteen

No kids shrieked while playing carnival games, no teens jostled each other back and forth, no adults mourned the loss of every dollar in their wallet. This early in the morning, the festival was empty.

My stomach twisted at the quiet. It reminded me too much of *that* morning.

I led Theo through the vendor booths and around the food court to the back of the festival where I'd met Cindy the previous day. She'd give us our instructions—and probably a pep talk—with the rest of the volunteers before the gates opened.

"Imagine this place at night." Theo spoke in a low, growling voice. "Carnival lights blinking off. The final dozen cars driving down the road. And you, the last to leave, crossing to your car in the empty parking lot, led only by the light of the moon. And you hear an eerie cry that echoes across the lake."

I turned and socked my brother's arm. "Really? Ghosts again?"

He ducked my next swing and raised his arms in defense. "I can't help it! The subject fascinates me. There are so many stories of credible people seeing—"

"Have you ever thought you're in the wrong field? Maybe you should lead ghost tours instead of study forensics."

A flush crept up his neck, and he lowered his gaze. He mumbled a response so quiet, I couldn't hear it.

I frowned. Why the sudden nervousness? My brother always jumped at the chance to defend his beloved ghosts.

"What's going on?" I crossed my arms over my chest and narrowed my eyes at him. "You're hiding something."

He jerked his head up. "Me? Hiding something?" His cheeks burned brighter than the festival lights. Definitely hiding something. "Why would I be hiding something? I don't have anything to hide from you."

And now he was babbling. I poked his arm. Who was this awkward, bumbling brother of mine? What didn't he want me to know? We shared everything—well, almost everything.

"Oh, the volunteers are gathering. Mustn't keep them waiting." He skirted around me, projecting an air of innocence that his face betrayed.

"Mustn't?" I laughed and followed, one step behind him. "You really are hiding something!" I reached for his arm. "Come on, Theo, you can—"

Cindy broke through the back of the half circle of volunteers that had formed around the little shack. She waved her arms at us, bracelets jangling on her wrists. "You're late! It's sixteen minutes past! We need to get started."

I quickened my steps and came up to Theo's side. "Don't think I'm going to forget you have a secret."

"I wouldn't think you could," Theo muttered, and we joined the crowd.

Half an hour later, Cindy escorted my brother and I to the blue booster tent. Three white folding tables had been set up underneath, and plastic blue tablecloths flapped in the soft breeze coming off the lake. A handwritten posterboard sign boasted: HOMEMADE GOODIES. BROWNIES, COKIES, CAKE, PIE.

"Cokies?" Theo snickered. "What kind of snacks are you selling here?"

Cindy planted her hands on her hips and sighed. "Can no one else do anything right around here? I'll scrounge up a Sharpie somewhere." She marched into the tent and around the tables, then pulled a metal lockbox out from under the middle table. "Cash box is here. We're cash only since the town won't invest in a card reader. Which is why we probably won't make our fundraising goal."

"What is this?" Theo peered down at one of the dozens of clear plastic containers that littered the tables. He picked it up, shook it, and it sounded like rocks clunking inside.

"Oh, those are my brownies." An older lady hobbled up next to my brother and grinned up at him. "Every time I make them for family get-togethers, they disappear in minutes. I donated them for the fundraiser, but . . ." Her voice trailed off as she perused the offerings. The wrinkles around her lips tightened, and she tapped her walking stick against the ground twice. "Cindy, there must be some mistake here. I dropped off a dozen brownies yesterday morning, and they're all still here."

"That's because this"—my brother shook the box—"is not—"

"Those look scrumptious." I hurried forward and butt-bumped my brother out of the way. "Is the recipe a secret, or are you willing to share?" I beamed down at the small older lady.

"These don't—"

"Yes," I turned so my face was away from the older lady, "they look even better than dear Aunt Margaret's, don't they, Theseus." I placed added emphasis on his name. Then I mouthed, "Shut up."

"Oh. Right. Yes." He quickly set the brownies down and took a step back.

"But I don't understand why no one bought them yesterday." A quiver shook the older woman's voice, and she traced a finger over one of the plastic boxes. "They usually do so well."

"That's because I placed them on hold," Cindy said. "I'm having some friends over for tea after the festival, and I couldn't serve tea without your brownies, dear Hazel."

The woman's shoulders relaxed and a smile returned to her face. "Well, I'll get the others from the car then. I baked a batch just this morning for the fundraiser."

"Theo, will you help Hazel carry them here?" Cindy asked.

My brother nodded, confusion still tugging down his brows, but thankfully, he didn't comment on the rock-like brownies further. He escorted the older woman back toward the parking lot, and as soon as they were out of earshot, Cindy blew out a breath.

"She's as sweet as a good brownie, but gracious, the woman can't see a recipe to save her life. And hates sweets so she has no idea what garbage she makes." Cindy gathered up the boxes of brownies and stowed them under the table. "As soon as Theo brings the others here, hide them. It's why her brownies disappear at family gatherings so quickly—her daughter whisks them away before someone can break a tooth."

I couldn't help but chuckle.

Cindy dragged a hand through her hair and muttered, "It's no wonder sales are doing poorly with these being the donations."

I reached over and rested a hand on Cindy's. She sucked in a shuddering breath. I quickly rounded the table and dragged over one of the metal chairs for her.

"You need to rest. You've been doing too much."

She tried to wave me off, but I gently pushed down on her shoulders, and she lowered herself into the chair. Tears glinted in her eyes, and she swiped them away with the back of her hand.

"It's lack of sleep." She forced a laugh. "Your poor grandfather and I have been up late chatting with everything going on, and even before the festival, if I'm honest, as we prepared details. It's just catching up with me."

"You're doing a wonderful job, Cindy." I crouched in front of her and gave her hands a squeeze. "This town couldn't have asked for anyone better to coordinate this festival."

She sniffled and waved a hand in the air, her bracelets jangling. "I'm just afraid it won't be enough." Her gaze grew distant, and her grip on my hands slackened somewhat. "I can't lose this town. My husband—" She shook her head and focused back on me. "I can't lose this town."

An image of the boarded-up ice cream shop I'd so loved as a child came to mind. I couldn't lose this town either. It was the home I'd found every summer. A haven of safety and peace I never wanted to leave.

And I still didn't want to leave it.

The thought startled me almost as much as my idea to start my own business. There must've been something in the air or perhaps it was an effect of too much fair food. I was letting dreams and ideas take over. But when I answered Cindy, I couldn't keep the passion out of my voice, "We won't lose this town."

Theo's return with the packaged brownies ushered in the opening crowd. Kids and adults flocked to the few carnival rides and lined up for boat tours down the docks. No one approached our table.

After nearly an hour of no customers, Theo balanced on the back legs of the metal chair he'd sprawled in. He picked at a loose thread on his jeans and moaned. "Why are we even open? No one wants crummy desserts at nine-thirty in the morning."

"Not all of them look bad." I picked up a carrot cake coated in a one-inch thick cream cheese frosting. "This one's all right."

"Yeah, but why get homemade baked goods from here when you could buy fried ice cream down the way? Or a crisp elephant ear? Or an oversalted pretzel with the gooiest cheesy dipping sauce?"

I crossed my arms. "I can see your mind is on the task at hand."

"What task? No one is here." He dropped his head back and groaned. "I'm so bored."

"They say being bored is a good thing. It can grow creativity and boost mental health and all that."

"I think my creativity is draining from my soul as we speak. At this rate, I'll lose my sense of ghostly smell by noon."

Ah, the perfect in to repeat my question from earlier. I leaned against the table in front of my brother and stared down at him.

"Spill, Theseus Gonzalez Sawyer. You're hiding something from me, and we don't do that."

He wrinkled his nose and stuck his tongue out at me. "You're hiding something from me, too, so you can't put all the blame on me."

Okay, I was hiding something from him, but it was something I wasn't even sure about myself. Starting a business took a lot of work and time and money—money that I didn't have.

"I will tell you my secret if you tell me yours," I said, then added under my breath so he couldn't hear, "Although when I tell you my secret is up for debate."

He squinted at me, and the next several minutes passed in silence except for the squeaking of his chair as he adjusted his position several times.

"Come on, Theo, we don't keep things from each other."

"I'm afraid," he whispered.

I snorted. Liar. He'd never been afraid of anything in his life—which probably fueled his fascination for ghosts. But the longer the silence stretched on, the more I realized that he'd spoken the truth.

"You're afraid of me?" I swallowed hard, and a knot twisted in my chest. I'd betrayed my brother, somehow. I must have, if he was afraid of me.

"Promise you won't tell anyone. Even Mom and Dad? Not till I'm ready."

What would he be so scared to tell me that he'd hide it? I gasped. "You've got a girlfriend."

"What? Ew, no!" Theo let his chair drop to the ground and he swatted at me. "What is wrong with you?"

"When you start off saying not to tell Mom and Dad, what am I supposed to think?"

When Theo didn't respond, I frowned down at him. He stared vacantly at the tent ceiling. I wanted to push him to tell me what he'd been hiding for so long, the words right on the tip of my tongue. But I stayed silent too. While we didn't keep secrets, we didn't push. We waited. We listened. It's what he'd always done for me, and now, I'd do the same for him.

After several more long beats, he burst out in a rush of words: "I'm thinking about dropping out."

I blinked, the words taking a moment to register, but then I gaped at him. "Of college?" Hearing my brother might be following in my footsteps would not go over well with my parents. They'd been so proud when he'd announced his intention of becoming a Forensic Investigator. Of course, they'd been proud when I'd enrolled as a nursing student at OSU. But that hadn't lasted long. "I thought you loved it?"

"I do. Did." Theo groaned and rubbed his hands over his face. "I don't know. Mom and Dad are going to kill me."

Questions broke through the dam of shock that had built inside me. "What do you mean you want to drop out? To do what? Have you signed up for fall classes yet? I thought Mom and Dad paid the bill already? Why didn't you tell me sooner?"

"You're struggling too, Beatrice. It doesn't take an investigator to know that. I couldn't ask you for anything."

"That's a bunch of lies, and you know it. What am I for if not to be your sister?"

He sighed and lifted his hand, palm out, toward me. I scrutinized the small square of cardstock in his palm. Theseus Sawyer,

Paranormal Investigator was written in a haunting script across the top. My brother stared sternly at me from the picture on the card, arms crossed and blond curls slicked to perfection. He looked like he could take down the most devious of ghosts.

A smile blossomed on my lips. Holding this business card—my brother's paranormal investigating business card—felt right. For as long as I could remember, this is what he loved.

"I'm crazy, I know," he muttered, drawing the card back to clutch to his chest. "But—"

I ran around the table and pulled him into an awkward hug, his bony elbows digging into my ribs and my frizzy hair covering his face. "But you want to do what you love."

"I shouldn't," he whispered, stiffening in my arms. "But classes are so stifling. All professional and procedural and everything I'm not. It's not that I hate it, I just . . ." He pushed away and wrapped his arms around himself. "I used the money Mom and Dad gave me for the semester to get new equipment—but I'll pay them back. I swear. But I don't want to go back to school. No one appreciates creativity there. They want facts and figures and no imagination."

"I feel you." I huffed a dry laugh. "Try nursing school. All they want is blood and feces and whatever else they can throw under a microscope. But I don't think you should drop out. Not yet."

"What do you mean?"

"You've got a year left." He opened his mouth to protest, but I held up a hand. "Hear me out. You've got one year of classes left, yes. Stifling classes, I know. But think about the credibility your degree will give you. Ghost hunt on the side, build your business while you take your classes, and when you're finished, you can add "Forensics Investigator" to your business card. I don't know about you, but I'd feel better hiring a Forensics Investigator to take a look at my ghost problem than anyone else."

He huffed. "Since when did you become so good at dishing out advice? That actually makes sense."

"You don't have to sound so surprised. Just don't do anything yet. Think about what I said. You can always enroll late if you need to."

"All right. I will. If you do one thing for me?"

I pursed my lips. "And that would be?"

"You're turn. What's *your* secret?"

I pulled out another metal chair and slowly lowered myself onto it. While I trusted my brother, speaking my desire to start a small business seemed too final. Too much like a commitment. I knew, if I uttered my candlemaking dreams aloud, Theo would push me to pursue them. And I wasn't sure I was ready for that.

But what would happen if I took the leap? If I finally let myself dream a little? If I finally let myself do something that many would call crazy, but it was something that I felt was right deep in my bones?

I straightened my shoulders and set my gaze on my brother. Fear of what other people thought was what made me enroll in college to be a nurse. Fear was what made me drop out—although with a fear of blood and needles, I shouldn't have even started the degree. And fear was what kept me working dead-end jobs ever since. I needed to stop being afraid.

"I want to start a candle business." I let my dream fly and braced myself for panic, for second-guessing myself. But a sense of rightness settled on my shoulders. "It would be called Mimi's Memories, and it would be a business dedicated to making candles that remind others that there is light in the darkness. That there is good even when the bad overwhelms."

My brother stared at me. I gripped the bottom of my chair until the metal dug into my palms.

"I have no idea what I'm doing. It's been years since I've made candles with Mimi and I'm going to have to relearn everything and maybe I'm crazy—"

Theo leaned over and grabbed my hands.

"What?"

"It's brilliant, Beatrice. It's absolutely brilliant."

"Please don't mock me." I covered my face with my hands.

"I'm not mocking you!" Theo wrenched my hands away. "Why would I mock you? I'm not that mean, am I?"

I pretended to wipe a fake tear away. "Well, if you want the truth—"

"All right, all right." He gave me a playful push away. "Stop that or someone really will think this is the worst food booth ever."

I laughed and pushed to my feet. The crooked block letters and misspelled word on the booth's sign caught my eye again. Theo had been right. It was no wonder people weren't stepping up for homemade baked goods. I wouldn't trust the baking skills of people who couldn't spell "cookies."

Colorful flags, kitschy fish, and flashing lights decorated the booths across from and surrounding us. They screamed "fun!" and "festival!" and "try us!" Not only did our booth display a blatantly misspelled sign, but the boring blue tent did nothing to make us stand out. If we were going to help save this town, we needed to up our game.

"I'll be back. You're in charge." I started out of the tent.

Theo's chair thunked on the ground. "You're leaving me? Where are you going?"

"We need a new sign." I tossed over my shoulder. "And a bit of pizzazz if we're going to draw customers."

"Then I should be the one leaving," he said. "You wouldn't know pizzazz if it smacked you upside the head!"

I melted into the crowd. I'd show him—I did too know pizzazz. Grab a couple of paper lanterns, maybe some multicolored tulle fabric to drape around the sides of the tent. We could even hang some solar-powered Edison lights around the inside to create a sort of magical haven for those who wanted a brownie and rest. Maybe we could drag in a few comfy chairs, offer people a place to sit and a bottle of water.

I did feel slightly bad at leaving Theo by himself—hopefully he still remembered how to count back change without a calculator—but I didn't really expect many customers to show up and he could whine without me present.

I wove through the vendor booths and smiled at a woman manning a small craft booth. Soaps and whipped sugar scrubs were displayed on the table in an enticing, colorful array, and a sign announced the products as handmade with local goat's milk. If Thisbe survived and if I could make my dream come true, perhaps I could share a booth with her next year.

I imagined a wooden shelf stacked with delicious-scented candles, all handpoured and blended by me. A crowd gathered outside my booth and oohs and aahs filling the air as lids were unscrewed and the aromas revealed. Maybe I could partner with the town and create a special Thisbe Harbor candle—I couldn't bear to call it "Smallmouth Bass Festival." No one would trust a candle with that kind of name.

My candle would be scented like the town in summer. Lake breezes, sandy beeches, and something spicy like gossip. My childhood favorite place wrapped up in a candle.

"You!"

Chapter Nineteen

I froze at the all-too familiar blustering voice. He'd found me. Closing my eyes, I sucked in a deep breath and slowly released it. I had a right to be here. Cindy needed my help, and Joel had okayed it. I had a right to be here.

Straight shoulders, chin up, hands clenched at my sides, I turned to face the mayor.

He stalked down the aisleway, arms swinging like clubs at his sides, lips pursed, and gaze firing bullets. I hunched my shoulders and shrank into myself. I hated conflict, especially when the other person was so unpredictable. He certainly looked like he could kill someone with his bare hands.

He was only three yards away now.

I swallowed and prepared to deliver my defenses. I had a right to be here. Cindy needed me.

I opened my mouth. "I know you said—"

The mayor strode right past.

My jaw dropped, but he didn't even cast a glance in my direction. Instead, he made a beeline toward the soap and sugar scrubs craft booth. The woman behind the table rose, glanced around for a moment, then focused back on the mayor. She pointed a finger at herself as the mayor neared.

"Are you needing me, Mr. Mayor?"

"I need your table." He jabbed a finger at the table, prettily decorated with a fringed robin's egg blue table cloth and golden signage with the prices and item ingredients written on it. Elegant dark-stained wooden stands lifted up the woman's goods, giving the table a clean, minimal, yet refined feel.

"My-my table?" The woman frowned. "But the festival has already begun, and I need—"

"My people forgot that I'd be having a meet-and-greet today, and I need a table to sit behind. I've chosen yours."

She pressed her lips together and swallowed hard before responding. "Mr. Mayor, I mean no disrespect, but I own this table. I brought it from my own home, and I need it to display my bath—"

"I've been watching. Not a single customer has come up in the past hour. No one wants soap and sparkles that you have to spend an arm and a leg on when you can go to Walmart and get the same thing for a buck or two."

Her cheeks reddened, and she ground her teeth together. I started forward. This mayor had no idea what it took for a small business owner to survive in the current market of fast and cheap. The woman had probably spent hours and hundreds of dollars perfecting her craft before she even sold her first bar of soap or sugar scrub. And according to her signage, she even purchased local goat's milk to handcraft her soap—which would be a heckuva lot more expensive than whatever knock-off ingredients the chain grocery store used to make their soaps.

"My meet-and-greet lasts only an hour—from noon to one. You can have your table back afterward." The mayor rested his hands on the table and leaned toward her. "I'd hate to see your application to next year's festival be denied."

Color drained from the woman's face, and her shoulders drooped as the fight swept out of her. "Give me twenty minutes to pack up my products, please."

The mayor's lips twisted into an ugly smile. "My people will be back then." He patted the table once then strutted away.

The woman's lower lip trembled, and she tilted her head toward the sky for a long moment. So this was how small business owners were treated in Thisbe. If this interaction was any indication, my candle journey would be an uphill battle.

"Excuse me?" I called out. "Do you need any help?"

She startled and gripped the edge of the table. "Oh!"

"I couldn't help overhearing," I said and motioned to the multicolored sugar scrubs. "I'd been admiring your products and I'm sorry for what he said. These are worth every penny you charge." I lifted a blue and purple scrub swirled with hot pink glitter: Mermaid's Song, according to the label. Even through the plastic lid, I could catch a whiff of the ocean mist, raspberry jam, and underwater lilies scent. "They're beautiful."

Her lips turned upward. "Thank you. It's been my life's work, building this business." She sighed and patted the top of her table. "Thanks to inflation, though, I'm struggling. All small businesses are struggling. Costs are rising and customers are holding tighter to their money. Although he didn't have to be so rude about it, the mayor is right—very few have been willing to part with their hard-earned cash for luxury bath products."

She pulled several boxes out from under the table, and I moved to help her safely repackage her products.

"How long have you been in business?"

"Eight years this Christmas. A while back, I sold on consignment through the marina. Did pretty good business that way. But when Owens stole the place, he didn't care about helping a small business out."

I paused, holding one of the soft jars of Unicorn sugar scrub above its box. She knew Owens? "What do you mean stole the place?"

"A sweet couple owned and ran the marina for decades—Vincent and Sophie. But when Sophie passed, well, Vincent . . ." She shook her head. "He fell back into old habits and started gambling again. Owens took advantage of that and manipulated Vincent into betting the marina. I swear the jerk somehow cheated, but Vincent's an honorable man. He kept his word and handed the deed over." She must've realized the anger in her voice because she forced a laugh. "Not to speak ill of the dead or anything. What happened is terrible."

A puzzle piece clicked into place. Vincent wanted the marina back from Owens. That's what his proposal was about. It was a contract. Which, now that I thought about it, made sense. But if Owens refused to sell, how far would Vincent go to take it back?

"Do you know Vincent well?" I asked.

The woman laughed. "Everyone in town knew Sophie. If you needed anything at all, you could always count on her to help. It's thanks to her that my business grew like it did. Sophie hosted parties and spread the word like none other. I owe her everything."

I folded the flaps of the box in front of me and grabbed another empty one. "How long did they run the marina?"

"Oh, the marina was in Sophie's family for decades. It was her great-great-great grandfather that first opened up the place as a fishing dock. When Sophie passed, her family was furious that she'd left it to Vincent. They'd never had kids, see, so willing it to her husband took it out of the family."

"And then he gambled it away?"

"I don't think they know." She shot me a quick look. "They kind of cut him off after the funeral, or so I've heard."

"Oh." I forced nonchalance as best as I could, but inside I was screeching in victory. While I didn't know Vincent's opportunity yet, he definitely had the means to strangle Owens and the motive. I pretended to zip my lips shut. "The secret is safe with me."

"Right." She focused back on the box in her hands, and a heavy silence descended between us.

Ugh, I didn't want to ruin the relationship between us. I could learn so much from her, if she'd allow me to.

"Can I ask one more question?"

She narrowed her eyes for a moment, then nodded. "Okay."

"If you could give your younger self one piece of advice before starting your business, what would it be?"

The tension in her stance dissipated, and she tilted her head. "Are you thinking of starting your own business?"

"Candlemaking. If I can make it work."

"Then that's my advice. Don't doubt yourself." She took the half-full box from my hands and set it on a cart behind her. "File for your LLC, buy your domain, and don't quit. Not when you only make one sale and it's your mother. Not when you get your first negative review. Keep working hard and keep believing in your business' mission." She handed me a watercolor business card, colored by the sunset and complete with light blue sketched seashells and seagulls surrounding the name Seascape Soaps. "My name's Vivian. If you do start your business, feel free to reach out with questions."

I gaped at her and took the business card like it was my lifeline. "Really?"

"I wouldn't be here today if someone hadn't reached out and helped me. So I like to do the same when given the opportunity. But you have to promise me something."

"Yes?" I clutched the card to my chest.

"Promise me you'll start your business. Take a chance and do it."

Heat hummed in the air, and sweat dripped down my neck and dampened my armpits by the time I reached Cindy's shed. If anyone had a permanent marker around, it'd be her. I only hoped she'd be inside. And maybe have a spare bottle of water. Fewer people seemed to be milling about compared to yesterday's opening. With tomorrow being Monday, however, many tourists were probably heading back to the city and their jobs. That did not bode well for tomorrow's festival finale.

Boats sailed around the harbor, and at least a dozen people stood in line for the next boat tour. If we could clear Aunt Penny's name in time, it'd be nice to take a victory lap around the harbor.

"Will you leave her alone!" A woman's bellow rose above the crowd.

I stopped and glanced around. A few others around me did the same, casting uneasy looks about before continuing on.

"She's clearly hurting." While softer, the woman's voice was no less menacing. "And you're doing nothing but increasing her pain."

I moved to the left and slipped between two booths that backed up to the docks. Several feet away, the mayor stood in front of Maeve and her sister. I should've guessed. He, apparently, was on the hunt for blood today.

Maeve's sister pressed a finger against the mayor's chest, while she swept one hand behind her to keep Maeve back, as if shielding her.

The mayor smacked Maeve's sister's hand away. "Unhand me, brazen woman. This has nothing to do with you."

"I'll show you brazen." Wren's cheeks flamed. She heaved in a breath and started toward the mayor, raising a clenched fist.

Maeve leaped forward and slid between her sister and the mayor before anything could happen. She faced her sister and pressed her palms against her sister's shoulders. "Woah, woah, woah, calm down, Wren."

"Calm down?" Wren growled. "Calm down when he's pestering my grieving sister? Calm down when he's insulting me? Calm down when he's—"

"I don't have time for this." The mayor took a step back and spluttered for several seconds. Then he gestured toward Maeve. "When you're ready to call off your guard dog, we can talk. And while you wait, you might want to think about your son. This kind of money can work miracles for him."

My jaw dropped. Was he really going to stoop so low as to use Maeve's son for leverage to get what he wanted? And calling Maeve's sister a guard dog? Could he be any more of a jerk? She was only trying to protect her sister!

Wren shouted a curse at his back, then turned as Maeve slumped against the side of a dock brace and slid to the ground. She dropped to her knees next to her sister and clasped both her hands in her own.

"Ignore him," Wren said. "You don't have to do anything you don't want to do. He thinks he can get whatever he wants if he bullies people enough, but—"

"But he's right." Maeve's voice is barely a whisper, so I step closer to catch her words.

"He's—"

"Could you get me a lemonade?" Maeve squeezed her sister's hands. "I'm parched."

Wren bit her lip, and hurt flashed through her eyes, but she wiped it away with a blink and gave a sharp nod. "Of course. Want to split a funnel cake? I know you love those Buckeye ones."

"That'd be great."

Wren pushed to her feet and scanned the surrounding booths. I ducked next to a fry and sausage food truck. Thankfully, if my faulty memory served me right, the nearest lemonade stand was several trucks down the line. This could be the opportunity I'd been waiting for to ask Maeve a few more questions.

When Wren stepped out of view, I scurried from behind the truck and slowly approached the former receptionist. She sat on the ground, head tilted back against the pole, a single tear rolling down her cheek. A deep, shuddering sigh slipped from her lips, and she swallowed hard.

My heart broke for her. She may have despised her husband, but she didn't deserve this. Enough burdens weighed on her shoulders without having to deal with the fallout of Owens's death.

"Your sister's right, you know," I said.

Maeve startled, and she jerked her head in my direction. When she spotted me, she relaxed slightly and a sad smile turned up her lips. "You heard all that, huh?"

"The mayor doesn't deserve to be mayor. Not when he wields his power like that."

Maeve reached down and plucked a few blades of grass from the ground. She rolled them between her fingers, not speaking for a long moment.

I lowered myself to the ground in front of her and waited. As much as my questions wanted to burst from me, I knew she needed space. Someone to listen and to just be there.

"It's been a long time since I've loved Owens. A long time since I've been anything but afraid of him." She gave a harsh laugh. "I'd been in the process of trying to divorce him, but he kept refusing to sign the papers and any money I had to pursue the matter was long gone. So I settled with knowing he'd always be a thorn in my side.

"I hated the sway he had over me." She fisted the grass. "Hated the way he treated me and the way he knew he could because I had no other choice but to work for him." She finally lifted her gaze to mine. "But I never imagined he'd be gone. Oh, how I wished for it. But to happen like this . . . I can only think of my son." Her voice broke, and she ducked her head. "How he could be gone in a moment too."

"We're not going to let that happen." I reached over and gripped her hands. "We're going to keep fighting with him."

"I need the money, Beatrice," she whispered. "I don't want to sell to a man like him, but I don't have a choice."

Aunt Penny popped into mind. I wanted to offer her as a solution—solve two problems in one—but with Aunt Penny's historical treatment of Maeve, I couldn't imagine the receptionist thinking her much better than Owens.

"What's he want with the place anyway?" I asked. "I wouldn't think the mayor would be interested in running a marina, or the town taking kindly to him doing something that would take so much away from his mayoral duties."

Maeve shrugged. "Beats me. But I could do with a million dollars to pay off some debts."

I bit the inside of my cheek to keep from gaping. A million dollars? Where was the mayor getting that kind of money in this run-down town?

"Wren insists it's a lowball offer. And in any other town, it would be. But no one comes here. Not anymore. I'm honestly surprised it'll go for that much."

My thoughts whirled. A lowball offer and a dead body. Coincidental? Maybe, but I had a hard time convincing myself it was.

"Did the mayor ever approach Owens about this?" I asked.

"Not that I know of. The first I heard of it was yesterday." She snorted. "He'd barely said, 'Sorry for your loss' before he was stumbling over his offer on the place. I'd just found out myself that the marina was mine."

"But he knew?" I wrinkled my nose. This mayor was sounding more and more suspicious to me.

"Word gets around, I suppose."

Yes, word spread fast in a small town. But not that fast.

"When does the mayor want an answer?" I asked.

"Before the end of the weekend."

"Would you hold off a little longer?" I rubbed the back of my neck. "I know you need the money and you don't have any reason to listen to me, but can you give me a few more hours? I want to check something."

"I haven't decided if I'm even selling to him or not, so a few more hours is the plan. Vincent had also asked to buy the place before Owens passed, but . . ." She bit her lip, then leaned forward and lowered her voice, "If I'm being honest, I'm not sure he's in a state to run the place. This town needs a bit of life injected to it, and Vincent, well, he's held onto the past for so long that I don't know if he could let go of the memories enough to do what it takes. I want to do right by the town—because that's something my husband never did."

"I understand." I rose to my feet, pressing my lips together before I told her that Vincent was also under suspicion.

"Why are you so interested in all of this anyway?" Maeve asked. "You're not even from around here."

I bit my lip. I knew Maeve didn't like my aunt. Probably was even a little happy that Aunt Penny was in prison. But I also knew that Maeve valued family.

I sucked in a deep breath and said, "Because this is the one way I can try to save my family."

"Your family?" She tilted her head to the side, then understanding dawned in her eyes. "Your aunt? You're trying to get your aunt out of jail?"

"My family's been broken for years. And if my mimi were alive, it would devastate her. I'm doing this for her. If I can figure out who did this and clear my aunt's name, perhaps my family can find peace again."

"Are you with the police?" Wren's voice came from our left, and both Maeve and I startled. Wren stood only two feet away, a large lemonade in one hand, and a plate topped with a funnel cake oozing with melted chocolate and peanut butter in her other hand.

"What?" I asked.

"You said you're investigating. Are you police?"

"No." I laughed. "And I doubt they appreciate my efforts to help."

"But isn't it dangerous?" She glanced between her sister and me. "I mean, if you really think you're aunt isn't a killer, doesn't that mean a murderer is out there? What if they come after you?"

I swallowed hard. In all honesty, I'd been trying to avoid that line of thought. I hadn't wanted to think about the fact that the real murderer might not like me coming after them. Especially if they were content to let Aunt Penny take the blame.

A shiver trailed down my spine. If I poked too far into this case, how would they kill me? Clearly they didn't mind getting their hands a little dirty—strangling someone took guts. Which meant they also had to have some semblance of a workout routine. While a rounder man like the mayor may look like he prefers cupcakes to the weight room, adrenaline could do wonders.

Did the mayor have the strength to kill someone?

I thought of his blustering attitude when Julian and I had caught him snooping in the marina. Anger could make the gentlest of men strong.

My thoughts caught up to me, and I wrinkled my nose. Here I sat trying to analyze the mind of a murderer. No wonder I was single.

"Beatrice?" Maeve murmured. "If poking around is going to get you hurt, I don't think it's a good idea."

I batted her concerns away. "I'll be okay. Just like you're willing to do anything to save your son, I want to do whatever it takes to save my family. It's been a long time since anyone has fought for my family. So I'm going to try."

She took in a breath and studied me for a moment longer, then nodded. "If you're sure, I'll wait to give the mayor my answer."

I exchanged numbers with Maeve so I could share any new information with her or so she could let me know if she decided to accept the mayor's offer. Then I started back toward the middle of the festival.

"Hey!" Wren called after me.

I turned to see her jogging up behind me. I steeled myself. She didn't appreciate it the last time I'd tried speaking to her sister, so I could only imagine the vitriol she'd have for me now.

"I wanted to say thank you," she said.

My eyebrows shot up. That was unexpected.

"For helping my sister." Wren bit her lower lip and brushed the toe of her shoe through the grass. "She doesn't have a lot of friends here in Thisbe. After everything that's happened, well, not many people would give her a chance. So, thank you. For being someone who'd give her a chance."

"O-of course," I stammered. This was the opposite of the Wren I'd previously met, but with her softer words, I understood her better. Her love for her sister drove her fierceness. She'd walked with her sister through hardship before, and she wasn't about to abandon her now.

"But be careful." Wren reached out and lightly touched my arm. "I'm thankful you're putting yourself out there for my sister, to give her closure, but I'd hate seeing something happen to you."

"Don't worry, I've got my brother and best friend watching my back. And we're just asking some questions. The police will do the actual hard work of making the arrest."

She didn't look convinced, and I wasn't really convinced myself. Because if the killer did find out we were asking questions around town to give information to the police, I couldn't imagine them liking that. But I wouldn't stop now.

I waved and walked back toward the booster tent.

A mayor with a million dollars. And three different people who wanted the marina from Owens.

Perhaps it was time I finally visited my aunt a second time.

She might've known that the mayor wanted the marina property and might have insights on why. Was the mayor taking out all of his competition to ensure he'd get the marina?

Talking with Aunt Penny might also give me the chance to convince her to be nice to Maeve. My aunt would certainly give Maeve a fair price for the marina, and Aunt Penny and Uncle Rob's investment would help the town.

But did I want to subject myself to my aunt's smoldering, judging gaze? I would've hoped that being in jail for over 24 hours would've calmed her down some—maybe given her the time to think of how she'd been acting—but it'd been years since the family split. Years for her to think about her words and actions, and it'd done no good.

My words to Maeve rewound in my mind. Just like she was willing to do anything to save her son, I wanted to do whatever it took to save my family. Even visit my aunt.

Chapter Twenty

I blew out a breath and headed back toward the booster tent. More questions than answers accompanied me. I now had two very plausible suspects, and no ideas on how to find out and prove the real murderer.

As I neared the booster tent, the crowd thickened until I found myself having to push my way forward, excusing myself over and over again as I navigated between tightly packed bodies. One of the booths must've been having some sort of event to attract this crowd. And quite the event it must be with this many people.

I rose on my tiptoes to peer over the shoulders of the people in front of me. Six booths down, my brother stood on top of a metal chair right in front of the booster tent. Dozens of people jostled in front of him, most of them laughing. A middle-aged woman near the front was red-faced and laughing hard enough that tears streamed down her face.

Theo grinned at his place in the spotlight and reached down to clap the woman on the shoulder.

"You gave me such a fright!" she cackled. "I haven't laughed like this in ages!"

Familiar dark dreadlocks wove in and out of the crowd, and Julian passed out containers of cookies and cakes to willing customers. Ah, Romeo had arrived. I let out a little gasp at the thought. I needed to stop letting Cindy's ideas invade my mind. Julian was not Romeo.

I scanned the area for anything else to concentrate on and spotted Joel lounging against a nearby food truck. Even he was snickering. What on earth was my brother doing?

"Excuse me?" I turned to the person pressed next to me. "What's going on?"

"Oh, he told the most spine-tingling ghost story!" the middle-aged man said. "When he got to the part about happening upon the ghost, that woman up there shrieked, and it was so funny! I've never laughed so hard in my life." He cupped his hands around his mouth. "Tell another one!"

"Yeah, we didn't get to hear it!" another person added.

More shouts joined in, all clamoring for my brother to weave the next story. A flush colored my brother's cheeks and he straightened in the chair. A gleam sparkled in his eye. He was finally doing what he loved so much—making others laugh and screech with his haunting tales. The stories afterward were why he pursued ghosts so much. Because if he had a story to tell, he had a chance to bring joy to someone's day.

Theo's gaze landed on me, and his smile only widened. I lifted two thumbs up. Apparently sharing our secrets had sparked something in both of us.

Theo clapped his hands, then held them up until the crowd quieted. "Ghost stories will resume at noon today. If you are interested in more haunting happenings, I highly recommend taking a boat tour and checking out some of the houses overlooking the cliff sides. Watch closely, and you may see something . . . otherworldly."

I couldn't help but chuckle and shake my head. I knew for a fact my brother was making everything up. He had no clues to anything regarding Thisbe Harbor's history much less its haunted history. Yet the crowd buzzed at his words, and at least a dozen people raced toward the docks to get in line. So despite my utter dislike of anything ghostly, I had to admit my brother was doing a stellar job boosting this town.

The crowd started to disperse, and I wedged my way up to the front. Julian joined his brother and winked at me as I came up.

"We're almost sold out of booster goodies," he murmured. "Which means we might be able to fund a new playground at the park. All thanks to Theo's marketing."

Theo hopped off his chair and joined our small huddle. "Sorry about that, Joel. I didn't mean to cause a fuss."

"No harm done." The police chief chuckled and shrugged a shoulder. "Although I have to say . . . Ghosts?"

"What can I say? It draws a crowd." My brother laughed, but I didn't miss the slight twitch of his left eye. Although I knew Joel didn't mean to make fun of my brother's passion—and although I didn't believe in ghosts myself— it bothered Theo to hear others dismiss him.

Joel pulled out his phone and glanced at the screen. "I'll remember to ignore anymore screams around noon." He tipped his head toward my brother, then glanced toward Julian. "See you tonight?"

Julian agreed, and the police chief strolled away.

"Did you find the marker?" Theo asked.

I gave him a blank look. What did a marker have to do with our investigation?

"The marker," he repeated. "You know, the whole reason you left the tent to begin with."

I opened my mouth once, twice, then shook my head. I'd completely forgotten my earlier errand.

"I was thinking of reworking the sign to advertise the ghost stories," Theo was saying. "I could create a ghost scavenger hunt around town. Maybe get other businesses to participate and—"

"That's a wonderful idea, dear brother of mine, but way too much for a three-day festival. Besides, we have other new developments to worry about."

"Other new developments?" Julian asked.

I explained everything I'd discovered while on the search for the marker I forgot, ending with my new complication—whether I should pursue Vincent or the mayor. I shared both of my theories: first, that the mayor knew Maeve would inherit, so he bumped off Owens to lowball Maeve and get the marina. And second, that Vincent killed Owens because he was desperate to get his wife's marina back.

Both Julian and my brother stared at me. I swallowed hard in an effort to keep the smug smile from my face. I'd stunned them with my theories. Yes, yes, even I could be brilliant sometimes.

"One problem with your theory about the mayor." Theo, of course, broke the silence. "Means, motive, and opportunity." Theo ticked them off on his fingers, then crossed his arms over his chest and leaned back with a satisfied smirk.

Julian and I blinked at each other then focused back on my brother to await his next words. They never came.

"What are you saying?" Julian asked.

"We need to figure out the means, motive, and opportunity. That's how we'll know who did this."

"We already know that."

"Theo." I rubbed my forehead. "Anyone who is anyone knows that. It's repeated across every crime show, podcast, and book in existence."

"You didn't let me finish," he protested, and I rolled my eyes again. Another thing that drove me nuts about my brother—he loved to use "clickbait" sentences to draw in listeners, add a dramatic pause, then act like you were the one who interrupted him. "In your theory, you've got someone who has the means—I could easily see the mayor strangle someone—and I suppose he has the opportunity, but the motive?"

"The property," I said. "He wanted the marina property."

"But why?" Julian spread out his arms. "He's the mayor of this town. What's he need with marina property?"

"That's exactly what we need to find out. And we also need to find out where Vincent was the night of the murder."

"And how do you propose we do that?" Theo asked.

"You're going to do some snooping, and I'm going to call Mom."

Chapter Twenty-One

"I don't think this is such a good idea." Mom shifted in the passenger seat and rubbed her hands up and down her arms.

I unbuckled my seatbelt then reached over and popped the button to do the same for her. "We've already discussed this. The worst she can do is say no."

"But it's been years, Beatrice."

"Which is why it's time we do this. Think of what Mimi would want. What she always said."

"Family is important," Mom murmured.

"Exactly." I hopped out of the car, ran around the side, and opened the door for my mother. I extended my hand. "So let's go get our family back."

We entered the police station together, and after explaining our mission to the desk sergeant, we were led back to the small room my aunt was being held in.

"You have ten minutes," the police officer said.

I nodded, and he unlocked the door. Mom clutched my hand and pressed against my side. Her entire body trembled against mine. I squeezed her fingers and gave her a gentle nod. We'd talked for nearly half an hour in the car outside the police station and we both knew it was time to face this. Together.

The door swung open to reveal my aunt sitting on the side of her cot once again.

Her mouth opened but no words came out. She watched us shuffle into the room and didn't blink when the door shut behind us.

"Hello, Aunt Penny." I bit my lip. Every question I'd wanted to ask her fled my mind.

"Helene?" she whispered.

I sucked in a deep breath, then released it in a whoosh. "Uncle Rob told us about the marina. About you trying to save Thisbe. And we want to help."

"You . . ." Aunt Penny rose to her feet and looked between my mom and me. "What?"

"We want to help you, Penelope." Mom's voice cracked. She swiped at her eyes, then released my hand and took a step forward, head held high. "This whole experience has helped me realize something. Family is worth fighting for. *You* are worth fighting for. And I've been blind to that for too long."

My aunt's shoulders shook, and she gasped back a sob. "I've done so much wrong. I abandoned my family."

Mom lurched forward and nearly knocked her sister over with the force of her hug. "Penelope," she whispered, her own tears dripping off her face and landing on my sweater, "it's not only your fault. I didn't understand after Mom was gone. I didn't give you a chance. And I'm so sorry it took this awful situation for me to realize how wrong I've been."

They clung to each other and cried for another two minutes, blubbering every few seconds yet another apology. When they pulled apart, Mom was beaming in a way I hadn't seen for a very long time.

Aunt Penny reached out a hand toward me, and with barely a thought that I hadn't hugged my aunt in ages, I crossed the room and wrapped my arms around her.

"I've missed you, my dear girl," she whispered against my hair. "And I'm so sorry for everything. The things I've said to you. The way I left you." She cupped a hand against my cheek. "Can you ever forgive me?"

Her harsh words about my appearance filtered through my mind, but I pushed them to the side. Words spoken through anger, while they cut deep and I'd have to work through them, could still be forgiven.

"I forgive you, Aunt Penny."

Her hand trembled against my cheek, and she inhaled through her nose. "I don't deserve this family."

"None of us do." I winked at her. "But it's the one God gave us, and for that, I'm grateful."

She rubbed her face on the bottom of her shirt and took a deep breath. "Thank you for coming. I didn't realize how much I needed you until I saw you in the doorway."

"I actually have a question for you, Aunt Penny. Two questions."

"Anything."

"The morning you found Owens..." She visibly shuddered at the name, but when she didn't speak, I continued, "did you see anyone else there?"

"The police asked me the same question." She shook her head. "There weren't any other cars in the lot. Not other than Owens's, that is."

I sighed. Of course the police would've asked. I should've thought of that.

"But I was surprised at the number of people on-scene when your brother caught me." She frowned. "As I told the police, anyone could've blended in rather quickly. What's your other question?"

"It's a bit morbid. But was the body warm?"

"Beatrice!" Mom gasped. "What kind of question is that?"

Aunt Penny wrapped her arms around herself. "Another question the police asked. But no, it wasn't. Yet the body was..." She shivered again. "It wasn't stiff. When you walked in, I thought I could save him. I had no cell service inside that blasted building, so I was trying to get him outside so I could get him help. Then when you accused me, I-I panicked."

"Why are you asking these questions?" Mom crossed her arms over her chest. "You sound like the police."

"I'm just asking." I gave her an innocent smile. "Curiosity and all that."

"Beatrice Ophelia Sawyer, don't you lie to me."

"Mom, I'm only asking some questions. It's—"

"What do you mean asking some questions? Who else have you been talking with?"

I opened my mouth, but I had no reply. If I admitted that I was investigating, my mom would never let me out of the house again. But when it came to my mom, lying never worked. She always saw through it.

"Beatrice, this is a murderer we're talking about. If you ask the wrong person the wrong question, you could be killed! Haven't you seen those cop shows?"

"Aunt Penny is being wrongly accused. I'm not doing anything dangerous. I'm only searching for any information that could help."

"Don't do this for me," Aunt Penny whispered. "The police have matters well in hand."

A knock thumped on the door and saved me from anymore of Mom's interrogation. For now. "Time's up," the officer called.

"Come back." Aunt Penny leaped forward and snatched my mom's hands. "Please come back and see me."

"As soon as they'll let us," Mom promised. "And next time I'll bring Dad. It would do him good to see you."

"Tell him it'll be all right now. No matter how this turns out, things will be better."

After one more tight hug, we bid our goodbyes, and the officer escorted us from the room and to the front door of the station. For the entire car ride back to the festival, Mom argued against my investigation. Her imagination ran rampant with ideas of what could happen to me if I encountered the true killer—beheaded, stabbed, and poisoned, just to name a few. I kept silent to avoid revealing Theo and Julian's involvement as well. If she knew both of her kids were playing detective...

Not that I'd fooled myself into believing hunting down a killer was a safe endeavor. I knew it'd be a risk, but it was a risk someone needed to take. When we arrived at the festival, I tossed Mom the keys and hopped out of the car.

"Want to meet here for dinner tonight? Then you don't have to cook."

"You're changing the subject."

"But you don't have to cook?" I wiggled my eyebrows at her like my brother always did when he was trying to avoid getting in trouble.

She shook a finger at me. "You're not getting out of this conversation, young lady. I'm going to tell your father, and we'll see what he says."

"Love you, Mom," I said in a singsong voice, then kissed her cheek. "And I'm happy for you. And Aunt Penny."

Her stern face softened, and she pulled in a deep breath. "Part of me can't believe it's true. That I'll wake up and this'll all have been a dream. It's been so long since I've had my sister, but now there's hope." She focused back on me. "We still have a lot to work through, emotions and hurtful words said over the years that aren't simply erased. But I have hope that we can be friends again."

I waved her off, then sent a quick group text to my brother and Julian to find their locations. Determination swelled within me. My mother and aunt needed time together. To talk and cry and share and heal. But they could only get that if my aunt was released. If her name was cleared.

My phone buzzed, and a message from my brother popped up on the screen. "By the booster."

I jogged over to the tent, but when I was a few yards away, I stilled. My jaw dropped.

Ethereal ghosts and black-sequined bats hung from the sides of the tent roof and fluttered in the gentle Lake Erie breeze. Black and orange pumpkins flickered with light despite the sunlit area, and a mist swirled around the ground, writhing into the air so that if you saw only out of the corner of your eye, you might think you saw a spirit.

Julian strolled out of the booster tent, holding a frappucino, and grinned at me.

"Where did you get all this?" I shook my head.

"When you ask the resident Halloween-obsessed Cindy for ghost-hunting decor, well, she delivered."

The misspelled "Cokies" sign in front of the tent had also been transformed. In slasher-horror writing, it now read: "Ghost Stories with Theo Sawyer at noon. Come learn the hidden history of Thisbe Harbor."

Theo trotted up to us and took the melty frappucino from Julian. "Cindy lent me a grim reaper's costume, too, but I thought it might be too much."

"This is incredible." I shook my head. "You are incredible."

He ducked his head but that couldn't hide his pleasure. "It's all thanks to Cindy. But that's not important right now. Did Julian tell you what we found?"

I perked up. "Wait, you found something out?"

"I don't think it's that helpful, but your brother was strutting around like we solved the case. So maybe it's more important than I think."

"Well, Julian finally did what we hired him to do"—Theo propped his hands on his hips—"and used his contacts."

Julian snorted. "I don't recall hearing anything about a salary or hourly wage."

"You work for free." Theo waved a hand at him, then continued, "Vincent recently sold his house—the house he and his wife spent their entire married life in."

"O-okay." I didn't see how Vincent's living situation had anything to do with his alibi or with our case. Who cared if he sold his house? Perhaps it held too many memories for him and he was working on moving through the grieving process.

"Really?" Theo facepalmed. "Neither of you get it?"

Julian and I both shrugged.

"Where's he been living? Julian's librarian friend didn't seem to know that."

"I don't know, Theo." I patted his shoulder. "It doesn't seem like a big deal. The guy can live wherever he wants. We really need to know where he was at on Saturday morning, not where he's living."

My brother deflated like a balloon, but I nudged him with my elbow. "Chin up. The ghost hour is approaching, and you're going to knock their socks off. Afterward, we can regroup and figure out what to do next."

"How did the visit with your aunt go?" Julian asked.

Theo wrinkled his nose. "I'm glad you took the lead on that one, sis."

"There's a chance for them now—for Mom and Aunt Penny." I drew in a deep breath, still hardly able to believe it myself. "Miracles might really happen." Which meant there might be a chance for me and Julian too.

The thought nearly caused me to trip. What was wrong with me lately? Julian and I were just friends.

But there was something about his easy, calm manner, the way he thought through situations, the way he checked on others and truly cared...

I couldn't help but find him attractive.

Not that I was going to admit that to anyone.

"She didn't have any information for the investigation, though. She didn't remember anyone else here. Although she did mention rigor mortis hadn't set in yet. Which means he couldn't have been dead for too long."

"That or he'd been dead long enough for his body to relax again," Theo said.

My nose wrinkled, and I shuddered. "I suppose she wouldn't know the difference. I certainly wouldn't."

"Sometimes, I wonder about you two." Julian snorted. "No one—at least, none of us normal people—would know that."

"We have arrived!" Cindy's singsong voice called out.

She marched through the crowd, an army of older ladies toting hundreds of desserts in plastic containers.

Cindy had called in the Ladies' Baking Society of Thisbe Harbor or Lisbeth (LBSTH) as they liked to call themselves. And they'd delivered dozens of extra banana breads, cookies, brownies, and cakes. And, Cindy's favorite, Hazel brought her rock-hard brownies as well.

"Slip those under the table for now," Cindy hissed. "We'll get rid of them later. She's not the type to stay for ghost stories, but you never know with the residents around here. We all have our quirks." She winked at me, then scurried off to intercept yet another delivery.

Residents of Thisbe were quirky indeed—Cindy leading the charge of eclectic tastes with her obsession with Halloween decor.

As soon as fall hit, you could find her dressed in her witches' robes and black pointy hat and draping fake spiderwebs in her trees and headstones in her yard.

If nothing else in this weekend had gone as planned, I was at least happy to see a bit of hope in her face.

Fifteen minutes later, I once again stood at the back of the crowd watching my brother captivate everyone with yet another one of his haunting tales. This time, thanks to word of mouth, the crowd was even larger, and Julian and I passed out dozens of treats to listeners. Cindy waited near the back, her smile growing with each passing minute. After passing out the last of our chocolate chunk cookies, I shuffled around the crowd to her.

"Your brother is a natural," she whispered. "What a turnout!"

"He's in his element." I grinned at where my brother stood on his makeshift stage—a metal chair. He bent forward, arms spread wide, everyone locked on him. "People doting on him. Telling ghost stories." If only he looked this happy all the time. I recalled our conversation earlier that morning. The haunted house he'd so giddily showed me, his confession of joining me in the starting-a-business club, his dream of becoming a ghost hunter.

I drew in a breath and tilted my head back to take in the bright blue sky above. It'd been a long time since I'd felt a sense of peace and belonging in the place I'd lived. I certainly didn't feel it in my parents' basement. But here in Thisbe Harbor—well, Mimi said it best when she said that Thisbe Harbor had a kind of magic to it. And after spending the weekend here, I never wanted to leave again.

Biting my bottom lip, I slipped my phone from my back pocket and searched for the listing my brother had discovered. Two acres of property overlooking the beautiful lake. Four bedrooms, 2.5 bathrooms, a wraparound porch, a butler's pantry, parlor room. And that tower. The home was everything I'd dreamed of as a child.

I clicked on the auction information. Zero bids so far, but a starting bid of $55,000. I doubted a bank would give us a loan for the property, not with the house's condition. Besides, Theo and I had no construction experience. But we could learn.

One impossible dream was enough for the weekend. I pocketed my phone again and focused back on the crowd. Columbus welcomed small businesses. It was a great place to begin my candlemaking journey.

But it wasn't Thisbe Harbor.

"Is something bothering you?" Cindy rested a hand on my arm and I jerked back to the present.

If I told her what was really on my mind, she wouldn't be able to keep it a secret from my grandfather. And I didn't want to raise his hopes. Yet.

Although, if I were honest with myself, my hopes were high enough that I wasn't sure anything could stop me from staying in Thisbe.

I lifted my almost-empty tray of boxed cookies. "I'm going to refill this. Theo should be wrapping up soon, but there's time to sell a few more."

"Don't work too hard, dear. This is supposed to be a fun weekend for you!"

"Saving Thisbe is the best thing I could be doing." I shrugged then rounded the crowd to the back of the booster tent. While the crowd for Theo's talk had grown from this morning, many of the festival goers had already snagged greasy burgers and fries or corn dogs for their lunch and weren't interested in baked goods. Not that I blamed them.

I inhaled the scent of fried food and my stomach growled. After this, I wouldn't mind snagging one of those deep fried sausages with peppers all loaded on a hot dog bun. Then maybe Julian and Theo would want to share a bucket of fries with extra salt and drizzled with as much ketchup as could fit.

Reaching the back of the booster tent, I set my tray on the edge of a table then arranged some of the plastic dessert containers on it. The crowd out front laughed and applauded. My brother must be wrapping up his presentation sooner than I thought.

Well, might as well clean up a bit then. The next set of volunteers would be here soon, and it wouldn't be fair to leave them with a mess. I crouched and lifted the tablecloth hiding the many boxes of Hazel's brownies. Even if she were in the crowd, she'd hopefully be too distracted by my brother to see me throwing them out.

I pulled out the first stack of plastic boxes, and a white paper floated off the top and fluttered to the ground. Huh. I hadn't noticed Hazel leaving us a note. Hopefully it wasn't a sob story about the brownies. I was a sucker for sob stories and Cindy would never forgive me if I didn't throw these out.

Five words were scrawled across the page:
BACK OFF OR YOU'RE NEXT.

An icy shiver drenched my body like I'd plunged into the depths of Lake Erie in winter. This was no sob story. This was a warning.

My hands shook, and the paper slipped from the grasp. It drifted back to the ground, but the words continued to glare up at me. The killer had found me out.

I gulped in air. Okay, think, Beatrice, think. If the killer was sending us a warning, that meant we had to be close. Had anyone seen the mayor around here? Or Vincent?

I'd been so focused on selling goodies and watching my brother that I hadn't bothered to pay attention to anyone loitering behind the booster tent. Which gave the killer the perfect opportunity.

I swept my gaze across the crowd and found Julian. I motioned for him mouthed, "Come here."

He immediately hurried toward me, and when he was a few feet away, he asked, "Are you okay? What happened?" He reached up and cupped my cheek. "You look like you've seen a real ghost."

I leaned into his touch and let myself savor his warm fingers on my cold skin. I wanted nothing more than to throw my arms around him and bury my face against his neck. Have him whisper in his deep baritone that everything would be okay. For the first time, this investigation scared me.

But I needed to put that aside. The killer could still be around. Could be watching to make sure we received their message. We needed to get Joel here to manage the crowd and question everyone.

"You need to call Joel." I pointed a shaking finger at the message.

Julian crouched and reached for the paper. I lunged forward and pulled back his arm, the force sending him to his butt. "Don't touch it! There could be fingerprints."

His eyes widened. "Is that . . . ?" He yanked his phone from his back pocket. In seconds, he lifted his phone to his ear and waited for Joel to pick up.

I swallowed hard and stole a glance around the area. But there were so many people. Any of them could have done this. Any of them could be watching me. The hair on the back of my neck rose. Any of them could be waiting to make me the next victim.

Chapter Twenty-Two

Red and blue police lights swarmed my vision. Julian, Theo, and I stood outside of the marina, awaiting our trial by Joel's fury.

He'd thankfully answered Julian's call on the second ring and had rushed to the booster tent per our request. Now, officers were swarming the festival, questioning Theo's crowd and collecting evidence. They'd already bagged the warning note as well as the tablecloth and Hazel's brownie container for fingerprints. At least Cindy didn't have to get rid of Hazel's brownies herself this time.

Three police officers exited the two vehicles and crossed the parking lot toward us. None of us even bothered trying to protest. The anger simmering underneath Joel's words when we'd talked to him told me everything I needed to know. Joel knew we were investigating when he'd told us not to, and we were in big trouble.

"Chief has requested you come into the station for a chat," the tall officer explained. He glanced toward Julian. "Even you."

The shorter officer snorted. "You mean, 'especially you.'"

The officers unhooked handcuffs from their belts.

"Is that really necessary?" Julian crossed his arms.

Tall shrugged. "Chief's orders."

"You can tell him I think he's petty. This is ridiculous."

"Obstructing an investigation is a legitimate crime," Short said.

I sighed and held my hands out in front of me. Several people from the crowd lifted their phones and snapped a few photos, excitement and disbelief tinging their whispered gossip. Maybe I should ask them for a copy when this was all over—the candlemaker who couldn't keep her nose out of everyone's business and went to jail before she could launch her dream.

The officer cuffed my hands behind my back and led me to a waiting car, where I unceremoniously and quite clumsily climbed into the backseat. I'd never worn handcuffs before. And after a twenty-minute drive, in which I'm pretty sure he took the long route, I never wanted to wear handcuffs again.

We arrived at the police station, my wrists already sore from my scramble to keep from being knocked around in the backseat as we passed over every pothole on this earth. The dispatcher raised an eyebrow from behind her desk. "The boys are already in the chief's office. He's on his way, and he's fit to be tied." She clucked her tongue. "You kids always were troublemakers. I told your grandfather to keep a closer watch on you."

I snorted. What would she say if she knew Papa had encouraged us "troublemakers?" He was, after all—because of my promise to him to clear my aunt's name—why we were here.

The officer nudged me from behind and steered me toward an office down a short, narrow hallway. Three wooden chairs stood in front of a large cherry desk in the middle of the room, and a golden nameplate on the desk read: Chief Joel Laurent. Stacks of papers scattered across the desk, and the pencil holder had been knocked over, pens and papers littering the papers and some on the floor in front of the desk.

Julian and Theo sat in two of the three wooden chairs in front of the desk, both their hands cuffed to the back rungs of the chairs. I walked forward and plopped into the remaining chair between them. The officer behind me secured my hands to the chair. Completely unnecessary, but Joel probably wanted to teach us a lesson.

"Welcome to the party," Theo said dryly.

The radio on the officer's belt squawked. "Chief's arrived. Incoming."

The voice had barely fallen silent when Joel marched into the room and jabbed a finger toward his brother as he rounded the desk. "Start talking." He smacked his hands on the top of the desk and leaned over it, gaze smoldering at us. "Didn't I ask you to stay out of this?"

"I—"

But the chief wasn't about to give me a chance. "Yes, I recall specifically asking you to leave this investigation to me. The chief of police. Yet here I find you encouraging my brother to act like a common criminal—breaking and entering, obstructing a crime scene, causing a public disturbance."

"She didn't encourage me to do any of it." Julian barked out a hollow laugh. "I volunteered."

"If it's any consolation, he did tell us we were nuts." Theo shrugged and rocked back in his chair, as if being handcuffed and interrogated in the chief of police's office was a normal, everyday occurrence.

"That's no consolation at all. He should have listened." Joel glowered at the three of us. "You're lucky that it was simply a warning. Do you not realize there is a murderer out there? That a man has already been killed? You have a target on your backs now. They easily could've shot you first instead of giving you a warning."

I squirmed in my chair.

Being shot was not on the list of ways I wanted to die. Based on my brother's descriptions from what he'd learned in his classes, death by bullet sounded horribly painful. And if the shooter missed a critical body part . . . Bleeding out sounded like an even worse, more agonizing death.

But then I frowned. Joel thought the murderer was still out there. Which meant—"Is Aunt Penny free?" I interrupted whatever argument Julian and Joel had started into.

Joel blinked and stared at me. "What?"

"Is Aunt Penny cleared? You said the murderer is still—"

His scowl deepened and darkened his face further. "As the mayor has continually reminded me, my duty is to keep our town safe."

Meaning the mayor didn't want Aunt Penny freed. Not when he was about to take the marina for himself. I straightened in my chair and tried to lean forward, but my handcuffs knocked against the chair and tugged me back. "Did you know the mayor offered a million dollars for the marina?"

Joel's eyes narrowed. "What do you mean?"

Hope swelled in me. We'd found something he didn't know. "Apparently, before he died, Owens had three offers on the marina."

"I know of your aunt and Vincent. Maeve told me of those herself."

"Well, the mayor is one of them too. Maeve said he knew she was inheriting the marina before she even did and approached her about it. Her sister says it's a lowball offer, but Maeve needs the money—which the mayor would know."

"What exactly are you saying, Miss Sawyer?"

"I think the mayor found out Owens wasn't going to sell him the marina because he was trying to leverage his position to get the property for cheap. So the mayor offed him and framed my aunt to get two of his competitors out of the way. Then he would convince Maeve to sell the place to him."

Joel groaned. "Miss Sawyer, are you accusing the mayor of murdering Mr. Owens? Because that's a serious charge to level against him."

"I'm not accusing him of anything." Yet. "But I thought you should know—"

"Please stop." Joel scrubbed his hands over his face. "Please stop investigating and let me and my men do our jobs and keep you safe."

"Have you even looked into him?" I asked. "He—"

"Miss Sawyer." Joel folded his hands on his desk.

"Wouldn't you defend your family?" Julian asked. "If Aunt—"

"I'm the chief of police," Joel snapped. "My job is to defend my family and my community. Which includes the three of you. So, please, let me do my job. And you do yours. Stop butting in."

"Just think about it," I tried one last time. Why wouldn't he at least consider my idea? Didn't he find it a little suspicious that the mayor wanted the marina? That he was targeting Maeve so soon after Owens's death?

Joel pushed to his feet. "I know this is disappointing. But investigating often isn't as fun—or as rewarding—as they make it look on TV. In real life, police have to not only figure out whodunnit, as the shows like to say, but we have to have solid evidence proving the fact. And getting that evidence takes time. Especially in a small town like this where we don't have the crime labs and forensic teams at our disposal. Autopsies and lab results take weeks because we have to send things to bigger cities for their resources. So please understand. I have to investigate a certain way in order for a judge not to throw the book at me. And investigating the right way takes time. Okay?"

"Yes, sir," I muttered.

"Good. Now, Miss Sawyer, can we have a word in private, please?"

I snapped my mouth shut, and my cheeks flamed. What had I done this time? The officer behind us stepped up and unlocked my hands. I rubbed my wrists, the hour they were bound enough to leave a red ring around them. Then I dragged in a deep breath and followed Joel to the hall.

The minute we stepped into the stark white room, he shut the door behind us and growled, "Stay away from my brother."

Blood drained from my face. I'd known he was going to say something like that. Joel never had liked me. But knowing something was coming and hearing it happen were two different things.

Because I didn't want to stay away from Julian.

I didn't want to lose our friendly banter.

Didn't want to lose the tentative trust we'd built again.

"Julian was doing fine without you. He's worked hard to get into grad school and will be very busy this fall with classes and working.

I care about my brother, and I'm not going to let him throw away all he's worked for because of you. Don't ruin his life again."

I staggered back like he'd slapped me. Ruin his life again? We were kids when we'd parted before. I couldn't have ruined his life. Kids didn't do that.

Dread and guilt curled in my stomach. Because the voice in the back of my mind told me it was true. Julian and I had promised to be friends till doom or die. And I hadn't been there when he'd needed me most. Simply left because my own life was spiraling out of control and I could barely stay afloat.

Tears burned the backs of my eyes. But I couldn't cry now. I couldn't let Joel see how much his words hurt me.

"I—" The words to apologize, to try to explain myself, stuck in the mess of tears that threatened to break forth if I didn't pull myself together soon. I bit the inside of my cheek until I tasted blood.

"I'm glad we understand each other now." Joel reached for the doorknob behind me, his gaze never leaving my face. He shoved open the door and barked, "Take the brother and sister home. And warn their parents to put them under surveillance. I don't want them getting any other bright ideas."

Chapter Twenty-Three

Explaining our investigation efforts to Mom and Dad and Papa wasn't how I wanted to spend the next two hours. Especially not when Joel's words were still ringing in my ears.

By the time they'd finished grilling us and demanding we forget our sleuthing efforts, a headache pounded through my skull. I kneaded my knuckles against my eyes and shuffled down the hall to my shared bedroom with my brother. At this point, I wanted nothing more than to throw myself onto my bed, have a good cry, then maybe take a nap.

"What are you doing?" Theo jogged after me.

I pushed open the bedroom door. "Having a moment. You're not invited." I started to shut the door, but he squeezed his skinny body through before it closed. "Theo," I moaned, but I crossed the room and flopped down on the bed.

He didn't answer, but I could hear the shifting of blankets and the creaking of the floor as he presumably dragged his own pillow and blankets closer. I wasn't about to start the conversation. Not since he'd been the one to butt into my pity party.

"What did Joel say to you?" He broke the silence after another minute.

"Considering he shut the door, I don't think it was meant to be any of your business."

"That's exactly when he made it my business."

"It was nothing, Theo—"

"It's about Julian, isn't it?"

I buried my face in my pillow and prayed the pressure would keep any threat of tears away. I didn't want to cry. Being in Thisbe had brought to light so many things I'd wished away, feelings I'd buried so deep inside me I thought they couldn't hurt me. Yet here they were.

"Why did you two stop talking?" Theo asked, his voice muffled by the pillow on my head.

I didn't want to have this conversation. Not now. Not when Joel wanted me to leave Julian again.

"Have you told him how you feel?"

"He told me to stay away," I blurted. "That Julian was doing fine without me and didn't need me ruining his life again." The pillow whipped off my face to be replaced by Theo glowering down at me.

"Give that back." I lunged for the pillow, but Theo held it just out of reach.

"What do you mean ruining his life? You're not ruining anyone's life."

I picked at the edge of the comforter without even bothering to respond. Because no matter how much I hated to admit it, Joel was right. I was a bad influence on his brother. First I'd abandoned him, then I'd gotten him nearly thrown in prison.

But Theo didn't seem to notice my silence. "Who does he think he is anyway? He's telling us to butt out of his business; well, I'll tell him. He's got no business butting into your or Julian's relationship."

I couldn't help but give a small smile at my brother's indignation. The exact indignation Joel probably felt at me for getting his brother in trouble with the law.

My humor faded.

Because the fact remained: I had gotten Julian in trouble—could've even gotten him killed. And I'd never forgive myself if that happened. Maybe it was best I stayed away. I could keep my head down, focus on my business...

An image of the bystanders snapping pictures of me in cuffs popped into my mind. It was going to be even harder to start a business here in Thisbe now. No one would want to buy candles from someone who couldn't stay out of trouble with the police.

"It's going to be okay." Theo's voice dropped, softer now. "We'll free Aunt Penny and we're going to make your business work."

To anyone else, the change in topic would've been surprising. But my brother always knew me better than anyone else. I rarely had one problem whirling around in my mind at a time.

I stole my pillow back and hugged it to my chest. "How?"

He lightly punched my shoulder. "With a little of that good ole Sawyer magic."

Perhaps Mom felt bad about her earlier interrogation. Or maybe she really did just want a night off cooking. Either way, we found ourselves back at the festival that evening to gorge ourselves on greasy fair food. A funnel cake, a soft pretzel dipped in cups of cheese, a whole bucket of fries, and a corn dog or two sounded like a great idea to help me feel a bit better after this afternoon's events.

And no, I would not be sharing with my brother.

We walked under the colored flag awning at the festival's entrance, and I adjusted the collar of my jacket. I'd changed into jeans, a t-shirt, and one of my brother's oversized jackets in hopes no one would recognize me from earlier. But since I'd be walking around with my unforgettable brother, the attempted outfit change probably wouldn't do me much good. At least it made me feel a bit more inconspicuous.

Dad led us to the side of the pathway and dug in his back pocket for his wallet. He handed two twenty dollar bills to both my brother and me. "For food or whatever else you'd like to spend it on."

"You're letting them go off by themselves?" Mom frowned and crossed her arms. "I don't think that's a very good idea."

"Do I have your promise to stay out of trouble?" Dad gave us both a stern look.

I nodded. "I want to avoid Joel as much as you want us to."

"Take a boat then. Enjoy the island. And eat as much as you want." Dad pulled my brother and me into side hugs. "We leave tomorrow afternoon, so maybe you should think about enjoying yourselves for once."

"Yes, Dad," Theo and I chorused like we used to as kids.

He gave us one more squeeze then reached out a hand for Mom. "And we will go enjoy ourselves. Sawyer, you joining us or the kids?"

Papa glanced over from where he sat in his wheelchair observing the festivities. He winked, then motioned toward my parents. "I'll stick with you old party poopers. I'm too old to go with the kids nowadays."

Mom pursed her lips and frowned. Papa had defended us this afternoon, claiming we'd done it all for family and we hadn't gotten hurt so it wasn't a big deal. Mom had not appreciated his perspective. I had a feeling she'd be exchanging more words with him after they were out of earshot.

Dad tugged her forward. "Come on, Helene."

"Do you want me to push you?"

Papa shook his head. "Nah. I want to go slow and take everything in. Don't worry about me."

My parents exchanged a look but nodded and started forward. The moment their backs turned, Papa shot his chair forward and skidded to a stop in front of us.

"Do as your parents said and stay out of trouble. But that doesn't mean you can't keep your eyes open and your eyes peeled, eh?"

Theo laughed. "Nothing will stop us from that, Papa."

"But only if you can be safe." He wagged a finger at us. "I don't need to be losing anyone else, ya hear me?"

"I'll keep us safe." Theo puffed out his chest and pretended to flex his biceps.

Papa laughed. "That is what I'm afraid of."

Theo cackled and gave Papa a hug. The two of them were peas in a pod, always ready with a joke or a snarky comment. They both lived to make others laugh.

Papa rolled away before my parents realized they weren't being followed, leaving Theo and I to ourselves.

"Corn dogs first?" I asked.

"Actually, wait." Theo grabbed my wrist to keep me from walking away. "I wasn't kidding when I told Papa I'd protect you."

I raised an eyebrow and looked him up and down. "We both know that I hit harder."

"Ha ha. Well, you may sing a different tune when you see this." He lifted something from his front pocket and tossed it toward me.

I caught the little tube, barely the size of my palm.

"There's a pocketknife on one end and a pepper spray that's useful for ghosts and people on the other."

I peered closer at it and noticed the small nozzle on one end and the slider button on the other end for the knife. "What do you mean useful for ghosts and people?"

"It's made of capsaicin, which is in pepper spray; salt; and liquid iron. Pepper spray to repel humans, if need be, and the salt and iron to repel ghosts."

"Where did you get this?" While I didn't believe in ghosts, having this on hand wouldn't be a bad idea. Walking around the festival, a murderer watching our every step. But I could do some damage with a knife and pepper spray.

"I made it," he mumbled.

My mouth dropped open. Now I was really impressed. I shook the canister and leaned forward. "*You* made this? How? When?"

"Last semester." He shrugged. "I made it as a joke in my forensic chemistry class, but it's actually proved useful, so I've kept it around."

Why my brother would be pepper spraying anyone, I didn't know. But who knew what went on in the boys' dorm of a college? "Let's go get something to eat."

"Can I join?"

Chapter Twenty-Four

I whirled around at the sound of Julian's casual tone.

He stood no more than a dozen paces away, hands shoved in his pockets, and a lazy half smile on his lips.

I shot my brother a narrow-eyed look.

He raised his hands and shook his head. "I didn't call anyone."

"I've been sitting here for . . ." Julian glanced at his phone. "Three hours now. And I've eaten way too many of those random fish-flavored crackers that sound awful but taste amazing."

"You're not supposed to be here." I crossed my arms and glared at him. If Joel caught me with his brother, I'd be dead before the end of the day. I winced to myself. Okay, maybe not dead. Dead was too real. But he certainly wouldn't let us get away with it.

"Nice to see you too." Julian smirked. "I know I wasn't invited, but this has kind of been our place. You know, to discuss everything. And after this afternoon, I figured we had things to discuss."

"Like your brother," Theo muttered.

I groaned, but the set of Theo's eyebrows told me nothing would sway him from what he saw as his holy war.

"For your information," Theo plowed onward, "your brother—"

"Has no business dictating my friendships."

I blinked and stared at him. "You know?"

"I'm not an idiot to think that my brother rudely pulled you into the hallway to have a little heart-to-heart with you." He wrinkled his nose. "Although perhaps that was his version of a heart-to-heart. Either way, he never should have placed the blame of everything on your shoulders, and he absolutely should not have told you to stay away. I choose my friends, and I choose you."

Warmth filled me at those words, and I tried to ignore the feeling that danced in my stomach. He chose me. As his friend.

"Well"—Theo blew out a breath—"glad that's already straightened out. Anyone want to find something to eat?"

"But what will Joel say? If he finds out—"

"If he finds out, you can remind him that his job is to protect the citizens of Thisbe Harbor, not threaten them."

Theo whistled and reached out a hand to fist bump. "I knew I liked you, man."

Julian tapped his fist against Theo's. I shook my head at the two. It was all well and good to be brave and speak my mind right now, but when staring down the face of the law? I didn't think I'd ever have the courage to tell Joel that I was going to be Julian's friend whether he wanted me to or not.

But I did finally have the courage, and the opportunity, to say something I should have a long time ago. I sucked in a deep breath and focused on Julian. "Joel is right, though. I ran. You'd lost your mom and needed a friend, and I wasn't there."

The first year of high school had been brutal. Since I'd spent most of my childhood summers in Thisbe, I'd never developed many friendships in middle school. And freshman year, no one wanted to befriend the frizzy-haired, I've-got-no-idea-what-I-want-to-do-with-my-life girl. But that was no excuse for not being there. A good friend would've, no matter what.

"I'm sorry, Julian." I wrapped my arms around myself. "And I hope that you will give me another chance to be a better friend."

His gaze softened and he reached over and lightly brushed his fingers over my shoulder. A spark shivered up my spine at his touch. "We were young and scared and going through things we didn't know how to handle."

"That's no excuse for what I did." I swallowed hard. "But I hope you can forgive me, and we can try again. And maybe, this time, Joel might even come around too."

I honestly wasn't sure I wanted to be friends with the goody-two-shoes police chief, but he was Julian's family. If Julian didn't like Theo, I didn't think we could be friends, so I needed to offer him the same courtesy.

His fingers traced up to my cheek. "I forgave you a long time ago, Beatrice Sawyer."

The world seemed to still around us. Julian's fingers dropped to my chin and tilted it up ever so slightly. I breathed in his scent of cedar and mint soap.

"All right, all right." Theo's voice cut through, and I jerked away from Julian. My brother pretended to gag. "I didn't come here to see you two gush all over each other. If that's what you're going to do, get a—"

"Theo." I ground out, my cheeks on fire. "Sometimes I hate having you as a brother." Although I don't know what I would have done if I had kissed Julian. So much for staying away.

Theo slung an arm around my shoulder and pulled me against his side. "The pleasure is all mine, Sister Dearest."

"Anyone want coffee?" Julian asked. "My treat?"

"Well, if you're paying!" Theo skipped ahead a few steps. "Let's go!"

I snuck a peek at Julian to find him looking down at me with that gorgeous grin and tender gaze. My mouth went dry, and I forced myself to hurry after my brother. I needed to figure out my own life—if I could live in Thisbe, if I could start my own business—before I added a relationship to the mix. But oh, at this moment, I wanted nothing more than to turn and throw myself into Julian's arms.

We walked to the opposite side of the festival where the coffee truck sat near the front doors of the marina building. A half-dozen people formed a jagged line in front of the truck, and we filed in behind them. I swallowed back a groan. Miss Flirty—Julian's wanna-be-girlfriend—once again manned the truck. At least Theo was with us. Not that my skinny, lanky brother was much compared to Julian. Maybe I could slip out of line before we reached the front. I didn't really want anything, after all.

As we moved forward in line, I studied the people around us, catching snippets of conversation as people jostled past. Most seemed excited to be here and enjoying their time, although a few complained about the rest of the town and there being nothing to do.

Hopefully that would change if this festival continued going well.

My gaze landed on a thin, balding man striding through the crowd, gaze leveled on the coffee truck. He wore a black suit and tie, which was in stark contrast to the shorts and t-shirts others wore around him.

"Who is that?" I whispered to Julian.

He followed my gaze and shook his head. "I have no idea."

The man shifted a black leather briefcase to his other hand.

"What's he doing?" Julian frowned.

Fancy Pants rolled back his shoulders, adjusted his suit coat, and barged into the front of the line without a glance at those behind him. I leaned forward from our place as fourth in line. Something told me this guy wasn't here just to enjoy the festival.

Miss Flirty gave him an obvious once-over then asked, "What can I do for you, sir? Passing through town?"

I sniffed. Apparently, if you dressed to the nines, you got a free pass for cutting the line. Wish I'd known that yesterday before she'd yelled at me for thinking I'd cut in front of Julian. But as much as I despised the barista, at least she managed to succeed in asking a leading question. Thisbe Harbor wasn't exactly the place many people stopped when "passing through town." Especially not well-dressed businessmen.

"I'll have a small black coffee." He fished a wallet from his pocket and tapped a credit card against the card reader. "And some information, if you have it?" He slid a business card from his wallet and held it out to the barista. Miss Flirty peered down at it, and when she nodded, the businessman tucked it and his wallet back into his pocket. "I'm looking for a Mr. Gilberth. We have an appointment, but I did not realize that this, uh, gathering would have such a turnout, and we neglected to set a meeting place. Do you know where I can find Mr. Gilberth?"

I clutched Julian's arm and nodded my head toward the patron. This businessman had a meeting with the mayor?

Miss Flirty shrugged a shoulder. "The mayor finished up the opening ceremonies not that long ago. I don't know where he went after that."

A frown pulled down the businessman's lips. "I don't think you understand. It's very important that I find him."

"And I don't know where he is." Miss Flirty flapped a hand toward the line. "Sir, you're holding up the line and you didn't even wait your turn. You'll have to ask someone else for help."

I bit back a chuckle. Apparently I wasn't the only one she didn't mind being rude to.

The second barista in the truck slid a Styrofoam cup of steaming coffee onto the counter. "Order up."

Miss Flirty pushed the cup toward the businessman. "Enjoy the coffee and the festival. Hope you return to Thisbe Harbor."

He jerked the cup off the counter, and some of the hot liquid splashed through the lid onto his starched shirt. His knuckles whitened around the cup. "Oh, I'll return." He gave a mirthless laugh. "This place needs me."

I nudged Julian. Whoever this was had just written himself onto my suspect list.

The well-dressed man stormed out of line and barged through the crowd toward the parking lot.

"Should I follow him?" Theo whispered.

"Should you what?" Julian frowned at him.

"I want a large salted caramel frappucino with an extra shot of espresso and extra caramel."

"Theo, we promised not to!" I hissed.

But my brother was already hustling after the suspect.

Julian shook his head. "You Sawyers are something else. Shall we see if we can get information a different way?"

"What do you mean?" I asked.

He sauntered up to the coffee truck as the person in front of us took their order and left.

Miss Flirty's gaze landed on him, and her face lit up. She tucked her hands under her chin and purred, "Hey, Julian. It's so wonderful to see you again. Two times in two days. You must really like the coffee here, huh?"

I swallowed a gag. Did she really think this was how you snagged a boyfriend? This girl really was stuck in high school.

"Who was that guy?" Julian jerked his chin in the direction the businessman had stalked off. "He seemed pretty upset."

Miss Flirty flicked her long hair over a shoulder. "Oh, some real estate guy. A Mr. Taylor something or other." She bit her lower lip and rested her elbows on the counter between them, one finger spinning a strand of her hair. "He wanted to talk to the mayor, but how am I supposed to know where he is? I'm stuck in this truck all day."

"Right." Julian flicked me a quick glance. A real estate guy? Interesting. "Did you happen to see where he worked?"

"No." She snorted. "He wasn't very nice, was he? I sure hope we don't see him around here again."

"What'd he want with the mayor?" I shuffled forward a step.

She curled her lip and wrinkled her nose, barely flicking me a glance. "How am I supposed to know that? Didn't you hear me say I don't know who he is?"

"He mentioned meeting with the mayor. Do you know what kind of meeting? Was it for real estate?" I pressed. Considering I'd overheard their conversation, I doubted she knew the answer, but I'd hoped my questions would prompt her into remembering the man's company or what type of real estate he worked in.

Her gaze slid up and down, giving me another once-over that wasn't any kinder than the first. "Who are you again?"

"Beatrice Sawyer." I wanted to ask what that had to do with my question, but I could guess. She wanted to size up her competition. Well, joke was on her, because I wasn't competition. I was not looking for a relationship with Julian. One hundred percent not looking.

Something flashed in her eyes, and her lips turned upward in a smug smile for a split second. Then she pressed a hand to her chest and drew back. "Oh my goodness." Her voice rose two decibels louder than it needed to be. "Aren't you the girl whose aunt was arrested for the murder of that marina guy?"

Anger simmered in my stomach. Really? She was trying to gang everyone up on the new girl so she didn't steal the popular boy from the popular girl?

"My aunt didn't kill anyone." I lifted my chin in defiance.

Julian rested a hand on my back, his lips pursed. "Thanks for your help, Lydia. Let me know if you see that guy around again, yeah?"

"Of course, anything you need, Jules." She reached out and grabbed his sleeve. "Do you want any coffee or anything? It's on the house, you know."

"Large salted caramel frappucino with an extra shot of espresso and extra caramel?"

He flicked a glance in my direction and winked. If Miss Flirty was going to be a jerk, I supposed my brother might as well get a free coffee out of it.

Chapter Twenty-Five

I opened the lid of my chai cup to let the aroma wrap around me. I hadn't been able to resist after all. The strong scents of ginger and clove felt like a warm blanket settling on my shoulders. This smelled like homemade chai—not the nasty store-bought stuff. Whoever owned Beans & Leaves knew how to make a good chai.

Sipping my drink, I let the warmth of the spices work all the way to my toes.

If chai was always made like this, it might rival my current matcha obsession. Perhaps I'd make a custom line for Beans & Leaves inspired by their customer's favorite drinks. Chai would smell heavenly in candle form. And despite my aversion, coffee in candle form always made me want to try the drink again. Maybe I could do a series of coffee candles for each season—a pistachio, whipped cream, and espresso for summer; pumpkin and maple for fall; peppermint mocha for winter; and a raspberry mocha for spring.

Mm, there were so many delicious coffees that would make equally delectable candles. They couldn't say no to that, right? I'd have to ask Julian who owned the local coffee shop so I could meet them and develop a candle plan to pitch to them.

"She's really harmless," Julian said. Condensation dripped from the frappucino and spattered the front of his t-shirt. You knew it was hot when a frozen coffee started melting immediately.

I turned toward my childhood best friend and raised an eyebrow. She? As far as I knew, I hadn't said anything about a girl. Just wax and wicks and business plans.

"Lydia," he continued. "She's had a rough life, and I don't think she realizes how she's coming across, so—" I pressed a hand to my mouth to keep from laughing. He was bringing this up now? He cut off his sentence with a "What?"

I shook my head. This was not the conversation I thought I'd be having at this point. "You don't have to explain your love life to me."

"Beatrice! That's not what I'm saying!" He reached over to swat my arm.

I ducked, a grin twisting my lips, then retaliated with a playful punch to his upper arm. Julian tried to lean out of the way, but I successfully landed my strike with a laugh of glee.

"If you make him drop my coffee, I'll never forgive you!" My brother jogged toward us, a hand in the air and a huge grin on his face.

"No luck?" I asked.

"He hopped into his car before I could catch him." My brother shrugged. "White Tesla. Should stand out in this town."

"Well, we—"

"You didn't let me finish." Theo stuck his bottom lip out in a pout. "It wasn't all for naught."

I swept my hands out. "By all means, tell us in the most dramatic way possible what you found then."

"He had this huge bumper sticker on the back of his car in this fancy font: The Sinclair Group. Aaaannnddd..." He clasped his hands together and glanced between Julian and me.

"And tell us already!" My goodness were brothers annoying. Did everything have to be a drama filled with suspense?

"I looked them up online. It's a company owned by Taylor Sinclair, and they focus on luxury real estate for less. How that works, I don't know. Luxury doesn't ever come cheap. From what I could find, TSG has been snapping up land along Lake Erie for the past few months. The closer to the lake, the better."

"Why?" Julian asked.

"Isn't it obvious?" Theo snorted, and I rolled my eyes. It wasn't obvious or we wouldn't have asked. "You can charge a lot more money for a place with a lake view than one without."

"But that's not really a motive for murder," Julian said. "Developers buy land all the time."

"They don't usually promise that land to someone first, though. Especially not when that land is owned by someone else."

I tightened my grip on my chai cup. "What? How do you know that?"

"I'm good at research, thank you very much." My brother never was one for shying away from complimenting himself. "My theory is the mayor sealed the deal with TSG before he secured the land from

Owens. Which means he'll be liable for whatever TSG has already spent on the project if they don't get the land."

"Liable? What do you mean liable? The mayor or the town?"

"Depends on how he signed the contract."

Julian massaged the back of his neck. "If he ruins this town further . . ."

"What if he found out that Maeve was Owens's beneficiary?" I said. "Owens refused to sell to the mayor, and the mayor killed him because he thought Maeve would be easier to convince. After all, she has her son to provide for."

"But how can we prove that? We can't go to Joel—he'll tell us to butt out again," Theo said. "We need proof before telling him."

We stood in silence for several moments, racking our brains for some idea to gather evidence for Joel.

Finally, Julian shook his head. "Sometimes my brother has to take a step back to see a case in a new light. If you get too close, too wrapped up in it, it can make the details fuzzy, and it's those details that you need to solve the case. Or, at least, that's what he's told me before."

"So why don't we keep good on our promise to Mom and Dad?" Theo suggested. "I could go for some smothered ribs and tater tots. And one of those ultimate milkshakes."

"Let's do a boat tour too. It may give us a new perspective," I said.

I tried to push the puzzle from my mind as we let the festival sounds and smells wash over us. My stomach growled, and I realized I was in fact hungrier than when I'd entered the festival. A funnel cake, a soft pretzel dipped in cups of cheese, a whole bucket of fries, and a corn dog or two still sounded like a plan.

We hopped from food truck to food truck until we were laden down with smothered ribs and tater tots, two buckets of fries, a bag of three soft pretzels and cups of cheese, and four corn dogs.

"Elephant ears or funnel cakes to finish it off?" Theo asked. "I am not missing out on dessert again."

"How about one of Hazel's brownies?" Julian teased.

Theo visibly shuddered. "Ugh, don't remind me. I'll never be able to see a brownie the same way ever again."

I laughed and nudged Theo with my elbow. "Aw, too bad. That means I'll have to eat all of Wilmena's brownies." Our cousin on my dad's side was legendary for making the chocolatiest, fudgiest brownies on earth. Made with melted chocolate bars, sprinkled with chocolate chips, and slightly underbaked. There was nothing more heavenly.

I'd need to give her a call after this weekend was over. Although it might be too late to avoid begging for forgiveness. She'd scream when I told her that not only had I reunited with my childhood best friend—whom she'd never met but I'd shared all about—but we'd investigated a murder. Hopefully I could also add that we'd solved the murder.

"How about we snag a boat tour, eat all the food, then we grab dessert?" Julian asked.

The Lake Erie sky was already turning from blue to orange and yellow, the setting sun a blaze on the horizon. Julian was right. If we didn't want to miss out on the tours, we'd need to go before the sun gave way to the moon. Which, since it was the middle of summer, would still be a few hours, but I didn't want to miss a golden hour boat tour.

Ooh, that'd be a good candle name. The label could be a picture of a pink and yellow sunset over deep blue seas. Shadowed sailboats could dot the landscape, and in a beautiful, curling script the label could read "Golden Hour on the Lake."

"Sounds good to me." Theo shrugged one shoulder. "As long as I get my dessert."

We hurriedly devoured our food then headed to the boat tour line. This late in the evening, only a half dozen or so people stood in front of us. Another tour boat had just pulled into the dock, and the tourists climbed off with the assistance of the captain. They chattered about the gorgeous views and the breeze cooling their sweaty faces. All seemed to have enjoyed their time.

The captain jumped aboard the ship once again, and after straightening a few things, he motioned the line forward. "All aboard for the sunset tour of Thisbe Harbor!"

We moved with the rest of the group, and the captain greeted each one as they boarded. When Julian stepped up, the captain grinned.

"Well, this is a pleasant surprise! It's good to see you, young man." He helped Julian onto the boat, then reached a hand to me.

"Good to see you too, sir. This is my friend Beatrice and her brother Theo. Guys, this is Captain Turner. He's been a captain for as long as I can remember," Julian said.

"Nice to meet you." I flashed the captain a quick smile then squeezed his hand tightly and stepped onto the seat. My brother hopped down next to me, and the boat rocked with the sudden addition of his weight. I squealed and pulled out of the captain's grasp to pinwheel my arms.

Julian leaped forward, and I fell into his outstretched arms. Heat flooded my body as his muscular arms circled protectively around me, and I slammed against his chest.

He took a step back for balance but held me firm. Since when had my stick-figure friend become so toned? I shoved away the thought and pulled my feet under me.

"You all right, Miss?" Captain Turner asked.

"Yes. Sorry," I muttered and dove for the seat nearest us. "It's been a long time since I've been on a boat. Guess I forgot my sea legs."

"You can fall for me anytime." Julian winked and lowered himself to the seat next to me.

I blinked. Was he flirting with me? Was that a pick-up line? Or was he being silly like my brother? Why did this have to be so complicated? I opened my mouth once, twice, but I didn't know what to ask. Theo would tell me to be blunt—to come out and ask if Julian liked me, but I didn't want to wreck the friendship we had.

I swallowed a groan. What was this, a Hallmark movie?

"Everyone comfortable?" Captain Turner asked.

Once everyone nodded, he unraveled the knot anchoring the boat to the dock, then hurried to the captain's seat. He revved the boat's engine and maneuvered us from the docks. This was what I remembered as a kid. The breeze rippling through my frizzy curls, the taste of lake water on my lips, and the rock and dip of the boat as it pushed through the waves.

I sucked in a deep breath of the fresh air and leaned into the bounce of the boat. My heart twinged at the thought of leaving this place again.

The sun's darkening rays flickered on the horizon, outlining the triangular flags, the pointed booth tops, and the squares of food trucks and the office building. What would I do if I had to say goodbye to Thisbe Harbor—to Julian—again? Would I still have the courage to start my own business in Columbus?

In the big city, people rushed to and fro, horns honked late into the night, and no one had time to stop and smell the candles. Rarely did people stay home for a cozy day to light a candle, tuck under a blanket, and enjoy a moment of quiet.

Thisbe Harbor, however, seemed a place wrapped in magic. A place away from the hustle where you could breathe and where life seemed truly alive.

I chewed on the inside of my cheek and stared at the rocky outcropping we neared. I didn't know how, but I would return to Thisbe Harbor to call this place home. And I'd do it as soon as possible.

"Hey!" Theo pointed up at the cliff. "There's that haunted house."

Everyone on the boat turned at his statement. Rocks climbed up out of the water and created a slippery slope up to the grassy clifftop. The waves crashed against the bottom of the rocks and tossed white foam into the air. Sure enough, a dark Victorian-style house towered above us. From this distance, it appeared stately enough for a lord and a lady, although I knew from the pictures it was in disrepair.

I could imagine a lovely pergola perched near the edge of the cliff, complete with a fire pit and a half circle of chairs overlooking the lake. Grape vines would encircle the legs of the pergola and drape through the slatted roof. Then wildflowers and roses would create a colorful walkway to welcome visitors into the lush interior of the cozy home. Inside, I'd restore the estate to its heritage with jewel-toned walls and vintage furniture. Brass and gold fixtures would complete the look with a touch of elegance.

"Julian, do you know anyone who could pull some strings and let me get a look at the place?" Theo asked.

"It's been on the market for ages," Julian said. "But I don't know who'd you ask to view it. No one wants the place because the locals say something terrible will happen to anyone who steps foot inside."

My brother was practically drooling now, and even I had to admit my interest was piqued.

"So it is haunted?" Theo asked.

"Story says that a young woman used to live in the house. One day, the woman's brother-in-law went missing. They searched everywhere for him, but then they discovered the young woman was also missing. When the police went to her house to investigate, they found his blood spattered everywhere in the parlor. After a few years, they closed the case as unsolved. Rumor says that he wanted to have an affair and she killed him to keep him away from her then fled when she realized what she'd done. But no one really knows what happened. All they know is no one would buy the place, and it's sat empty ever since."

He lowered his voice. "They say that his blood still stains the carpet in the parlor."

Theo sucked in a breath, and the fading sun sparkled in his eyes. There'd be no keeping him away from the place now.

"I really don't know if any of it is true. But it's been a story the townsfolk love to share."

"Are you interested in touring the place for purchase?" A prim but firm voice asked. An older woman with graying hair tucked into a severe bun angled toward us. She wore a navy suit jacket, blouse, and pencil skirt and peered at us through thick-rimmed gold glasses.

"Well, um, I mean . . ." Theo swallowed hard and gave me a panicked look. I knew he wanted to say yes, but I also knew he didn't have the money for the place.

"It's up for auction, if you're interested," she continued. "I—" She paused and adjusted her glasses. "Julian?"

He startled next to me and focused on the woman across from us. Then he grinned. "Mrs. B! I didn't recognize you until now! How are you doing?"

"Oh, I'm doing well. Looking forward to this weekend being over. The mayor and I have spent too many hours on this."

"The mayor?" Julian asked, then exchanged a quick glance with me.

"Yes, yes." She chuckled. "I retired from high school English two years ago, you know. Couldn't handle the pace of you youngsters anymore. But, with Bill still working, I needed something to occupy my mind. So I work with the mayor three days a week as his secretary."

Julian slowly nodded. He faced me and said, "Mrs. B, this is my friend Beatrice. You probably know her grandfather, Sawyer? Beatrice, this is Mrs. B, my high school English teacher. Nothing ever got past her. Nothing."

Mrs. B laughed again and batted a hand. "Oh, you exaggerate. I'm sure you lot pulled all sorts of pranks under my nose. Those were some happy days, weren't they? But that's beside the point. It's lovely to meet you, Miss Beatrice. I know your grandfather well and he's a lovely gentleman. He talks about you and his other grandchild, Theo, quite often."

"Nice to meet you as well. It must be busy working with the mayor. Especially on events like this. But it's been a wonderful festival. Worth all the hard work, I hope."

"We'll count the cost and benefits after tomorrow," she said. "And hopefully that'll be our last all-nighter of the week."

"All-nighter?" Theo shifted in his seat. "Did you have a lot of those leading up to the event?"

"Oh my, yes. Friday night there was an issue with a few vendors and their placement. It took us until six in the morning on Saturday to iron out the details, and then we had to spend the next two hours writing his festival welcome speech. Then that awful murder happened, and well, I hardly had time to breath on Saturday much less handle all my other duties."

I felt like all the air had been sucked from my lungs. This wrecked everything. "You were up all night with the mayor on Friday?"

"When you say it that way, it sounds all naughty!" Her eyes widened. "It wasn't like that at all. We were reviewing contracts and invoices and—"

"No, no, I'm sorry, I didn't mean it that way. I'm sure you were just working."

"Did the mayor leave at all? For food or anything?" Theo asked.

"We called one of those dash people to bring us something. And breakfast was forgotten in the rush."

Well, so much for my idea of the mayor murdering Owens. No wonder Joel refused to investigate him anymore. He must've known the mayor had an ironclad alibi.

Julian scooted to the edge of his seat. Mrs. B copied his movements and cocked her head.

"We heard"—Julian glanced from side to side—"that the mayor was planning on purchasing the marina property?" A good question. At least one of us was thinking clearly. Perhaps Taylor Sinclair had something to do with this whole situation and my theory about the mayor's involvement wasn't completely off.

Her eyebrows shot upward, and she shifted even closer. "Where did you hear that from? That's confidential information."

"We had a run in with a Taylor Sinclair. He mentioned he was meeting with the mayor to discuss the property and contract," Theo said.

I wrinkled my nose. That was more than a little stretching of the truth.

Mrs. B huffed. "I'll have to discuss that with the mayor. We're trying to keep things under wraps until we know what's going on."

"What do you mean?" Julian asked.

"The contract's gone missing." She massaged her forehead. "One of the things the mayor and I spent ages working out on Friday night were a few modifications to the contract that Owens requested, may he rest in peace. We managed to negotiate with The Sinclair Group and reach an agreement, and the mayor and Taylor Sinclair signed the contract that evening, which I then personally dropped off at the marina. Owens was supposed to sign it that next morning, which the mayor was heading over to oversee when he heard the news."

"What happened to the contract then?" Theo asked.

"That's what we don't know. We alerted the police to the matter, and they scoured the office building and couldn't find any trace of it. The mayor is furious."

"What will happen if they don't find it?" Theo asked.

She shook her head. "He's requesting Maeve sell the place to him, but you know how he can be. When he's frustrated, he doesn't come across the best and I'm worried she won't agree."

It suddenly struck me the difference between this older woman and the mayor. He was blustering and easily frustrated while she was calm and gracious. How she stood working for him, I had no idea.

"I probably shouldn't have said anything." She lightly touched her lips with her fingers. "Please don't repeat this to anyone."

"Of course not," Julian assured her. "We wouldn't break your confidence."

She reached over and patted his knee. "You always were such a good boy."

"You must be far enough removed from freshman year English to think so." Julian chuckled. "Back then, you called me a mischievous squirt who didn't know what was good for him."

She flushed, and Julian laughed with her. I forced a smile to keep from looking out of place, but laughing was the last thing I felt like doing. It seemed like I could cross off both the mayor and Taylor Sinclair. Everything we'd done the past two days had been for nothing.

I sat back and bumped against Julian's arm, which had curled around the back of the seat. Warmth spread through me at his familiar touch, and I breathed a quick prayer of thanks for the wind that should have already whipped my cheeks pink. The last thing I needed was for Theo to point out my attraction to Julian.

I probably should've scooted away just in case Joel somehow spotted us, but I settled against Julian's arm and breathed in the freshwater air. As the boat sped along the harbor and the yellows and pinks in the sky deepened to orange and red, I chewed on my bottom lip. What did we do now? We only had one more day left in Thisbe Harbor. Then the festival would end and we would return to Columbus—the stifling busyness of Columbus.

My throat constricted at the thought.

I may have told my parents that we'd give up the investigation. But I couldn't do that. It'd been my life's trajectory to give up when things got hard, to let go of dreams because they seemed out of reach.

If I wanted to stay in Thisbe Harbor and start my own candle business, if I wanted to bring my family together once and for all, I needed to solve this mystery. I needed to show myself that I could do hard things and succeed.

Chapter Twenty-Six

We disembarked from our boat tour journey both windswept and invigorated to continue the search.

At least, I felt windswept and determined to continue.

Ruling the mayor out, while I wouldn't have minded seeing Joel lock him up, brought us that much closer to the real identity of the murderer. Or that was what I was telling myself to keep from giving up.

With only one more day left in Thisbe Harbor, I didn't know how much we could accomplish. But one more day in Thisbe Harbor meant one more day to show my aunt that she was worth fighting for. So fight I would.

"Dessert?" Theo asked once we'd stepped off the docks back onto the festival grounds. "I could smell the delight of fried food when we were still miles out."

"You were quiet on the boat." Julian nudged my arm.

"Probably too busy snoozing under your—"

I swatted the back of my brother's head. "Dessert sounds great. Lead the way."

Theo's face brightened, and he galloped ahead of us toward the food truck alley. Julian fell into step next to me, and I could feel his gaze on me as we walked.

"Funnel cake for your thoughts?" he asked.

"My encouraging thoughts or my doom-and-gloom thoughts?" I asked.

"Both?"

"I'm frustrated because I wanted it to be the mayor. I thought my theories were pretty good and it wrapped up the case in a nice little bow and also helped out your brother by getting rid of his nasty boss. It also would clear my aunt's name and might help my aunt, too, because maybe I could convince Maeve to sell her the marina." I sucked in a deep breath then plowed on. "But as discouraged as I feel about starting all over, after all that legwork we just did, I also don't want to give up. I'm tired of giving up on everything.

"My whole life I've given up. And I can't do that to my aunt. I *won't* do it to my family. If I won't fight for them, who will? I just . . . I just don't know what to do next. And we leave tomorrow. And I'm trying not to panic."

I swallowed hard and stared down at the ground, awaiting Julian's verdict that I was either crazy or insane for wanting to continue this investigation. But I'd gotten vulnerable enough with the "my whole life I've given up," and that was deep enough for now. I couldn't admit that I needed me to keep going, to keep fighting.

I needed to prove to myself I could do this. But I was scared I wouldn't be able to.

Julian paused and reached over to take both my hands in his. I stiffened, but I forced myself to look up at him. Face the feedback head-on.

"If anyone could solve this murder, if anyone could save your family, it would be you, Beatrice." He tightened his grip on my hands, and warmth spread from his touch all throughout my body. "You're the kindest, fiercest person I've ever met. And I'm with you to the end."

If that'd been a marriage proposal, he'd rival Mr. Darcy.

Leave it to my bookish side to come out when I least expected.

I tugged my hands away but smiled so he wouldn't think I was upset at him. "Thank you, Julian. That means a lot."

"What kind of funnel cake do you want?" Theo popped up beside us. He shimmied his shoulders and gave me a grin that let me know he'd seen the whole exchange. Oh for a brother that didn't love to tease so relentlessly. But I loved him anyway.

He motioned toward a white truck that was nothing to speak of. The size of a tiny U-haul truck, it's only decoration was the block letter stickers spelling "Funnel Cake" on the side. If it weren't for the long line of people standing in front of it, I'd think this was the sketchiest funnel cake truck I'd ever seen.

But we stepped up to the back of the line, and I caught a whiff of the most heavenly buttery, crispy scent. Theo had chosen well.

As we stood in line, I closed my eyes and took the opportunity to review my mental notes of the case. There had to be something—something important that I was missing.

I imagined a piece of notebook paper and created three columns scribbled with the headings: Suspects, Motives, Clues. Underneath Suspects, I wrote down Maeve, Mayor Gilberth/Taylor Sinclair, and Vincent. Over the mayor's name, I drew a red slash, and I hesitated over Maeve's name as well. I really didn't think she was a plausible suspect.

Did I believe she wanted out of her marriage with Owens and did I believe she hated him?

Yes.

Did I believe she'd do something as awful as murder and ruin her chance at saving her son?

No.

Besides, there was the detail of the missing contract. Maeve wouldn't care if the sale of the marina went through because the money would go to Owens's estate, which meant it would go to her.

But that left me with only Vincent. I didn't really know enough about him to pin the murder on him; however, I did know that he was desperate for the marina.

And wasn't that the entire point of this investigation? To uncover the secrets that had led to Owens's murder?

Well, it was time to unearth Vincent's secrets. Whether he wanted us to or not.

"Hey, isn't that Maeve and her sister?" My brother's question dragged me from my thoughts, and I watched as the two women scooted out of line, each balancing a funnel cake.

They walked around to the condiments table set up at the side of the truck. Bottles of extra chocolate sauce, whipped peanut butter spread, honey, caramel, and even cans of whipped cream lined the table as well as a plastic container stuffed with napkins and forks.

Wren whispered something to her sister, which made Maeve throw back her head and laugh. It was good to see her happy again.

"I suppose I should tell her about the mayor." I sighed. I really didn't love the idea of her selling to the mayor. But what would she say if I brought up my aunt and uncle? "I'll be back, okay?"

My brother shrugged, and I hurried over to the two sisters. Maeve glanced up when I was a few feet away, and she waved.

"Beatrice, hello. Are you enjoying your time?"

"Yes, we are. Had a boat tour a bit ago and are now on to dessert!"

"That's what Wren and I are doing tomorrow. The boat tour, that is. She is going to rent a boat for us to take out tomorrow. It's been forever since I've been out on the lake!" She peered around then leaned forward and asked, "Any news?"

"You're clear to sell to the mayor. If you want."

"I sense a 'but?'" Maeve raised an eyebrow at me.

"But I do have to agree with your sister that he's lowballing you. And I know someone who's willing to give you a fair price for the place."

"You do?" Wren moved closer. "Who?"

"My aunt and uncle." Maeve recoiled, but I raised my hands and pleaded, "Hear me out. Please."

Wren rested a hand on her sister's shoulder. "Your aunt was nothing but cruel. She's no better than that mayor."

"That was true."

"Was?" Maeve asked.

"I believe this, uh, experience has changed her. For the better. She doesn't even know that I'm doing this, but I can guarantee you that she and my uncle will be more than fair with you. And they have good motives, which I can't say for the mayor. They want to see Thisbe Harbor grow. Thrive, again. They do love this town. They—well, my aunt—just has a weird way of showing it, I know. But if you'd be willing to give her a second chance?"

Maeve dragged in a shaky breath, then slowly released it. "I was given a second chance when I didn't deserve it. So I can try to give her one too."

"Who are you talking about?" A shaky voice came from behind us.

Vincent stood two feet away clutching a manila envelope of papers in his hands. His gaze bounced from Maeve to me. The skin between his eyebrows pinched, and a frown darkened his face.

"Vincent." Maeve sighed. "Did you need something?"

"Are you selling to her?" he growled.

"Did you need something?"

"I-I—" He glanced at me again, his hands shaking. "You're considering proposals?" Before Maeve could answer, he shoved the papers at her. "The marina belongs to me, and you know it. Your husband promised it to me."

"Vincent, I—" Maeve broke off and shook her head.

"I have to get it back." He ground out.

I shifted from foot to foot. Owens must've lived a truly terrible life to have no one mourn his passing. To think how things might've been different if he'd only taken the time to be kind. "How did Owens get it?" I asked.

"He stole it from me. Took advantage of a man mourning the loss of his sweet wife with a few beers and stole it from me." His entire body was shaking now and anger flushed his cheeks. "I begged him to give it back. But he was a regular ol' Laban. Making promises he had no intention of keeping. Can't say I'm sad he's gone."

I pulled back a step and grimaced at the statement. With the slightly manic look in his eye, I could absolutely believe Vincent was capable of killing someone.

"Vince." Maeve laid a hand on his shoulder. "Why don't I take you back to your home? I think you need some rest."

He gave a half-crazed laugh. "My home? My *home*? Your dear, darling husband took that away from me too." His laugh suddenly cut short. He jabbed a finger toward Maeve. "I'm tired of people taking things away from me. If you don't—"

"Woah now." Wren shoved her way between the two and held her hands up in front of Vincent. "You'd better watch what you're saying or I'll call that police chief up for harassment."

"It's okay, Wren. He's been having a hard time for a while now. He and his wife were lucky enough to love each other," Maeve murmured.

"Then I sure don't think his wife would appreciate him acting like this," Wren snapped.

Vincent sucked in a breath and opened his mouth to spout something back, but he paused. He stared at Wren for a long moment, then he blinked. "I-I know. You're right." He ducked his head and stumbled back a few steps. "I forgot myself. Forgive me."

Before either Wren or Maeve could say anything else, he scurried away like a wounded puppy.

"That was strange." Maeve wrinkled her nose and crossed her arms over her chest.

"He must've remembered his dear, darling wife and been embarrassed by his actions." Wren snorted. "What a guy."

I watched Vincent disappear around the side of another food truck, taking a brief glance over his shoulder only once more, eyes wide. What an odd interaction indeed.

But I couldn't help recall his vicious words to Maeve. If he wanted the marina that badly and knew Owens wouldn't sell to him, then he might be desperate enough to get Owens out of his way.

My first step should be figuring out if he had the opportunity Saturday morning. After my experience with the mayor, I needed to find out if I could rule Vincent out with his alibi.

What had my aunt said?

Something about how the murderer could have blended in the crowd. I hadn't noticed Vincent in the crowd, but with so many people milling about and my attention elsewhere, it was possible. I thought of the flash of the many cameras as the officers escorted Julian, Theo, and me to the police station to be berated by Joel. If there were cameras then . . .

I bid a quick goodbye to Maeve and Wren, then hurried back to my brother and Julian. They were only three people away from the front of the line now.

"Does Thisbe have a newspaper?" I asked.

"A newspaper?" Julian asked. "Is that what that was all about?"

"You that desperate for a job?" Theo wrinkled his nose. "No offense, but I don't think—"

"I'll explain later, but I need pictures, Theo. Pictures of Saturday morning."

"What do you want pictures for? You saw the body yourself."

"Not of the body. Of the crowd. We need to see if Vincent was in the crowd."

"Oh, so we're back on him." My brother tapped a finger on his chin. "Hm, if I recall correctly, wasn't it I, Theseus Gonzalez Sawyer, who suggested him as a suspect in the first place? And wasn't it you, Beatrice Ophelia—"

"Can we stop with the dramatics for two seconds?" I planted my hands on my hips. "We're running out of time. We need to focus."

"Um, we have the Harbor Community News. It's printed every Sunday morning. There's also the online gossip group. It's mostly the older ladies at the various churches around here posting whatever tidbits they find the most fascinating, but sometimes they share something interesting."

"Where can we get a copy of the paper?" I asked.

"They're delivered to every house in Thisbe Harbor every Sunday morning. There should be one in your BnB's mailbox."

"We need to find Mom and Dad then." I hopped out of line and stalked down the aisleway.

"Hey, wait a minute!" Theo raced after me. "What about my funnel cake?"

With my earlier sort-of promise not to investigate, we decided Julian's presence at the BnB would be too suspicious. Even so, Mom and Dad were still doubtful when we found them and asked to return to the BnB. But Theo, despite his bad attitude at leaving behind his funnel cake, faked an upset stomach, and we piled back into the car.

My brother curled up on the back seat next to me and moaned and groaned with all the theatrics he could muster so that the moment we arrived home, Mom sent him to the bathroom with a promise to scrounge up some ginger tea—which I knew my brother hated.

With their attention diverted, I slipped out the back door and made for the mailbox. Sure enough, a newspaper and several days' worth of mail had been shoved inside. I extricated the newspaper, making sure that everything else was securely inside—the last thing I needed was to be arrested for stealing mail—then hightailed it back inside where I dove safely into my room.

Aunt Penny scowled at me in an overlarge black-and-white photograph on the front of the paper. Dozens of people filled the rest of the page, all gawking at the paramedics and police officers as they performed their duties. I squinted at the blurry faces and tried to pick out anyone I knew. But with the camera's zoom onto my aunt's face, everything else had been blurred out.

I skimmed the article detailing the events of Saturday morning and Joel's statement regarding it. Unlike the mayor, who'd loaded his statement with as much political speak as he could (such as "As mayor, I'll do everything it takes to keep that woman behind bars and keep this town safe."), Joel had declined commenting on any suspects or information regarding his investigation. At least my aunt had that going for her.

At the bottom of the article, in bold lettering, the paper instructed me to flip to page four for more details. I shuffled through the pages. A dozen or so photographs littered a two-page spread, and the captions underneath several of them were credited to different citizens of Thisbe.

Well, I supposed this was the perfect example of a small town in action. When nothing much happened, a murder deserved three whole pages in the paper.

I tore the paper in half, six pictures on one side and six on the other, and snuck out to the hallway. Creeping up to the bathroom, I shoved one half of the paper under the door, then gave a light rap on the door. "Text me if you find anything."

A grunt was my brother's only response, then I tiptoed back to the bedroom.

I spread my page onto the floor then laid on my stomach to peer down at it. The first picture was of my brother's flying-leap tackle. I couldn't help chuckling. My brother's limbs were splayed outward, and the horror on Aunt Penny's face as she looked over her shoulder at him was priceless. I'd need to cut this one out and save it for future brother blackmail.

The next several photos were different angles of the front-page picture, all without a focus on the crowd. The last picture sent my stomach churning. Julian, Theo, and I stood with Joel. My arms were wrapped around my chest, and a helpless, listlessness twisted in my gaze. Theo's flying-leap tackle might have been a bit amusing, but it also was a reminder of that awful morning.

An image of my aunt holding Owens's body popped into my mind again, and I squeezed my eyes shut. I didn't want to remember that—had been thankful for the investigation to keep my mind off that awful sight.

How did police handle seeing the evil in the world every day? How did they not break at the heaviness of what they witnessed?

My phone pinged, and I snatched it, grateful for the interruption.

A slightly blurry phone photo loaded onto my screen. Another black-and-white still of my brother's tackle, but this one was more zoomed out. And right at the edge of the docks, Vincent stood, arms crossed, at the corner of Cindy's volunteer shack.

Chapter Twenty-Seven

"Just because he was there doesn't mean he did it."

"Maybe not, but it means he's worth looking into."

Monday morning dawned with gray storm clouds and a darkened sky threatening rain. Even the lake had grown black and waves churned into a white froth. This was not a good omen for the festival's final day, nor for my investigation.

Theo shrugged one shoulder then shoveled another bite of cold cereal and milk into his mouth. We'd risen bright and early on our last day in Thisbe Harbor, and our parents and Papa were both still snoring away in their rooms.

"Investigating him was your idea to begin with. Why the hesitation all of a sudden?" I asked.

My brother ducked his head and scooped up another spoonful of cereal. Milk dripped from the silver spoon and splashed back into his bowl.

I poked my brother's arm. "Theo?"

He mumbled something, but I couldn't understand his words over the mouthful of popping Rice Crispies.

"What happened to no secrets?" I crossed my arms. "What are you hiding now?"

"I was hoping you'd do something for me. Er, rather, with me," he muttered. "But you'll probably laugh at me and tell me I'm crazy."

I pursed my lips and sat back in my chair. It wasn't unusual for my brother to have crazy ideas. But he usually didn't mind sharing them with me.

"I can't promise I won't laugh, but I do promise to listen."

"I suppose that's as good as I'll get." He huffed, lifted his head, and said in a rush, "I scheduled an appointment for us to see that haunted house with Mrs. B and I want you to go with me."

My jaw dropped. "You what?"

"I know, I know." He held up his hands. "We need to investigate and pin this on Vincent and all that. But I thought, well . . . I thought . . . I just want to take a look."

"You're thinking about buying it?" My voice rose in pitch. Not that I hadn't had the same thought myself, but to hear my brother speak it aloud?

"Shh, you'll wake Mom and Dad," he hissed.

"What are you thinking? Where are you getting the money for that?" I asked.

"I don't know yet. But it doesn't hurt to take a look, yeah? I mean, think of the credibility it'd give me to live in a haunted house."

"It'd be more credible if you made the house not haunted anymore."

He rolled his eyes. "Well, yeah, that'd be the plan."

I chewed on my bottom lip and sat back in my chair, another idea surfacing. If Theo wanted to move to Thisbe, and I wanted to move to Thisbe, and we both were lacking money, but we both wanted to start our own businesses . . .

"I'll go. But—"

He groaned. "Why do you have to always add stipulations?"

"But I want to get in on the house deal if you do decide to buy it."

"Beatrice, come on, that's—wait, what?"

"I want to buy the house with you if we like it," I repeated.

"Are you being serious?"

I straightened my shoulders and sucked in a deep breath. I was tired of living with Mom and Dad, waiting for something to land in my lap. If there was one thing I'd learned this weekend, it was that didn't happen if you sat by and watched the days go by. I finally had a dream, and I wanted it to happen here. I wanted to help bring Thisbe back to life with my small business. Was I crazy for thinking I could do so? Yes. But was I serious? "Yes."

A slow grin spread across my brother's face. "Then let's be crazy together."

Gravel crunched under the tires of Theo's car as he swung the wheel and veered into the driveway of the house on the cliff.

The house on the cliff rose into the roiling gray sky, a looming Jane Eyre–type Victorian manor complete with vines twisting along the crumbling brick sides and a rickety porch. Six out of the nine windows on the front of the house were splintered, the glass most likely scattered across the lawn. Grass grew in tall reeds around it, giving the cliff house an even more eerie air as the wind rustled through the stalks.

Thunder rumbled, the sound rolling over the ground with a tremble. I clenched my hands under my thighs to keep them from shaking too badly. Perhaps the stories weren't all wrong after all. If any place was haunted, it would be this one.

"Don't tell me you're chickening out now," Theo said. "What happened to being crazy?"

Mrs. B stood near the sagging porch, her hands clasped in front of her. She cast furtive glances toward the house behind her and the sky above. Theo maneuvered his car next to her silver SUV, and we both unbuckled our seatbelts and hopped out.

The roar of Erie's waves filled the air, and the hair on my arms rose as tension built in the air for the crackle of lightning. This was going to be quite the storm.

"Welcome." Mrs. B waved a hand in the air.

We crossed the overgrown gravel driveway, and Theo stuck out his hand for her to shake.

"I hope the rain holds off for a bit longer," Mrs. B said, "but we may need to rush through this."

"Thanks for meeting us on such short notice. You must be busy with the festival," Theo said.

I bit the inside of my cheek. Neither Theo nor I had the money for this place, much less the money to fix it up as it deserved. We would only be wasting Mrs. B's time by touring the place. She had much better things to do—like figure out what to do with the approaching storm threatening to derail festival plans.

"The mayor insisted I meet with you. There's not many people willing to take on such a project, as I'm sure you can imagine."

"What happened here?" I asked.

Her lips twisted into a half smile, half grimace. "The bank repossessed the house years ago due to, um, unpaid payments. The former owners weren't able to take care of it anymore"—That was an understatement if Julian's story was to be believed—"but the town's been complaining for years that it's become an eyesore, so the mayor is trying to help the bank out with the sale. Which is why I'm here."

A few droplets of water splattered against my arms. I tilted my head up and another rain drop splashed on my cheek.

Mrs. B tightened her grip on her purse. She pursed her lips and stared up at the house.

"Can we go inside?" Theo asked.

"Yes, yes," she said, although her voice sounded distant. She slowly walked up the porch steps, testing each one as she approached the front door. "We had an inspector out not too long ago to ensure the house was stable enough for tours. He assured us that structurally—other than the porch roof—things were safe enough."

Keys jangled and she jiggled the front door. I took the opportunity to lean against my brother and whisper, "What are we doing? We can't afford this?"

"Let's see the inside," he whispered back. "We're already here and the sky is about to unleash."

I blew out a breath and rubbed my hands up and down my arms. My fingers tingled with the electricity in the air.

Lightning burst across the sky in a brilliant flash right as the front door creaked open. The light illuminated dark red streaked down the wood floors of the front hallway.

"Is that . . . ?" Blood roared in my ears and the sides of my vision fuzzed and darkened. It felt like seeing Owens's body all over again.

Mrs. B shrieked, and the high-pitched note snapped me out of my focus.

The lightning faded, and it felt like the entire world went dark.

My brother flipped on his phone's flashlight, and his eyes glimmered in the yellow glare. Once again, the adrenaline of the moment made him come to life. He raced forward as thunder rattled the entire house. My heart galloped in my chest and cold wrapped around me without my brother's presence.

I squeaked and pounded across the porch. "Don't go in without me!"

Theo paused in the doorway, one hand on the frame and his other aiming his flashlight down the hall.

A dusty, torn red hallway runner stretched from the front door into the darkened interior of the house. No blood. Only carpet.

I released my pent-up breath. A dark and stormy morning at a rumored haunted house was not a good combination. What had we gotten ourselves into?

Mrs. B was apparently thinking the same thing. She forced a laugh and pressed a hand to her chest. Her cheeks had gone white, and her lips trembled. "Sorry about that. Got a bit, uh, carried away."

"Do you believe the rumors?" Theo asked.

"The rumors?" she squeaked.

"About the killings here," Theo said. "Is there still blood on the—wait a minute." He took a step inside, then paused. "Bea, do you have your phone on you?"

I held it up and turned on the flashlight, knowing instinctively what he wanted. We shone our concentrated beams onto the runner. Sure enough, amidst the layers of dust and grime, footsteps trailed down the hall into a doorway on the right.

"Have you given a tour here recently?" Theo asked.

Mrs. B shook her head. "You're the first ones. But the house is a steal. All the furniture inside comes with it, and the mayor told me to tell you that he's open to offers. So if you want to make an offer, we'll consider anything." She seemed desperate to sell the place. Unfortunately for her, I didn't think any offer Theo and I could afford would be enough to satisfy the mayor.

My brother moved deeper into the house, and I followed on his heels.

"Do you keep the house locked?" he asked.

"Of course. Only the mayor and I have access to the keys." She paused, and both Theo and I looked back at her. "Of course, several of the windows are busted." She sighed. "I hate to say this, but we can't guarantee animals haven't gotten in."

"Or humans," Theo muttered.

We tracked the footprints to an ornately carved wooden door. Flowers and swirls had been engraved on the six wooden panels on the thick cherry door, and the golden handle shone in our flashlights.

"This has been used recently," Theo whispered. "It's not dusty enough." He gripped the doorknob. "Stand behind me, but be ready."

I fished in my pocket for the pocketknife-mace device he'd given me and twisted off the cap of the mace. "Ready."

"One, two—"

"Is something going on?" Mrs. B asked.

"Three!" Theo shoved open the door and sprang inside.

I raised my mace and gave the best warrior shriek I could muster. We pulled up short, and I gasped.

The room was completely furnished, a faded green-and-white striped couch against one wall, a coffee table with cabriole legs stood over an orange and blue oriental rug, and an overstuffed emerald wingback chair was tucked near the fireplace. Cherry wooden bookshelves filled with torn books lined the rest of the walls.

But despite my shock at the furniture, that wasn't what had caught my attention. Takeout boxes littered the coffee table and the stale smell of orange chicken and lo mein filled the air. A sleeping bag and pillow draped over the couch, and a camo-patterned duffel bag had been shoved halfway underneath the coffee table.

Someone had been living here. Someone without a home.

And although I knew there were millions of people across the world with no home to call their own, one name immediately came to mind.

"I-I don't understand." Mrs. B's voice trembled from the doorway. "What is all this?"

"Theo, do you think this is where . . . ?" I let the question hang in the air.

He crossed the room and yanked the duffel bag out from under the table. "See if you can find any clues."

"Has someone been living here?" Mrs. B asked. "Do you think they're still in the house?"

I poked through the plastic bags and takeout boxes of food but found no sign of a receipt. Then I knelt on the couch to peer behind in case the trespasser had dropped anything behind. Something crunched under my weight and poked my leg even through the sleeping bag. I pulled back the puffy nylon fabric and gasped.

Underneath sat a gold frame, the glass front shattered. Despite the jagged lines splitting the cover, I recognized one of the faces in the photograph. Vincent smiled up at me, one arm slung over a beaming white-haired woman, Lake Erie and the white marina office building in the background.

"Theo." I picked up the photo and frame and something sticky clung to my fingertips. Lightning flashed. The room lit up white.

Drying blood coated the side of the photograph and stained my fingers. My heart dropped into my stomach. We'd found Vincent's new home, but something had gone very, very wrong.

Chapter Twenty-Eight

Although he was less than thrilled to see us, Joel arrived at the abandoned house in record time. While he and the few officers he could muster scoured the house for clues, Mrs. B sat on the top step of the porch nearly in hysterics while Theo and I patted her back and tried to comfort her.

"I knew this was a bad idea," she wailed. "Nothing good ever happens at this house. Nothing!"

Theo opened his mouth like he wanted to question her about it, but I reached behind Mrs. B and pinched his arm. He startled, and I shook my head at him. As much as I wanted to hear the story behind the rumors, now was not the time. Mrs. B was certainly not in the headspace.

Floorboards creaked behind us, and I turned to find Joel coming out of the house. His lips were pursed in a grim line.

"Did you find anything?" I asked.

He pulled out his signature yellow notebook and #2 pencil. "If you could each, in turn, tell me what happened, I'd appreciate it. We haven't been able to locate Mr. Cross yet, but I have an APB out for him. Unfortunately, it seems his cell phone provider has disconnected his service so we're out of luck there as well. He could've simply dropped the picture frame and cut himself on it."

"You can't believe that," I said.

"There's no reason to believe that the killer would've struck again."

"Unless he found something out!" I pushed to my feet. "What if he found out who the killer was, so he had to be silenced too?"

Mrs. B gasped and nearly toppled down the stairs. "You think he's d-d-dead?"

The clouds chose that moment to let loose. Rain poured from the sky in a torrent, and both Mrs. B and my brother scrambled all the way up the steps to keep from getting soaked.

Joel looked me in the eye. "There's nothing inside indicating that anything more happened to Vincent than he cut his finger on an old picture frame. But my officers and I will do everything in our power to locate Vincent and ensure his safety. Now . . ."

One by one, Theo, Mrs. B, and I shared everything we could remember with Joel. He instructed those not being interviewed to wait in their respective cars, giving each of us an umbrella to walk without getting soaked.

When it was my turn, I told him how we'd been told that Vincent had sold his house to earn the money to pay Owens for the marina and how he'd called Owens a regular ol' Laban when he'd approached Maeve yesterday. I also told Joel how we came to be at the house and where I located the broken photograph.

When I finished, he asked me a few clarifying questions then dismissed me with a glance that said I was not to stick around like I wanted to.

"Please find him, Joel." I chewed on my lower lip. "Something bad happened to him. I can't explain it, but I just know it." There was no way that Vincent would accidentally drop and shatter a prized photo of his wife and shove it underneath his sleeping bag. Not when there was sure to be another picture frame somewhere in the house he could replace it with.

Rain pattered on the front porch's roof and spattered the now-muddy driveway.

"I promise you I will do my job," Joel said. "Goodbye, Miss Sawyer. And, please, keep this to yourself for now."

I blew out a breath, but I wrapped my arms around myself, ducked my head, and ran to Theo's waiting car.

The minute I shut the door behind myself, he said, "That wasn't the house tour I was expecting."

"And it leaves me more confused than ever." I dragged a hand through my hair to shake out some of the sprinkles. "And worried."

"Why worried?"

"We're missing something. Something big. And it may mean someone else gets hurt, or worse."

"What do you want to do?" He started the car's engine and backed out of the parking spot. "We don't have the resources the police do for a manhunt."

"And Thisbe PD doesn't have the resources for one either."

"That leaves us back with my original question. What now?" He flicked on his windshield wipers and turned the car down the road back toward town. "Maybe give your boyfriend a call. He sometimes has good ideas."

"Theo, this is serious." I groaned. "He's not my boyfriend."

"But you want him to be."

"Will you please concentrate? I swear, the day you finally notice a girl, I'm going to—"

"You didn't deny that you want him to be." His grin widened. "I mean, I wouldn't mind having him as a brother-in-law."

I closed my eyes and balled my hands into fists. "Theseus Gonzalez, someone's life is at stake and here you sit—"

"I know, I know." He blew out a breath. "But I don't know what to do, so I'm defaulting to humor while my brain scrambles to come up with an idea."

I blinked and stared at my brother. That was a rather astute assessment of himself. "Well, then, any ideas 'Oh Scrambled Wise One?'"

"Give Julian a call and let's save Vincent."

Julian suggested a visit to Cindy since she knew the harbor and the people here best. So we gathered inside Cindy's shack at the festival, the diva herself at the back of the group. Water dripped from my shirt and hair and goosebumps shivered up my back. While the rain had slowed on our way over, the minute we'd stepped out of the car, the clouds had decided to unleash on us once again.

Cindy set three steaming mugs in front of us then propped a hip on her desk and surveyed us all. "You look a mess."

I wrapped my hands around the warm mug and lifted it to my face to inhale the sweet mint and feel the steam on my cheeks.

"We need your help. Vincent's gone missing, and we think the killer might have something to do with it," Julian said.

"Missing?" Cindy frowned and crossed her arms over her chest. "Who? How can I help?"

"We need you to tell us everything you know about Vincent's activities yesterday," I said. "We think he found something out about the killer's identity and they struck to keep him silent."

Cindy rubbed her chin then chewed on her lower lip. After a few tense, silent moments, she shook her head. "I can't say I saw him yesterday. I've been spending so much time running around managing volunteers, though."

"Does he work? Who's his employer?" I set down my mug and drummed my fingers on the desk. Every minute we spent contemplating and questioning was another minute that something bad could happen to Vincent—or more time for the killer to get away after doing something to Vincent.

"You know . . ." She tilted her head and frowned. "I don't know. After his dear wife passed, I suppose I didn't think about it. He's always skulking around here, and since that's exactly what he did before Sophie passed, I never thought much of it."

Her cell phone buzzed, and she lifted it from the desk. A scowl twisted her lips.

"What is it?" Theo asked.

"The mayor. He's on a rampage due to the rain. Wants to move everything inside the local school and continue on with the festival." She pushed to her feet. "I have to take care of this. I'll give a few contacts a call, though, and see if anyone's seen Vincent or knows any information about him."

She grabbed her purse from the floor and swung it over her shoulder. Bending over, she lifted a black leather clutch and set it on the desk. "Oh. Wait. Maeve is supposed to drop by this morning and pick up her sister's purse. Someone found it after the festival closed and brought it to the lost and found. Would you mind waiting a few minutes to see if she shows up?"

Tension twisted like a knife in my gut, but I forced a smile and nodded. "Of course. Go do what you have to do." Without any further information on Vincent or any idea of who the murderer was, it wasn't like we could do anything anyway. And maybe Maeve would know something about Vincent since he hung around the marina a lot.

Cindy popped open an umbrella then waved a hasty goodbye as she ducked out into the rain. Theo downed the rest of his tea then smacked his mug on the desk.

"You had to say yes?" he asked.

"What else are we supposed to do?" I massaged the heels of my palms against my temple.

"I don't know," he grumbled. "But going around asking questions is a heckuva lot more interesting than this."

We spent the next ten minutes in silence except for the drumming of the rain on the metal shack roof. My mind whirled with possibilities of what could've happened to Vincent, but no ideas as to where he could be now.

Theo groaned and pushed to his feet. He reached across the table for the tea kettle. "Anyone else want any more? Guzzling tea and holding your pee is the only thing to do around here."

"I'll have some." Julian handed his half-full mug to my brother.

Theo must have not seen the tea inside because he grabbed the mug, and the warm liquid sloshed. My brother screeched in surprise and dropped the mug.

"No!" I jumped to my feet. "What are you doing?"

Julian leaped forward and snagged the kettle from my brother's hand. Theo scrambled for the mug, swiping the papers, pens, and Wren's purse off the table in his haste. The mug hit the desk and tea splashed.

We all stilled and watched the liquid slither across the desk top and drip onto the floor.

"Well, you can add spill the tea to your list of things to do around here," Julian said.

"Anyone have any paper towels?" Theo turned a sheepish gaze to me.

I shook my head. "Only you, Theo. Only you."

"Cindy might have some behind the desk," Julian said. "I swear it's like Mary Poppin's bag back there."

Theo sidled along the desk and crouched down behind it. "Oops. Wren's purse spilled when I accidentally threw it."

"Pick it up, please." I smacked a hand against my forehead. "Maeve could be here any minute."

Shuffling sounded from behind the desk, then an eerie silence. I waited a second, then two.

"Theo?"

My brother slowly rose, a white paper in one hand, his gaze locked onto the words.

"What is it?" Julian moved to peer over my brother's shoulder, then he gasped.

"What?" I reached over the desk and snatched the page from my brother's hand.

In neat, typewritten letters, the top of the paper read: Contract Between Harry Owens, Pritchard Gilberth, and Sinclair Investment Group, LLC. And underneath was the date—the night before Owens's murder, just like Mrs. B had said.

It felt like someone had punched the air from my lungs. In my hand was the missing contract. And my brother had found it in Wren's purse.

Chapter Twenty-Nine

"He recognized her," I whispered, the puzzle pieces all suddenly clicking into place.

"What are you talking about?" Theo jerked the contract back. "Do you realize what this is? What this means?"

"I know where Vincent is! Or, at least, who he's with. He recognized her yesterday. He must've seen her here that morning." I dragged a hand through my hair, but my fingers caught in the tangled curls. What was it Vincent had said? Something about Owens being a Laban. "Does anyone remember that Bible story? The one with Laban?"

"Yeah . . ." Julian and Theo exchanged a look like I'd gone crazy, but my best friend continued, "Jacob worked for him for seven years so he could marry Laban's daughter Rachel. But then Laban cheated him and gave him his daughter Leah to marry."

"I think Vincent was working here. At the marina. Trying to earn back his wife's marina. And he saw Wren that morning."

"But why would Wren kill her sister's husband?" Theo asked.

"Owens was awful to Maeve. Wren probably hated him for it."

"Owens has been cruel for years. Why kill him now?"

I bit my lip, then pointed toward the contract. "It has to have something to do with that. But that doesn't matter right now. We need to find Vincent. I only hope he's alive."

"What's the plan?" Julian asked. "Thisbe may not be Cleveland or Columbus, but it's still big enough that it'd take us forever to search everywhere."

"We need to split up. Cover as much ground as possible and sound the alarm."

Julian lifted his phone. "I've already sent Joel a photo of the contract and told him our suspicions. But no answer, so far."

"Go after him. Check the house on the cliff first, and if he's not there, call him until he answers." I pointed to my brother. "Go find Cindy. Have her call everyone she knows to join the search. And I'll wait for Maeve. She's got to know where her sister is, right?"

"I don't like the idea of leaving you alone," Julian said. "What if Wren herself comes to pick up her purse?"

"Then I'll give it to her and pretend I didn't see inside." I shrugged.

"That'd work great if you weren't a terrible liar," Theo said.

I waved toward the door. "Will you two please get going? I can take care of myself, thank you very much!"

After a nod from my brother, both men started for the door. Theo paused for a split second. "Got my handy-dandy knife-spray still?"

"Ready and waiting."

A sly smile turned up one corner of his lips. "Don't hesitate to use it if you need to. Got it?"

I pretended to salute. "Sir, yes, sir."

And then they both disappeared out the door.

I pulled in a deep breath to try to calm my racing heart. If Wren did indeed pick up her own purse, I wanted to be ready to lie. My current panicked, adrenaline-pumping state was not conducive to that. Lowering myself into Cindy's more comfortable office chair behind her desk, I breathed in through my nose and out through my mouth. I thought I'd read somewhere that that was a good method for calming oneself down.

Not that it seemed to be working.

I couldn't get the question out of my head: If I were Wren, where would I hide someone?

She wasn't from town, and as far as I knew had been staying with her sister during her time here. From the way she talked about her sister, I couldn't imagine Wren bringing a kidnapped person into her sister's home.

Where would she hide him?

I leaned my elbows on the desk and pressed my head against my palms. Think, Beatrice, think! I mentally thought of every single conversation I'd had with Wren. Mostly she was rather antagonistic, but yesterday—

That was it.

Yesterday, I'd told Maeve we'd gone on a boat tour. And she'd mentioned that Wren was renting a boat for them to take out today. That had to be where she'd stowed Vincent away. Depending on the kind of boat, there could be a myriad of places to hide a body.

I winced at the thought and sent up a quick prayer that Vincent wasn't a body yet.

But what boat? There had to be a record of the rental somewhere, right?

What if the boat was her escape route?

I shoved away from the desk and raced out the shack door. Thankfully, the rain had turned to a drizzle, and the sun was starting to peek through the clouds with its golden rays.

An old fisherman stood at the end of the docks. He bowed over the side of a white and maroon pontoon boat, then pulled a small metal box out from under one of the seats.

"Excuse me!" I shouted and waved my arms in the air. "Excuse me!"

The man startled and fumbled the box. It teetered out of his hands and hit the ground, then tumbled dangerously close to the water's edge.

I cringed and put on a burst of speed. Leave it to me to startle him. Thankfully, the man scooped up the box with quick reflexes and tucked it back under his arm.

His eyebrows rose as I neared and gasped out an, "I'm so sorry. I didn't mean to scare you! But this is an emergency!"

Although I deserved every bit of a lecture, the man smiled and motioned toward the box. "It's all right, ma'am. Just my tackle box. Wouldn't have been any big loss."

I recognized his slow, drawling voice from last night. He'd captained our tour boat—Captain Tucker or something.

"You said something about an emergency, ma'am?" he asked.

"Right." I dragged in a breath then gasped out, "Did anyone rent a boat this morning? Would've been early."

"Not many people wanting boat tours today." He glanced toward the sky. "The lake's a deceiver. Tells ya that she's done with her storms then whips another up when ya least expect it."

"No, not a boat tour. Just a boat rental," I said. "This is really important."

"Well, there was one, which I thought rather odd since you could—"

"Which dock?" I asked.

"Lemme think." He bit his bottom lip. "She wanted a boat with a cabin. Said she wanted some comfort for her sister. Which I thought was sweet of her."

I wanted to scream. Did this man have no sense of urgency? Couldn't he see I needed to know where this boat was?

"I asked her price range, and she said cost was no factor, so I thought why not give her the best." He gave me a sheepish look. "Thought it might help the town, at least."

"Please," I tried to keep as much frustration from my tone as possible. "Which dock is the boat at?"

"Y36. I gave her one of the nice sport yachts. A Gale—"

"Did that boat leave?"

"No. No one left in this—"

I was already running, arms pumping at my sides, lungs burning. I shouted over my shoulder. "Call the police and tell them get to that dock ASAP!"

The lake's gentle slap against the docks would've been soothing if I hadn't been running to save someone's life. Instead, the roar of air rushing past me and the thudding of my heart drowned out nearly everything else.

Please don't let me be too late. Please don't let me be too late.

I reached row Y and slowed. I didn't want my elephant footsteps to alert Wren of my presence and scare her away. White, mildewy signs marked each dock's name. I held my breath as I passed Y30, listening for any signs of life on any of the boats.

Behind sign Y36, a sleek white-and-black yacht bobbed on the water. The rope creaked and strained against its mooring and the waves splashed up against the sides, but no other sounds reached my ear.

Had the captain given me the wrong boat? Had my theory been wrong?

"It's about time."

My breath caught in my throat and my heart seemed to drop into my stomach. She'd found me already. I hadn't been quiet enough, hadn't been—

"W-where am I?" Vincent's voice croaked.

"What were you doing here that morning? I know you saw me!" Wren's voice increased in pitch, and I realized it was coming from somewhere on the boat. "I had my plans. You weren't supposed to be there!"

The boat bobbed in the waves and bumped gently against the dock. I ground my teeth together. Water sloshed between the dock and the low onboarding deck of the boat. I could easily make the jump, but then I'd really be interfering in Joel's investigation. If I waited for the police, however, it could be too late. Wren could exact her revenge on Vincent or take the opportunity of the clearing weather to speed away.

I couldn't let Vincent face her alone. Not when I had the element of surprise and the ability to help.

The lake pushed the boat toward me again, and I jumped.

My weight dipped the boat for a moment before the waves regulated the shift in weight once again. I held my breath and squeezed my eyes shut, praying Wren wouldn't notice the extra movement.

"Y-you killed h-him," Vincent said.

I crawled up the few stairs to the top deck, then peered down the open hatch to the hull. The yacht was clearly meant for someone wealthy, a silk settee, golden picture frames with oil paintings, and tasseled pillows decorating the space. Wren paced back and forth in front of the stairs, her brown ponytail swinging across her back. She must've reached the boat right before the storm broke. Vincent sprawled on a plush rug a few feet away from her, half propped up against a glass coffee table. A blood-crusted gash sliced across his forehead, and he held a shaking hand to the side of his head.

"What were you doing there that morning? No one is ever there that early except for him!"

The boat teetered to the left. The anchor rope must've pulled taut because the boat jerked right again. I lost my balance and slammed against the stairwell wall. I clung to the railing to keep from tumbling down the stairs.

Wren must have had better sea legs because she whipped around. And it was only then that I saw the gun in her hand.

All the blood drained from my face, and my vision fuzzed except for focused clarity on the nozzle of the gun. What had I gotten myself into? I'd never really thought of dying as a real possibility before. The idea didn't scare me—I knew where I'd end up would be a much better place than here—but I couldn't help feeling disappointed.

Here I was, in my midtwenties and I hadn't accomplished much of anything. I'd wasted years trying to become something I never wanted, then when I'd finally decided to launch my own business,

I'd ignored candles in favor of murder. I'd done nothing notable, nothing to make my parents proud when they viewed my body in the casket. If Wren would leave my body for a burial. Who knew what she'd do to hide this crime.

Wren shook her head and gave a big sigh like I was the biggest inconvenience in her life. "You couldn't leave things alone, could you." She pointed the gun at me, then used it to motion over to Vincent. "Go sit by him."

I held tight to the railing, my legs like melted candle wax as I stumbled down the stairs. At the bottom, I gave a small squeak as I shuffled past Wren and lowered myself next to Vincent.

The old man gave me a snort. "Some rescue you are."

"And you're still cranky," I muttered.

Wren resumed her pacing, and a scowl twisted her face. "Now I have two of you to worry about."

"What are you going to do with us?" I asked. I started to pull my knees up to my chest, then I froze. Something poked me in my back pocket. Theo's knife-mace weapon. Why hadn't I thought of that when I was coming down the stairs?

"This wasn't supposed to happen. No one was supposed to see me. But then the way that he"—she stabbed the gun toward Vincent—"looked at me yesterday. I knew he knew. But how? Why were you there?"

"I worked there." Vincent snorted. "Or, rather, Owens used me for free labor because I was too stupid to realize he would never make good on his word. I always knew he'd get his comeuppance one day. I suppose it surprised him to see it come from you."

"But your sister," I said. "Why would you do that to Maeve?"

What was taking the police so long? Julian or Theo or the boat captain had to have gotten a hold of Joel by now. The police station wasn't that far away, nor was the house on the cliff. Someone was supposed to be here by now. I had to keep her talking. Buy us a little more time until I could either shimmy my brother's weapon out of my pocket and use it in a way that wouldn't get someone killed, or the police showed up.

"I did it *for* Maeve! Nine years ago, I watched that jerk promise to love my sister in sickness and in health." Wren's pacing picked up speed. "To cherish her, care for her. And you know what he's done? Made her life miserable. He was going to sell the marina, you know. Sell it right out from under all of you. And do you think he was going to give any of it to my sister, who has taken care of their son for the last six years and gotten nothing from him?"

She gave a dry laugh. "He was going to take the money and retire in luxury. He was going to leave my sister saddled with debts she could never pay and no job to even try paying them. She's spent years trying to rebuild her life after he nearly crushed her during their marriage. And he had no problem stomping her under his foot again."

"So you took things into your own hands," Vincent said.

"I was saving my sister," she snarled. "I saw what he was doing to her. And he wasn't going to stop until he'd snuffed her out. He asked more and more of her while giving nothing himself. Guilt weighed down her steps as she slaved for their son, all while he was making a deal that would set him up for life and take everything away from her!" Her voice crescendoed with every word until she was screaming.

"So you killed him?" I wrinkled my nose. "How is that going to help your sister? If the police find out you—"

"The police won't find anything." She jabbed the gun in my direction. I scooted back. I needed to keep my big mouth shut before I got shot. "Vincent here is the murderer. He wanted Owens dead when he found out he'll never get his wife's marina back. Beatrice discovered that, and he shot her to keep her quiet. But then he felt remorse, so he turned the gun on himself."

Vincent huffed and curled his lip at her. "Stupid plan, girlie. Your prints are all over that gun."

"Stop that!" Wren screamed and pointed her weapon back at Vincent. "You're nothing but a bully. It'll be a pleasure to shut your mouth for good."

Rage flickered through me, boiling hotter and hotter like a candle whose wick was too long. Wren may have thought that killing Owens would protect her sister. That she was loving her sister by taking away the source of her sister's pain and grief. But instead, she'd allowed her bitterness and anger toward Owens to burn and bubble over until she'd committed an act that would hurt her sister forever.

Well, as long as I still had breath, I wouldn't let her harm another person. Not like she'd done to Owens.

A guttural scream tore from my throat.

I leaped to my feet and yanked my brother's knife-mace device from my back pocket. "Leave us alone!"

Wren started to turn toward me, but I was ready. I pressed down on the mace's nozzle and aimed at her face, lunging toward her at the same time.

The pepper-laced spray coated her cheeks and eyes. *BANG!* The gun discharged a split second before I body slammed her.

"Vincent!" I shrieked.

But I received no answer.

Wren and I hit the floor, both of us screaming. I wrenched Wren's arms behind her back, but I needn't have worried. Somewhere between me tackling her and us landing, the gun had dropped from her grip. Tears streamed down Wren's cheeks.

"My eyes. Let me go, you monster!" she wailed.

"She'll do nothing of the sort." From my peripheral, I could see Vincent crawling out from underneath the settee.

I blew out a breath. He'd survived. Somehow, that ornery man had survived.

"Police! Put your hands in the air and drop your weapons." Joel ran down the stairs, followed by several other officers, and for once, his voice was the most welcome thing I'd ever heard.

Shoving between two officers, Julian bolted toward me. I leaped to my feet as Joel knelt next to Wren, and Julian crushed me in a hug, his minty scent mingling with the freshwater air of the lake.

"You are under arrest for the murder of Harry Owens. You have the right to remain silent. Anything you say can and will be used against you in a court of law. You have the right to an attorney. If you cannot afford an attorney, one will be provided for you." Joel's voice faded as they advanced up the steps.

I buried my face against Julian's neck and held him tight. He'd come. Again and again, he'd come for me, and I never wanted him to stop.

"It's okay," he whispered. "It's finally okay."

Chapter Thirty

Gold glitter decorated every table in the BnB, twinkling lights graced the walls, and a huge cake sat in the middle of the dining room table. Anticipation and excitement buzzed around the room, and I grinned. This is what I remembered my childhood as. Family together, everyone relaxed and happy.

Mother and Aunt Penny had outdone themselves for this party on our final night here at Thisbe.

Papa welcomed the latest guest from his position next to the front door, and his laughter boomed down the hall as he took Cindy's hands in his own and gave them a squeeze. I smiled at the two, then turned back to watch out the window as my brother paced around outside. His hand flapped animatedly in the air as he talked, which I hoped was a good sign.

A broad-shouldered man squeezed past Cindy and Papa in the doorway. His brown-eyed gaze roamed about the room, and butterflies fluttered in my stomach. I stepped forward and waved.

Julian's face lit up, and he crossed the room to give me a tight hug. I wrapped my arms around his waist and breathed in his familiar scent. I could get used to his hugs.

"How are you doing?" he asked.

"Still in a bit of shock. This weekend didn't go as planned at all."

"I really am sorry—"

"It wasn't your fault." Joel planted himself in front of us, dressed in a white dress shirt and black slacks. "She has no one to blame but herself."

"Is that your way of saying, 'I told you so?'" My cheeks colored.

Joel rolled his eyes and bumped his brother in the shoulder. "Still hanging out with the girl who's tried to get you killed multiple times?"

"Har, har." Julian jostled back into his brother, then turned and wrapped an arm around my shoulders. "Maybe you should try having fun some time. You might find that you actually enjoy life more."

"I don't know that I'd call running into the den of a killer much fun. You should be thanking me for saving your butts."

"Did you know it was Wren?" I asked.

"Search warrants and proof take time to get." Joel laughed mirthlessly. "In a court of law, no one cares what I think, only what I know. But I had my suspicions. Her story didn't quite add up."

"So I suppose you should be thanking us for speeding things along." Julian flashed his brother a winning smile. "You know Judge Wright hates your guts."

"What's going to happen now?" I murmured.

"That's up to the judge. But Maeve has a lot to work through. Thankfully, I heard that her son is starting to be responsive to treatments, and the doctors are hopeful he will come out of his coma soon. She's going to need him in the coming days."

My lungs clenched and I found myself gripping Julian's hand. Wren had killed Owens in a twisted sense of love for her sister, and I couldn't help thinking of my own mother and aunt. For years, they'd fueled every ounce of bitterness at each other, and it'd destroyed their relationship. If left to fester, bitterness could make a person go to lengths they probably never thought possible.

I glanced over my shoulder to see my mom and aunt laughing in the kitchen, arms wrapped around one another. I mentally whispered a prayer of gratefulness that Papa's wish had come true. We were a family again. We weren't a family without cracks and sinkholes, but just like candles, those cracks and sinkholes could be fixed with time and care. I hoped Maeve could also heal given time.

"Attention!" Papa clapped his hands, and his voice boomed over the party. "Attention, everyone!"

Conversations quieted, and the partygoers politely turned toward my grandfather. I raised an eyebrow at Julian, but he only shrugged in response. This part had not been planned.

Papa glanced around the room and beamed when he saw me. He rubbed his hands together, paused, then twisted his chair to face back out the door. "Theseus, you are needed in the house, please!"

Seconds later, my brother slunk into the shadow of the doorway, face red. Now he understood my embarrassment when he shouted my nickname B.O. at the top of his lungs.

Papa turned toward the crowd again, and Theo slipped around him to come stand by me.

"What's he doing?" he hissed.

"Your guess is as good as mine."

We didn't have long to wait. Mom and Aunt Penny moved to stand on either side of Papa, and their matching white smiles could've rivaled the brightness of a three-wick candle flame.

"I first want to thank you all for coming here again. I know my dear wife is smiling down on us to see her friends and family gathered." Papa reached out and squeezed Mom and Aunt Penny's hands.

His next words filled with emotion, and his nose twitched as he struggled to control himself. "I wanted to take a moment to thank my grandson and granddaughter, Theseus and Beatrice Sawyer. Very few know this, but I asked them to help me in what seemed like an impossible task." Tears dripped down his cheeks, and his knuckles whitened as he clenched both of his daughters' hands. "Your Mimi would be so proud to see the adults you've become. I'm so grateful to be called your grandfather."

My lower lip trembled. "Thank you, Papa."

Aunt Penny stepped forward next. "And I want to give a public thanks to you as well, my dear nephew and niece. Without you, my life would look very different right now. But because of your tenacity—or rather, a good bit of that Sawyer stubbornness—I am standing here, and I have my family back." She swiped at her eyes and took a moment to compose herself, "And I'm so happy to announce that Maeve Owens has agreed to sell us the marina, so your uncle and I can continue our efforts to give back to the town that has given us so much. As soon as your uncle is finally able to arrive, we'll sign the paperwork."

Applause scattered throughout the hallway, and my aunt crossed the room to give my brother and me both a hug. When she wrapped her arms around me, she whispered, "Thank you for teaching me about forgiveness and second chances. I owe you everything, Beatrice." She kissed my cheek then moved to stand next to my mom once again.

"All I've gotta say is hopefully things will settle down and go back to normal now that you and your troublemaking brother are heading out of town," Joel teased.

"Oh?" I turned to my brother. "Did you hear that, Theo?"

Theo grinned. "Then you'll be sad to hear we're coming back."

Julian stiffened next to me. He pulled away, his eyes wide. "What did you say?"

Theo slung an arm around my shoulders, and I leaned my head against his. Buying a fixer-upper on a non-existent budget was probably not our best idea. But with one hundred pounds of soy candle wax and two hundred candle jars on their way, I needed someplace to store them and launch my candle business.

Maybe Mimi was right and the sea did contain magic. Maybe the sea had listened to my whispered prayers. Because I was finally following my dreams and coming home to Thisbe.

A Note from the Author

My deepest gratitude to you for reading *Beatrice Ophelia is Flickering Out*! This story sprouted out of a very hard time of my life where I just couldn't find laughter or joy in anything, and then God gave me Beatrice, Theseus, and Julian—best friends who sometimes (okay, often) get themselves mixed up in wild scenarios. If you've enjoyed this story, I'd so appreciate it if you left a review on Amazon and Barnes & Noble! Reviews really boost an author's books!

Also, if you ever wished for Beatrice's candles to be real, they are! You can find several of the candles that Beatrice mentioned (and others!) at lamplighterliterary.com. Being a candlemaker myself was a huge part of the inspiration for this book, and I had so much fun infusing my love of candles into Beatrice's character!

You can also follow my newsletter at megangerigauthor.substack.com or find me on Instagram @megangerigauthor to hear updates on upcoming Beatrice books! I am so grateful for your support of this series, and it means the world that you have enjoyed Book One of the Lake Erie Mysteries!

Megan Gerig | megangerig.com

Acknowledgements

Thank you, dear reader, for picking up this story and making it to the end! This story sprouted after a very dark time of my life, when I just couldn't find laughter or joy in anything. And then God, who never leaves us or forsakes us, gave me these three characters—Beatrice, Theseus, and Julian—best friends who sometimes got themselves mixed up in wild scenarios. These three characters made me laugh more times than I could count, and even after facing countless rejections from agents and editors, I knew that wasn't the end of this story.

Thank you, dear reader, for also loving stories filled with hope and laughter and a bit of murder. This story is here because of you!

I know I already dedicated this story to my parents, but I have to mention them again. Mom and Dad, you never wavered in your support for me. Thank you, Dad, for the countless questions you answered about police procedures and not thinking your daughter too weird for asking yet another "murder question." Thank you, Mom, for the countless hours you put in watching my two kiddos so that I could write this story. You've been the biggest encouragement and supporter in my life, and there are no words I have to convey how much that means to me.

Thank you to my husband. You read draft, after draft, after draft, after draft of this story. You picked me up when I wanted to give up. You brainstormed with me when I couldn't figure out how to plant a certain piece of evidence. You nudged me to run to a coffee shop and write whenever I could and watched the boys when POTS prevented me from driving and I could only write on the floor. I love you so much.

Thank you to my two boys. J + E, you make me laugh daily and are the sweetest boys that I could ever have asked for. Thank you for loving Mommy unconditionally.

Thank you to my brother, Brian. You are the Theseus to my Beatrice and the best brother in the world. Thank you for the dozens of meetings you had with me about marketing this book and helping me plan out my launch strategy. I had absolutely no idea what I was doing, and you so kindly stepped in and shared your knowledge. You are brilliant.

HUGE thank you to my street team! You guys took a chance on a nobody author and blew me away with your support and encouragement. Nadia, Lizzy, Suzie, Abigail, Katelynne, Morgan, Stephanie, Hailey, Abby, Becca, Lori Ann, Heidi, Lena, Rachel, Megan, Cathy, Ariel, Rebecca, Victoria, Catherine, Ashton, Sienna, Samantha, E. G. Bella, Logan, Moriah, Jennifer, Addison, a thousand thank yous. You truly are the best street team I ever could have asked for!

Thank you to the Book Babes Writing Group! You so generously and kindly accepted me into your group, and I so look forward to our meetings. Catherine, Wilma, Kay, and Kali, you are such amazing women, and you are daily reminders to me to write for the Lord. Thank you for your prayers and encouragement!

Thank you to Korina Moss and Ellen McGinty who helped me craft this story into the one it is today. Thank you to Lyndsey Lewellen for crafting the most GORGEOUS cover I could have ever imagined and to Mikayla Drewry for designing such a lovely interior for this book. The little yachts are my favorite. <3

Thank you, Sara Ella. Mystery isn't your genre, but you spent months discussing the pros and cons of self-publishing with me. Your own stories of Light and stepping out in faith are a huge reason why this story is here. You are such a light, and I'm so grateful to you for your friendship and your mentorship.

Thank you, Cathy McCrumb. You cheered this story on in its earliest stages and never let me give up on it. You are the best.

Thank you to Stephanie Morrill and Korina Moss who took the time to read a debut author's quirky book and write such lovely endorsements. Your words were encouragement I needed over and over again throughout this publishing process. Thank you so much for your kindness!

And lastly, but most of all, thank you to Jesus Christ my Savior. You gave me this story and these characters, and You gave me the courage to step out in faith and self-publish this story. I pray that Your love and Your joy is seen in these pages.

About the Author

Megan is a lover of tea obsessed with autumn days in her Spare Oom with a book in her lap. When she's not chasing her wildlings around the house, she's dreaming about stories of mystery and magic. Megan and her family live on a mini-farm in the country where they live out their homesteading dreams. Readers can connect with her on Substack and on Instagram @megangerigauthor.

www.ingramcontent.com/pod-product-compliance
Lightning Source LLC
LaVergne TN
LVHW040043080526
838202LV00045B/3467